KEHUA!

FAY WELDON was brought up in New Zealand. Writer of the first ever episode of *Upstairs, Downstairs* and current Professor of Creative Writing at Brunel University, Fay is best known for her novels *Praxis*, *The Life and Loves of a She-Devil* and *Worst Fears*. In 2001 she was awarded a CBE. She lives on a hilltop in Dorset with her husband.

KEHUA!

'There's simply no touching Weldon as a writer'
Observer

'A warmly exuberant metafiction... The chief delight of this warm-hearted, laugh-aloud book is the voice of "your writer" as she chats us through each day's work' ***Guardian***

'A melange of waspish satire and briskly drawn characters... Weldon can't write a boring sentence' ***Sunday Times***

'Weldon, like Dickens, can have her readers perched on the edge of their chairs with excitement by the end of the first page and hold them there riveted until the last words' ***Evening Standard***

'One of the most prolific, entertaining and provocative of contemporary women writers'
Sunday Telegraph

'Fay Weldon crafts beautiful characters and creates wonderful stories and *Kehua!* is an exceptional novel – even for her' ***Sunday Express***

'Wickedly stylish… as a study of fiction, femininity and family it is bursting with intelligence and fire' ***Daily Telegraph***

'A tale of murder, adultery, incest, ghosts, redemption and remorse. What more could you want? Weldon has form when it comes to she-devilry and she knows exactly how to entrance the reader' ***Tatler***

'Immensely sophisticated... Teasingly Weldon asserts her control… Equally teasingly she pulls the rug from beneath her own feet' ***Independent***

'I loved this novel. Idiosyncratic, unpredictable, feisty and funny... written with such verve and inventiveness' ***The Lady***

KEHUA!

FAY WELDON

A GHOST STORY

CORVUS

First published in Great Britain in 2010 by Corvus, an imprint of Atlantic Books Ltd.

This paperback edition published in Great Britain in 2011 by Corvus.

1 3 5 7 9 10 8 6 4 2

A CIP catalogue record for this book is available from the British Library.

ISBN: 978-1-84887-460-2
eBook ISBN: 978-0-85789-057-3

Printed in Great Britain.

Corvus
An imprint of Atlantic Books Ltd
Ormond House
26-27 Boswell Street
London WC1N 3JZ

www.corvus-books.co.uk

KEHUA!

May the Maori amongst you excuse this fictional foray into your world, for which, believe me, I have the greatest respect, having as a child in the Coromandel encountered both taniwha and kehua.

A glossary of Maori words is provided on page 325.

PART ONE

Scarlet blows the gaff

Your writer, in telling you this tale of murder, adultery, incest, ghosts, redemption and remorse, takes you first to a comfortable house in Highgate, North London, where outside the kitchen window, dancing in the breeze, the daffodils are in glorious bloom: a host of yellow male stamens in vigorous competition, eager to puff their special pollen out into the world. No two daffodils are exactly alike, nor are any two humans. We attribute free will to humans, but not to daffodils – with whom we share 35 per cent of our DNA – though perhaps rashly, when we consider the way some human families behave. It may be that DNA and chance is all there is. We can only hope that this morning the strong wind blows the brightest and best of daffodil genes abroad, so all the gardens around are blessed by yellow loveliness.

Inside the kitchen, Scarlet, a young journalist of twenty-nine, is in conversation with her grandmother Beverley. Scarlet is indifferent to the marvels of nature – how the tender, sheltered female pistil, all receptivity, is rooted to the spot, while the boisterous male stamen above yearns for something better and brighter than plain stay-at-home she. To Scarlet a flower is just a flower, not a life lesson.

Daffodils occasionally self-fertilise, but not often. Inbreeding is unpopular in nature, in the plant and animal kingdoms alike.

'I wasn't going to tell you now, Gran,' says Scarlet, as casually as she can make it seem, 'but I've decided to run away from home.'

To which Beverley, aged seventy-seven, closes her eyes briefly like some wise old owl and replies: 'That's not surprising. There's quite a breeze today. How those daffodils do bob about! Are you going to tell Louis before you go?'

Louis is Scarlet's husband; everybody thinks he is anyway, though they never actually went through with the ceremony. The couple have been together for six years and have no children, so they are entwined merely out of custom and habit, like ivy tendrils curling up a tree, but not yet grown into one another. The severance will cause little distress, or none that Scarlet can see. She is anxious to be off to her new life, with a hop, a skip and a jump, as soon as she has packed her grandmother's freezer with all the delicacies that a relative newly out of hospital is likely to favour. She reckons she can just get it done, and meet Jackson her lover in Costa's Coffee House in Dean Street, Soho, by twelve-thirty. He will wait patiently if she is late but she would rather not be. A tune is running through her head which bodes no good. It is a doomy song in which Gene Pitney gets taken to a café and then can never go home any more. Twenty-four hours from her arms and he met and fell in love with someone else. It's the kind of thing that happens, Scarlet knows. It's at the very last minute that the prize is wrenched from you. She will not be late.

'No,' says Scarlet to her grandmother. Beverley has had a knee replacement, and is temporarily holed up on the sofa in her large and well-equipped kitchen. 'I haven't told him. I hate scenes. Let him come back to an empty house.'

Already Scarlet regrets telling Beverley she is leaving. She can see she's in for a sermon. As if *Twenty-Four Hours from Tulsa* were not enough, now the hop and the skip will turn into a lengthy drama with the hounds of doubt and anxiety snapping at her heels.

'The house isn't exactly empty,' says Beverley. 'Isn't Lola staying?' Lola is a wayward nymphet, and Scarlet's sixteen-year-old niece. 'I daresay she will look after him. But do be careful, all the same. Leaving home can cause all kinds of unexpected problems. But I don't suppose Louis is the kind to go after you with the kitchen knife. And you haven't got any children he can put in the back of the car and suffocate with exhaust fumes. So I expect you're okay. But you can never quite be sure what manner of man you have, until you try and get away.'

Try to envisage the scene. The dancing daffodils: the smart kitchen: Scarlet, a long-legged skinny girl of the new no-nonsense world, with the bright, focused looks you might associate with a TV presenter, attractive and quick in her movements: a girl for the modern age, a little frightening to all but alpha males, in conversation with the raddled old lady, who, though obliged in her infirmity to rely on the kindness of family, is not beyond stirring up a little trouble.

'I know it is tempting,' says Beverley now, equably, from the sofa at the end of the long kitchen, 'just to run, and on many occasions I have had to, and thus saved my life, both metaphorically and literally. But a woman does have to be cautious. Are you running to someone, Scarlet, or just running in general?'

'To someone,' admits Scarlet. 'But it's only temporary, a really nice guy with a whole range of emotions Louis simply doesn't have. Louis is hardly the knifing sort. I wish he was. Jackson's offered me a roof over my head. I'll move out as soon as Louis sells the house and I can get somewhere of my own. Louis hit me last night, Gran, so there's no way I can stay. You wouldn't want me to.'

'Hit you?' enquires Beverley.

'On my cheekbone,' says Scarlet. 'Just here. The bruise hasn't come up yet.'

Beverley inspects her granddaughter for sign of injury but sees none.

'Leaving in haste,' says Beverley, 'may sometimes be wise. The first time I did it I was three. I wore a blue and white checked dress and remember looking at my little white knees going one-two, one-two beneath the hem and wondering why my nice dress was bloodstained and why my legs were so short. My mother Kitchie, that's your great-grandmother, had very good long legs, like yours and your mother's. They bypassed me, more's the pity.'

Scarlet grits her teeth. What have these toddler reminiscences to do with her? She has since childhood been incensed by her grandmother's – and even her mother's – 'when I was a girl' and 'in those days'. Why can't the old realise the irrelevance of the past? There can be no real comparison between then and now. People have surely moved on from the old days of ignorance, hate, violence and prejudice they are so fond of talking about. No, she should never have started the Louis hare running.

'I can't remember what my shoes were like,' Beverley goes on, relentlessly, 'it being such a long time ago – 1937, it must have been – but I think they were yellow. Or that might have just been the dust. We were in New Zealand then, in the South Island, on the Canterbury Plains. The dust on those dry country roads round Amberley was yellowy, a kind of dull ochre. You notice the colour of the earth more as a small child, I suppose, because you're nearer to it.'

Beverley too wonders why she has set this particular hare running: now she has, she can see it will run and run. But then she takes a pleasure in rash action, and always has, and perhaps Scarlet inherits it. There is something grand about burning one's boats. And Scarlet, bound by the tale of the family scandal, longs to get away to her lover, but like the wedding guest in *The Rime of the Ancient Mariner*, holds still.

'I was quite athletic as a child,' Beverley says. 'I even used to get the school gymnastic prize. And I was a really good little runner, a sprinter, until my bosom began to grow, and I developed an hour-glass shape, and bounced while I ran. That was one of the early tragedies of my life. I expect it was that early experience of one-two, one-two down this dusty road to Kitchie's best friend Rita that made me so value running. I wasn't otherwise sportive in any way. I ran because Kitchie, that's my mother, your great-grandmother, was lying dead on the kitchen floor. I wasn't quite sure at the time what dead was, I was only three, but when I tried to open her eyelids she didn't slap my hand away as she usually did. There was a lot of blood around; I remember thinking it was like the time when I blocked the basin with my flannel and the water overflowed and I thought that was funny. But this wasn't funny and it wasn't even water, which is a nothing sort of substance, but a strange red rather sticky stuff coming from my mother's neck.'

'They say you can't remember things that happened when you were three,' says Scarlet. She would rather not be hearing this. It is making her very angry. What sort of inheritance does she have? What has her grandmother done? As happens with many when they are shocked, their first instinct is to blame the victim for the crime.

'I was rising four,' says Beverley. 'They say anything that suits them, and I am bad at dates. But help was required and I was sensible enough to know it, which was why my little legs were going as fast as I could make them. And the reason my mother was lying dead on the floor, though I didn't know this until later, was because she'd told my father Walter, while he was cutting sandwiches, that she was running off with another man. So Walter cut her throat with the bread knife, leaving me, little Beverley, having my afternoon rest upstairs. Men do the oddest things when sex is involved. And fathers weren't very close to their children in those days. They supported them and that was that. If it happened today I expect he'd have come after me too. In times of desperation, the nearest and dearest get it in the neck.'

'You never told me,' says Scarlet. She could see the Alexandra Palace mast between the trees. She feels it was probably transmitting invisible rays of evil, jagged and ill-intentioned, cursing her designs for the future. 'What kind of genetic inheritance is this?'

Today Scarlet is a little pink and feverish about the cheekbones; perhaps her blood pressure is raised? If it is, it is only to be expected: last night she wept, screamed and threw crockery. A high colour suits her, brightening her eyes and suggesting she is not as self-possessed as she seems, and might have any number of vulnerabilities, which indeed she has. After she has had a row with Louis, and these days they are more and more frequent, men look after her in the street, and wonder if she needs rescuing. Today is such a day, and Jackson is indeed at hand. She has no real need to worry about losing Jackson. He would be hard put to it to find another more desirable than she, celebrity though he may be.

After last night's row Louis went to sleep in one of the spare bedrooms of their (or at any rate his) dream home, Nopasaran. The bedrooms are described in the architectural press, where they often feature, as alcoves, being scooped like ice cream out of the concrete walls of a high central studio room. Guests are expected to reach the alcoves of this brutalist Bauhaus dwelling by climbing ladders, as once the cave-dwellers of the Dordogne climbed for security. Changing the bedding is not easy, and the help tends to leave if asked to do it – there is other easier work around – so Scarlet finds the task is frequently left to her.

No one in this book, other than peripheral characters like 'the help' as the particular reader may have realised, is particularly short of money; that is all in the past for them. The need to avoid poverty, once both the reason and the excuse for improper actions, no longer dictates their behaviour. This is not the case for Jackson, who is in financial trouble and has his eye upon Scarlet's good job and general competence, as well as upon her face and figure, but find me anyone whose motives are wholly pure? He for his part could complain Scarlet loved him for his headlines, which once were large though they will soon be small. None so desperate as a failing celebrity.

Murder will out. Poverty was not the cause of the crime which was to so affect Beverley's future and that of her descendants, and concerning which she had stayed silent for so long; rather it was love. And Beverley's version of an event which happened on the other side of the world in 1937 may not be as accurate as she believes. A different truth may still come back to solve the problems of the present. Novels can no longer sit on shelves and pretend to be reality; they are not, they are inventions, suspensions of reality, and must declare themselves as such. By hook or by crook, or even by the intervention of the supernatural, we will get to the root of it.

Where they live

Where we live influences us, though we may deny it. High ceilings and big spaces make us expansive; cramped rooms and low ceilings turn us inward. Those who once lived where we live now influence our moods. A house is the sum of its occupants, past and present. People who live in new houses are probably the sensible ones; they can start afresh. They may seem shallow to us, hermit crabs that we are, these strange empty people, dwellers in the here and now of new developments; but perhaps a kinder word is subtext-less. How can our precursors in the bedroom where we sleep not send out their anxieties, their sexual worries to us? As you brush the stairs – should you condescend to do so – spare a thought for those who ran up and down them before you. Something echoing from the past, as she changes the sheets in Nopasaran's alcoves, tossing the soiled bedding down, dragging the fresh up, almost drowns out Scarlet's lust for Jackson.

Nopasaran, where Louis and Scarlet share their lives, was built in the 1930s when domestic help was easier to come by. It was designed to an advanced taste: hailed at the time as a machine for living in. Machines in those days had a better press than they do today. Louis loves the house; Scarlet hates it. Now she has resolved never to spend another day in it, let alone another night. She wants to go and live with her lover, who has atrocious taste and shagpile carpets – but livelier sexual habits than Louis. A row with Jackson would surely have ended with sex, not a disdainful exit to different rooms, let alone scooped and moulded alcoves.

A lot of people assume that Louis is gay but he is not: indeed he is most assiduous, in a heterosexual fashion, towards his wife. Two or three times a week is not bad after six years of togetherness, but there is nothing urgent about it any more and Scarlet is conscious of a shared falling away of desire, which reminds her that soon it will be her thirtieth birthday, that though she studied Journalism she is working in what amounts to glorified PR, and that her ambitions are somehow being stifled by Louis, who will not take her job seriously while taking his own extremely so.

Louis has a wealthy mother, and it is through her family connections that Louis and Scarlet own Nopasaran, a house-name Louis loves and Scarlet hates. No one ever spells it right: it frequently comes out as Noparasan in articles, and for some reason this enrages her. It can hardly matter, she tells herself. Louis agrees. Perhaps she has the same over-sensitivity to language that he has to design; she earns her living through words, as he earns his through the way things look.

Louis knows how to acknowledge difficulty, to soothe and disarm. He is a thoroughly reasonable, thoughtful and considerate person. Nopasaran – which is Spanish for 'they shall not pass': the battle cry in the Spanish Civil War of the Communists at the siege of Madrid – was designed in 1936 by Wells Coates, the Canadian minimalist architect. Enthusiasts come from all over the world – for some reason disproportionately from Japan – to cluster outside and admire, to peer in as best they can through billowing gauze curtains at the rough flat concrete walls.

Scarlet feels particularly bitter about the gauze curtains, which

Louis prizes. He managed to acquire some original gauze drapes from the Cecil Beaton set for *Lady Windermere's Fan*, the 1946 production on Broadway. Scarlet, unlike Louis, does not feel the pull of history. Nor indeed of the future. She sees in gauze curtains only the worst aspects of suburbia. Last night's row had started, as so often, with disagreements over Nopasaran. Scarlet argued that it was no place to bring up children – they needed a degree of comfort, and au pairs would never stay: Louis argued that it was entirely suitable for developing their children's aesthetic and political sensibilities, and talk of au pairs 'struck terror to his heart'. Surely she must bring them up herself? What was the point of having children if you handed them over to someone else to rear?

'You are going to say next,' said Scarlet, 'that my job is of no importance.'

'I wouldn't say that,' said Louis, 'just that any literate girl from a mediocre university with a 2: 1 could do it and you are worth more than that.'

He meant it as a compliment but she did not see it like that. He had been to Oxford, she to Kingston.

She said that one thing was certain: until they lived in a proper house she would not be breeding. Two-year-olds weren't any good at scuttling up ladders to bed. They tended to fall.

'This is a proper house,' said Louis. 'We are privileged to live here. What you really mean is that you've decided against having children.'

'No I haven't. I just want them by a man who isn't a total nutter.'

'I resent that,' said Louis. 'Have you been drinking? Wells Coates brought up his own children in this house. My grandmother used to visit him here.'

'Any minute now you're going to reveal that this is your ancestral home,' said Scarlet.

'No. I am just telling you that the only way I am ever going to leave this house is feet first.'

'Me, I'd leave it with a hop, a skip and a jump,' said Scarlet. 'And I may yet.'

Scarlet had been drinking caipirinhas, clubland's current favourite, snatching a quick drink with Jackson before getting home from work, and Louis had shared a bottle of champagne with a colleague before leaving Mayfair, where he works. Lola had been staying, though she was out late tonight, and that had disturbed their usual equilibrium, making them see each other as outsiders saw them, not necessarily to their advantage. Both were quicker to anger than usual. Starting a family was normally a subject they skirted around, but that evening they had both piled into it with energy. Louis maddened Scarlet further by raising his eyebrows and sighing as if to say, 'What have I done in marrying a woman so bereft of aesthetic understanding?' He should have refrained: it was this look from him that tipped her into defiance, making Jackson's tasteless shag pad and pile carpet seem not so bad after all, for all the module in Art History she had done at Kingston, alongside her Journalism degree.

But then Louis did not suspect Scarlet of having an affair; it would be too vulgar of her. That she would allow herself to become physically and, worse, emotionally involved with someone as flashy and uneducated as Jackson was not within his comprehension. That Scarlet could move from a lover's bed into the marriage bed within the space of an hour – as in the last couple of months she had, five times, on her way home from work – well, it shocks even your writer. Louis would be dumbfounded, undone. But Scarlet is good at hiding her tracks; it is part of the fun.

It occurred to her even now, mid-row, that without the deceit Jackson might not seem so attractive. She had loved Louis and lusted for him when hiding that relationship from her family. They would find him boring, etiolated like some rare, pallid, carefully nurtured hothouse plant. Scarlet, out of Beverley, being more the tough, all-purpose, all-garden, all-climate-growth, adaptable and robust kind. As it happened, when she did finally present Louis, they liked him and said he would be good for her (what could they mean?) and even seemed to be more on his side than hers.

Louis is tall and thin and gentlemanly; he has a cavernous kind of face, good-looking in an intellectual, sensitive, gentle-eyed, slow-moving kind of way. Observers tended to murmur about 'the attraction of opposites'. Beverley once remarked that theirs was the kind of instant unthinking sexual attraction that usually moves on to babies, as if nature was determined to get the pair together whatever society might have to say, but Scarlet, whose second three-year contraceptive implant is coming up for renewal, and who has already booked her appointment with the doctor to see to it, has so far thwarted nature.

'So what you are telling me,' said Scarlet, as the row moved up a notch, 'is that I have to choose between this house and you.' He was being wholly outrageous.

She heard the kind of chattering noises in her head she sometimes hears when she is about to lose her temper. It is somewhere between the clatter of cutlery in a kitchen drawer being rattled as a hand searches for something urgently needed that isn't there, and the chatter of a clutch of baby crows rattling their throats in a nest. It sounds like a warning to run away, but probably has some boring cause to do with plumbing – there is a pump perched up in the roof next to something called a coffin tank.

The rattle, now more like a smoker's cough, seemed to be coming from up above her and she looked up, but there was only the thirty-foot *chamaedorea* palm tree, planted by the architect seventy years ago and still growing up towards the atrium skylight, and a source of yet another dissatisfaction. Its leaves were stirred gently by the fan that switches on automatically whenever the lights go on to save the plant from too much condensation and consequent mould – Wells Coates left nothing to chance – and would at least turn itself off after an hour was up. Perhaps it was to do with the fan rather than the plumbing? The lower leaves of the palm were discolouring and needed to be removed but how could Scarlet get up there to do it? Why couldn't she have a living room like anyone else, with a couple of armchairs and a sofa and a telly?

'No,' said Louis, bluntly. 'What I am telling you is that you have to choose between no children and me.'

This was strong stuff. Scarlet was usually the one who issued edicts. Again, unwise of Louis; the balance stops wavering, tilts towards Jackson.

'Well, sorry,' said Scarlet, 'if you won't move house to somewhere more sensible and not out in the sticks, that's about that, isn't it? I like my life as it is. It's far too early for me to start worrying about having children and why should I have them with a man who cares more about a pile of crumbling concrete than me. Sorry, but there are other fish in the sea.'

What she meant, of course, was that she loved Jackson more than she loved Louis, and just at the moment if she wanted anyone's children it would be Jackson's, and when Jackson kissed her goodbye outside the BarrioKool club in Shoreditch earlier that evening, saying, 'Move out from him, move in with me, let him take his gauze curtains and go back to his mum,' the feel and promise of his arm across her back made her catch her breath. 'What have you got to lose? A house built seventy years ago by some tosser?'

So lightly had Jackson swept away decades of aesthetic aspiration, dedication and financial investment on Louis' part that a kind of shift took place in Scarlet's vision. If Nopasaran was not to be taken seriously, was Louis either? Louis could be seen by others not as an alpha male but as a pretentious wanker. At least Jackson had the respect of a lot of howling, enthusiastic, underdressed girls. The chattering from the tree dwindled into the kind of sparky noise which the cooker makes when you press the electric button to light the gas, but somehow suggested there was no time to be lost. *Run, run, run* was what she was hearing.

'If I was choosing between you as you are tonight and the house I'd certainly go for the house,' said Louis.

As you are tonight. He is hedging his bets; he is at his schoolteachery worst. Why can't he just commit himself and say: 'I hate you'? Scarlet despised him the more. He was like his mother, po-faced and prudent, bloodless.

'Pity you couldn't have married your mother,' said Scarlet, 'instead of her opposite.'

Louis launched a furious blow into the air, which Scarlet managed to be in the way of, so that his knuckles scraped her cheekbones, thus giving herself the more reason to do what she wanted without qualm. Truth, tears, rage, insults, hysteria, then blended into distasteful memory; all that was clear to Scarlet now was that Louis took her favourite pillow with him to the lower spare alcove in the hope, he said, of silence and a good night's sleep. Scarlet of course lay sleepless, while her husband presumably slept soundly, after the fashion of men, for the rest of the night.

So that was the row. And in an upper spare room, or scoop, or alcove, Scarlet's niece Lola, who had slipped in unnoticed after her night out, listened to and cherished every word and wondered how best she could use them to her advantage.

In the basement

For your information, reader, your writer is working on her laptop down here with the spiders in her basement, where she has set up office, away from e-mail, landline and winter draughts. Stone walls prevent contact by mobile. It is very silent, even lonely, and the only music is the sound of the boiler switching itself on and off, and the washing machine stirring and churning in the otherwise empty room next door.

Yatt House is on a hilltop, large, square, stone and respectable, typical of the kind built in the 1840s for the wealthy professional classes. There is an acre of garden, and crumbling outbuildings. My workroom is part of the old servants' quarters, and the hard blue-limestone stairs down to it are worn in their centre from their constant toiling up and down, up and down, labouring to keep those upstairs fed, watered and comfortable. For some reason I feel it to be my natural place down here, and I like it, but I reckon the last time anyone replastered or decorated was in 1914, when the young men of the house – three sons – went off to war, poor things, and only one returned.

Bits of plaster flake from the walls and dust collects from nowhere on the flagstone floors, as do fallen leaves, though I have no idea how they get in. Concrete filler crumbles into tiny black balls and drifts across the shiny white windowsill beneath the cracked shutters, where someone once bodged a repair. But my laptop works as well here as anywhere, thanks to WiFi, and it is warm, so the drama Scarlet is about to release into the world by her intemperate and imprudent action, her running away from home, can grow and blossom unhindered by fingers too cold to work the keyboard. Which is what happens in my proper, smart office upstairs when the prevailing south-west winds blow hard and cold.

The ground slopes away from the house quite steeply here, so that my window is at ground level. It overlooks a narrow concrete patio and then a stretch of green grass falls away, so it is far less sinister than the rooms at the front, where the old iron ranges and the locked wooden cage around the wine racks still remain. It is a kindness to call them rooms at all – cellars would be more accurate, lit as they are by tiny grated windows set into the brickwork. The room I have chosen to work in must have been the servants' sitting and dining room. The old bell rack is still here, and the rusty mechanism quivers when anyone rings the front-door bell, though I cannot find any wire that connects them.

The house above is safely bright, cheerful and light, and children love to open the door to the basement and look down the worn stairs to the dark space below where I lurk. Some venture down to explore, some don't. My little grandchild Tahuri came yesterday, shuddering with delighted fear. She's four, and half Maori, of a warrior tribe, and brave.

'Do I have to go down?' she asked first. I heard her.

'Of course not.'

'I want to, but suppose there are kehua?'

'Kehua live in New Zealand,' said her mother, 'on the other side of the world. They don't have them here in England.'

'They could come in an aeroplane'. She pronounces the word

carefully, aer-o-plane. She is proud of it. 'They could have come with us, in the luggage rack.'

'The kehua are just spirits who come to take you home after you're dead. They're perfectly friendly unless you've done something really, really bad.'

'Are they making that rattling sound I can hear down there?'

'No, that's just your granny typing on the keyboard.'

'I'm a bit scared.'

'Don't be,' says Aroha. 'Kehua live in trees, not houses.'

'Do they hang from the branches upside down like fruit bats?' Tahuri asks.

'I expect so,' says her mother.

Tahuri decides it's safe enough to come down. She is very brave. Aroha follows.

I ask Aroha to tell me more about kehua and she says they're the Maori spirits of the wandering dead, adrift from their ancestral home. They're not dangerous, just lost souls making themselves useful, though people can get really frightened. Transfer them to another culture and they'd be ghostly sheepdogs, snapping at your ankles to make you do what you should while scaring you out of your wits. Kehua see their task as herding stray members of the whanau back home, so the living and dead can be back together in their spiritual habitation. Kehua are the ones who come to collect your soul after the proper death rituals have been performed: the ones who make you homesick if you're away too long from the urupa, the graveyard, a beautiful place special to the tribe. Kehua put thoughts into your head to get you there, and not necessarily sensible ones. They're not very bright, just obsessive in their need to get the whole hapu back together in one way or another.

'The hapu?'

'The Maori are very family-conscious,' says Aroha. 'Hapu is what they call their kinship group, which is a subgroup of the iwi, or tribe. The taniwha, river monsters, who guard the iwi, are a very different matter. You don't want to meet them in a place you don't belong on a dark night. They have teeth and talons and can do you physical harm. Kehua just use mental and emotional pressure.'

I ask her what kehua look like and she says nobody quite knows, you hear them rather than see them, they're thought to have wings, which they rub together to make a clattering chattering sound. It registers with you as good advice but you're not wise to listen. They're like the grateful dead of Central European mythology, or the Jewish dybbuks, or the hungry ghosts in Japan. They try to return you a favour but they understand only what the dead want, not what the living need, so they get it wrong. Poor things. They haven't much brain. Why should they have? They're dead.

Aroha has a Master's in Anthropology from King's College London. She's a lovely, warm, rounded, vibrant creature and I am pleased to have her in my basement, and little graceful Tahuri too, who says she has just found the ghost of a daddy-long-legs on my unswept windowsill and holds it up by one fragile leg to examine it.

'Does this have a kehua?' she asks, but doesn't wait for an answer, just drops it into a dusty corner where it joins its family of assorted dried-up, dead-and-gone insects. We all go up for tea in the living world.

The next night it snows and it settles, so when I go down early to work and open the shutters, light streams in and for once the room is actually bright, so I don't have to turn on the overhead light. The early sun is making the snow sparkle, and the red spindleberries glow in the hedge the far side of the garden, so it's all white, green and red, like the Italian flag. And then I see a large rat run across the snow just in front of my window, leaving a trail where his belly dragged. Mice leave rather charming little footprints, rats leave runnels. Well, well, it's all metaphor.

Running into a trap

Let me remind you. Scarlet is our heroine, Louis her common law husband, and Jackson her lover. She is between her husband and her lover, but although we are already on page 23 she has still not got any further than her grandmother's kitchen where she has brought food for the freezer. It is this sort of novel, I am afraid. Like a river that overflows its banks, it spreads sideways rather than carves its way forward, plot-wise. Well, never mind. It is what it is. If Scarlet had lived in a more ordinary house we could have got on faster; had she only known, she could have blamed Louis for this too, for making her live in Nopasaran. Yet the unofficial wedding party was held in its garden and she was happy enough about it at the time. So much sexual guilt will do you in. Blame and opprobrium are hurled with abandon by the betrayer towards the innocent party.

Beverley is the grandmother with the new knee and the splendid kitchen in Highgate. So far referred to but undescribed are Scarlet's mother Alice, a staunch Christian, and Cynara, Alice's daughter, fifteen years older than Scarlet, who is a staunch feminist barrister. Staunchness runs in the family, though it does seem to have rather bypassed Scarlet. Lola, whom we met briefly pretending to be asleep in the spare room at Nopasaran. Lola, who is Cynara's daughter and Scarlet's niece, is a treacherous little bitch, staunch only in her desire to have Louis and Nopasaran for herself.

The goodies from Waitrose that Scarlet unpacks – should you have a yen for such detail – include creamy fisherman's pie, lamb biryani chicken with lime and coriander, oriental salmon with lima beans, steam-fresh broccoli, par-cooked croissants. (I am really hungry as I write this – I have had no breakfast and it is already lunchtime.) Scarlet, as we know, had hoped to be out of the house by mid-morning, but now that she has rashly blurted out the truth, her grandmother will clearly not let her go without further discussion. Scarlet wishes she'd stayed quiet and waited for news to seep through to friends and family in the normal way. As it is there will be uproar enough when they find out.

You can't do this, Scarlet, her mother will say. *Just stay where you are and see it through. You inherit instability from your fathers. Both you girls do. I will pray for you as ever – what else can I do? – but sometimes I feel I'm wasting God's time.*

You are, you are, Scarlet will want to say. *Not that there is a God. And Alice will want to reply, What are we then? A plague of woodlice on a rock hurtling through space?* So they will not have the conversation. The subject is too fundamental. Neither mother nor daughter is quite prepared to cut the other off. Both hope the other will recover their reason and believe as they do.

Scarlet's sister Cynara will roll her eyes sigh and say, *Out of the frying pan into the fire. Do think again, Scarlet. Louis isn't so bad, but isn't there some nice woman you can shack up with? Anyone can see you're a lesbian.* Which they can't. But then Cynara's specialty is seeing what she wants to see, not what is, and what she sees everywhere is the villainy of men.

But Scarlet does rather look forward to telling her friends of the severance of her bond with Louis. The more boring ones will no doubt protest briefly and say, *You can't do this to us. We've got too used to saying Louis-and-Scarlet.* The others, the fun ones in fashion PR, will say, *Jackson Wright? Wow! Go for it, Scarlet.* But all they know is that Jackson got a lot of column inches for his last vampire film, so their advice can't be relied upon.

Her uncle Richie, whom she seldom sees, but admires, and who is paranoid on the subject of gayness, will eventually call from Hollywood and say something along the lines of, *Oh so Louis finally decided to come out, did he?* And Scarlet will leap to Louis's defence, and in so doing lose her resolve to leave him. Scarlet likes Louis. She is fond of Louis. She just doesn't love him – at least not today – and certainly not in the carnal way she loves Jackson – and she hates living in Nopasaran – but she does not like others denying his heterosexuality. What would that make her?

She hates the way people just can't leave other people alone to live their lives in the way they want, but most of all she hates the way she cares what other people think of her. She feels resolve drifting away. She has to get out of here. There is twittering in her ears. She is just not where she should be. She has not run far enough yet.

It is her own fault. She should have kept her mouth shut and said nothing; she could already have escaped from Nopasaran at last, looking out over the Soho rooftops from Jackson's fabulous apartment in fabulous Campion Tower, in Jackson's fabulous bed, with Jackson's fabulous body beside her. Louis has narrow shoulders and few muscles; he is a life-of-the-mind man. Jackson, so far as Scarlet knows, is a life-of-the-body man. All these life-altering things happening, and here Scarlet still is, trying to decide whether *moules marinière* can be frozen or should be eaten before their sell-by date. Should she put the delicate little white cucumber sandwiches out for Beverley's tea or not? Will they dry and curl up? Life keeps leaping from the mundane to the cosmic and back again.

As for Beverley, she thinks the girl is looking decidedly shifty. I haven't described Beverley in any great detail. She looks much like any other seventy-eight-year-old, one who has seen better days and become, as the old do, somehow fuzzy round the edges. But she's not too bad; when she comes into a room she brings energy with her: she does not deplete it in those around. Her figure remains trim, her heels stay more high than flat, in spite of the recent trouble with her knee. She has a vulgar tendency to wear satins and velvets, and what the unkind would call bling: large pieces of gold and platinum jewellery better suited to evening than day.

The antique yellow-velvet sofa where she nurses her recovering leg is under a window, where tiny, elegant fronds of Virginia creeper, red and green, push in under the frame. In winter it is almost impossible to keep the room warm, in spite of the Aga's year-round, patient efforts. The north wind can blow in quite cruelly, but it's not too bad today. The other side of the daffodils the lawn runs down to a little stream that flows between reeds and marks the end of the garden. Someone once even saw a fish here, really tiny, but nevertheless a sign that the energies of nature cannot be denied for ever. In the 1730s a minor tributary of the River Fleet escaped when the rest of the flow was diverted into underground culverts, and has flowed in a trickle through the back garden ever since, to disappear from sight where the brambles and elders of Highgate Cemetery grow thickest, there where Karl Marx's massive bearded headstone stands.

Beverley's house Robinsdale too has its history, which should not be ignored. Its very bourgeoisity seems to have attracted to it revolutionaries of one kind or another. It gave them shelter and comfort even while they despised it. A very parental kind of house, in fact, late Victorian, solidly built, if in a rather gloomy Gothic style, double fronted and detached, complete with turrets and, apart from the problem with the windows, fortunate in that its owners and tenants have always maintained it well. But then revolutionaries tend to spring from the educated middle classes, and to keep their own houses in order, whilst undermining the structures that oppress the masses. A wealthy but radical owner of gold mines in South Africa had the house built for his American wife, Ellen, in the 1890s. Here, in the healthy air and light of Highgate, she ran a small progressive school for the daughters of aspiring professionals. She was the one who named it Robinsdale, after the birds who twittered to her on her first inspection of the site.

The school continued in her spirit after her death in 1925, and the famous free-thinker and educationalist Dora, wife to Bertrand Russell, was a frequent visitor in the twenties and thirties. The school closed during the Second World War and was converted in the fifties by its new owner – a founder member of the New Communist Party of Great Britain – into a private dwelling. Beverley, being of a no-nonsense disposition, sees nothing incongruous with the house name, though her children have always found it naff, and don't understand why she doesn't just take the name board on the gate away and call it No. 15 Elder Grove, which it is on the council records, or better still, sell it as an old people's home or a school and live somewhere more practical. But she won't.

Beverley, as it happens, has vague plans to marry again – she comes from a generation of women who like to be married – but the plans are still embryonic and she will not mention them to her family. Would they carp and agitate, suspecting her judgement and wondering what would happen to their inheritance if some new man, some fortune hunter, were to step in and claim it? They are all principled, in their different ways, and unworldly, not interested in gaining wealth, but they certainly do not want to see it disappearing.

Beverley's hair is in need of a wash. She likes to look her best, even at her age, in case a new man should walk through the door. She could well afford to hire someone to come in and do it, but when Scarlet suggests it Beverley is dismissive. It seems a needless extravagance. Beverley has seen hard times and good times, and is always fearful that the bad times may come again. She has been widowed thrice. Perhaps she attracts death, for it always circles her, while leaving her alone, other than to dump unexpected wealth at her door. Certainly she sees herself as 'prone to sudden events' as an astrologer once described it, something to do with Uranus and Aries being in the ascendant when she was born. Neither her mother nor father was around in her childhood to confirm the exact time of her birth – the father having killed the mother and then himself, as Beverley now relates.

'You're not concentrating, Scarlet,' complains Beverley. 'I tell you something I've kept hidden all my life and all you have is a mild worry about whether or not you inherit unfortunate genes. Well, you do, though two generations down they are quite diluted. God knows what your father brought into the family. But it's no use. You have sex on your mind. Just finish with the groceries and then fetch me my plant spray.'

Scarlet, surprised, gives up stacking Beverley's frozen-food chest, and fetches the ugly green plastic flask Beverley uses to mist her geraniums. Beverley lifts the blanket that keeps her warm, pulls up her skirt, and gives her still quite shapely bare legs – albeit the left thigh still badly bruised from the surgeon's efforts – a quick blast of water, and then asks Scarlet to come closer. Whereupon she aims a similar blast at Scarlet's cheek, just below the spot where Louis allegedly hit her.

'I get the water from the stream at the bottom of the garden,' says Beverley by way of explanation. 'In the old days the water from the River Fleet was thought to have healing powers. I find it works very well on the computer. When it crashes I give it a quick blast.'

Scarlet pushes back her damp hair in outrage. She presses her fingers where the bruise was meant to be, but feels no tenderness. She cannot think which is the worst conclusion: to suppose that there was no bruise in the first place, or that the water has done the healing. She decides the solution is not to think about it at all.

Down in the basement

I don't *think* it's haunted down here where I write. It's just that at night there's a general feel of busyness around me, a sense of movement, an urgency, a stirring in air that's never quite still. It's okay, I almost like it, it's company. Just sometimes, like now, when I'm working late at night and invention falters and I pause and become conscious of my surroundings; and the dishwasher upstairs in the scullery has finished, and the chandeliers in the library above me have stopped tinkling and I know this means Rex has gone to bed, only then do I feel in the least spooked. If I listen hard there is something near by interrupting the silence, and I wish that it wasn't.

It is a sound I can interpret only as an intent breathing too close by for comfort, and then a hissing and silence, hissing and silence, and a suggestion of the satisfaction of work well done – as if whoever's standing next to me is inviting me to share their pride. Which I would, I am sure, if only you, ghost, whoever you are, were meant to be here, but you aren't. You're out of your time, your time is way back then, when you were the laundress with your steam iron, down here where the basic work of Yatt House has always been done, at least for the longer part of its existence. What I hear is the hiss of steam as a hundred years ago you press the iron on to damp fabric and then lift it again. And press, and lift. It is perfectly possible that it's the radiators cooling down now the central heating has clicked itself off for the night, but I don't think so. Go away anyway. This is *my* room, *my* space, *my* year to occupy it. I have work to get on with.

All the same I am contemplating giving up for the night. But I am startled by a sudden dreadful banshee wail, and another, and another. The neighbourhood cats are going courting. But it's an eerie sound, less feral than human. And this one drives me upstairs fast. I remember what Aroha said about the kehua, the spirits of the homeless dead, and how they like to inhabit animals and birds: the screech of the morepork bird in the velvety Maori night is a case in point. I don't suppose the kehua can travel from the other side of the world, and why would they want to, but I close down my computer quickly, check the shutters are properly barred, turn off the lights and get to bed and human companionship as quickly as I can.

Scarlet's plan for leaving home

Where were we? Scarlet, the morning after the row, had woken alone in the double bedroom alcove, and heard Louis leave for work, half an hour earlier than usual. He did not come in either to apologise, say goodbye, or enquire after her bruise, so there was no obvious reason to amend her midnight decision to leave home, and at once. It was true she had a panicky moment or so. Supposing he was actually glad to see the back of her? Then she, not Louis, would be devastated. There was little point in leaving if not to punish him.

But he would no doubt call during the course of the day, having calmed down a little, and suppose things to be back to normal, only to find her mobile blocking him and no one at the end of the land-line. And serve him right. He had admitted he loved Nopasaran more than he loved her, and must take the consequences. She need feel no guilt. At least Jackson was prepared to say he loved her. The big gentle brown eyes that so entranced teenagers, especially for some reason when his vampire fangs grew and dripped blood, had gazed into hers as he spoke and had been impossible to disbelieve. It would not last – she was no fool – but it did not have to last. Whatever did, these days? Jackson would serve as the lever to prise her apart from Louis, put an end to the absurdity that was her life with Louis. Yet when Jackson said he loved her she felt vaguely embarrassed. What did he mean by it? He wanted to fuck her, obviously; more, he had fucked her, and wanted to do it again. But was it more than that? What was the difference between being motivated by love, and motivated by lust? She had certainly never said 'I love you' to Jackson, let alone to Louis, except sometimes she thought she had felt it.

So few people talked of love any more. Mothers were often saying *Remember I love you* to their children, especially when they were splitting up with the father and going off with someone else, but so few adults said it to each other. Possibly gays did but not heterosexuals. This was just not the age of romance. It seemed rather sad.

So when Jackson declared his love she subdued embarrassment and did her best to forget he was an actor and for all she knew merely parroting the lines of a scene in which he played some romantic lead. Stage rather than TV, perhaps some musical – he had a thrilling voice – stage plays being on the whole more sophisticated. I love you, I love you, I love you works well in song but nowhere else. If something seems too good to be true it may well be so, like investing your money in Icelandic banks. That you should meet someone like Jackson who was available, lived centrally, was sexual dynamite, had sufficient status not to worry about hers, earned good money – look at the Campion Tower penthouse – who did not play emotional games, was not a cynic, but actually rather simple, equating sex with love in an old-fashioned way, and on top of all this said he loved you. True, he didn't read books; but that would be a relief. Louis read so many.

So now, Scarlet pulls on her vintage Levis and a navy Prada stretch T-shirt – raising arms made sore from where Louis had grabbed and squeezed them – and is pleased to feel the pain because it reminds her how impossible Louis is, and how no one can possibly blame her for leaving. She goes to the kitchen where Lola is making some kind of herbal tea. She has forgotten Lola. What is to be done about Lola? Sixteen-year-old Lola.

Scarlet has offered Lola sanctuary and now can hardly just abandon her. Lola dropped out of school four weeks back, not before stirring up a perfect storm of bad publicity for her parents, had a big row with her mother and went straight round to her aunt and asked if she could stay for a couple of weeks. Home had become unbearable. She was, said Lola, expecting an e-mail on her iPhone about her passage to Haiti, where she had been accepted by a disaster charity as an aid worker. Lola wanted to make a difference, save the world. How could Scarlet say no? Except that getting out to meet Jackson might be more difficult if Lola was around.

She had checked with Cynara, rather hoping she, fearing Scarlet would distract her daughter's mind from serious issues by taking her to beauty parlours and Harvey Nic's, would say no. One way or another, Scarlet thought, Cynara would get Lola back to school and resitting her exams, and she, Scarlet, would be safe. But Cynara seemed to have lost all interest in her unfortunate daughter.

'I hadn't heard about the Haiti bit,' was all Cynara had said. 'And she'll have lied about her age. But I've had enough. Take her, keep her, and for your sake pray she leaves the country soon.'

Which Scarlet took as permission, which she would really rather not have had. She checked with Louis, assuming at least he would object.

'If it's okay by Cynara,' Louis had said. 'Take the poor girl in. She's family.'

Scarlet was surprised but on reflection supposes Louis can put up with Lola because she is so smart, smart enough to qualify for the Government's special needs subsidy as a gifted pupil. She is also quite ornamental, as he puts it. She has a teenage figure, skinny legs and middle, but a somehow blurry, fleshy face, with a jawline that is never quite clean and firm. It stays over-padded. She takes her features from her potato-faced father, not her mother, which as Louis observes is rather a pity. On the other hand Lola has a perfect polished dark-ivory skin, very large blue eyes beneath strong eyebrows, and an overbite that makes her full upper lip stick out in a surprisingly sexy way. Scarlet has every reason to believe Lola is a virgin. She has dismissed any fears that Louis might become sexually interested in Lola, though they have flashed through her mind. Louis has too great a sense of his own dignity not to feel and behave responsibly.

Besides, Lola speaks through her nose. When she gets excited she talks with a sharp whine that Louis admits to finding trying. Lola confided in Scarlet, as she was settling into the upper alcove, that recently someone at a party had told her the reason her voice was the way it was, was because she took too much coke and had damaged the tissues of her nostrils.

'But that's terrible,' said Scarlet.

'I haven't snorted a single line since,' said Lola. 'It's bound to get better. I'm only young.'

Scarlet reported the conversation to Louis in the hope that he might think better of having Lola in the house but no such luck. She wonders if Louis has a suspicion of Jackson's existence, and wants Lola around for the same reason that Scarlet does not, but dismisses that fear too. Guilt can make you paranoiad.

All he said was, 'You were the same at her age. You took Ecstasy, ran away from home and lived with Cynara. That's when you changed your name to Scarlet, just to annoy your poor mother. I expect now Lola's here she'll change hers to Mary. Don't fuss so,

Scarlet. It doesn't suit you. She'll be off soon enough.'

Scarlet had indeed started life with the name Joan, and Cynara's real name was Mary, but both daughters, at the earliest opportunity, had subverted their mother's domestic dreams for their futures. The romantic spirit which afflicted the rest of the family had bypassed Alice.

So here Lola was, it seemed, in Nopasaran until her ticket from Help the Harmed came through, which never quite seemed to happen. It had been three weeks already.

'That was quite a night,' Lola complained as she squeezed the juice from the last grapefruit. There was not even the most primitive electric juice extractor. The kitchen, state of the art in 1937, was short of power points. 'Why do you put up with it? You have these rows and when you have sex afterwards it usually goes on only for about ten minutes, shouldn't it be longer? My friends say half an hour is more usual. And last night it didn't go on at all.'

Scarlet is mortified. Of course Lola *hears*. So much for Wells Coates and his design for living in. There is no way Scarlet can go on sharing a roof with Lola, forget with Louis. All she wants is to be with the simplicity that is Jackson, away from Lola, away from Louis, away from the embarrassments of the past. But this would mean leaving Lola alone with Louis, and Lola, Scarlet suddenly perceives, has the gift for what Scarlet can only think of as manifold disruption. It may be one step down from having poltergeists manifest themselves around her, but somehow nothing in Lola's ambience ever quite goes smoothly. At the very least electrical impulses discharge themselves around her.

Lola finishes squeezing her grapefruit, and licks the pulped fragments in their shell with her very pink, vibrant tongue, and Scarlet wonders how her own life would have been different if Lola had not been born. Certainly the messy horrors of Lola's birth had been enough to put Scarlet off motherhood for life. If Lola had crept in unnoticed would last night's row have been so dreadful? Had Cynara's child turned out to be a boy, would D'Dora now be in Cynara's bed? D'Dora being Cynara's new lesbian lover.

Lola is the kind of girl, Scarlet sometimes thinks, who'd once have made the milk go sour when she passed a churn. The female equivalent of a Jonah: the unlucky one whose presence on board is enough to make the ship sink. And then she is ashamed of herself for thinking such uncharitable thoughts.

'When Mum did it with Dad, you could hardly hear when they had sex,' she goes on. 'Now she's with D'Dora there's more noise. A lot of giggling and slapping and dressing up. I think perhaps it's S&M. It can go on for hours. They never even think about my exams and how at my age I need sleep.'

'Too much information,' says Scarlet. 'Allow your mother some privacy.'

'Why? She doesn't hide anything. She's all for openness. She threw Dad out and invited D'Dora in. It didn't occur to her I might not want two mothers, I wanted a father and a mother like other people. I can't wait to get to Haiti.'

Lola had been tested for Asperger's but failed to make the grade – she was normal, just too bright for her own good, they said – but at least had qualified for the gifted category, which was a lesser grant but still useful.

'And it's even worse here,' Lola persists. 'Rows are even more upsetting than sex. And there's not even a proper bedroom to sleep in so I can close the door. Why do you stay with Louis? He hit you. Mother would die if I told her. Why don't you just move out?'

'There's you to look after,' says Scarlet.

'I've got friends,' says Lola. 'They have sofas. I don't need you. I can be out of here by this afternoon. I will be. Can I borrow your transparent white top thing?'

'No you can't,' says Scarlet, automatically.

'Why not?'

'It isn't decent.'

'You wear it,' says Lola, 'when you go and meet that man.'

'I don't meet any man,' says Scarlet.

'You are such a liar. And Louis never notices a thing. Or perhaps he does and doesn't say anything. What's his name?'

'Jackson Wright,' says Scarlet.

'Wow!' says Lola, impressed. 'So what stops you?'

'You,' says Scarlet. 'I can't abandon you.'

'Like I said, don't mind me,' says Lola. 'You go and I'll be out of here before Louis gets back.'

Scarlet thinks: well then, that's it, last obstacle to new life overcome. What was there to lose? She could work from Jackson's flat in Campion Tower as well as she could from Nopasaran. All you needed these days was a laptop and an iPhone and you could be anywhere in the world. She had to put in an appearance at the office two or three times a week max; and now she'd be able to walk from Soho, not have to make the tedious journey from Belsize Park. She was certainly not weighed down by possessions, having accumulated so few over the partnered years. Louis' taste reigned supreme. Early in the relationship she'd brought home a set of really pretty dinner plates she'd seen in a sale in Selfridges' window and he'd been so rude about them she'd thrown them at him one by one, and even then he had only worried about the walls, which was absurd because they were rough Bauhaus concrete anyway and the odd dent wasn't going to show. So if she travelled light, so light that home was merely a concept, like Nopasaran itself, not a reality, and there was nothing to bind her to it, Louis had only himself to blame if she cut loose.

She called Jackson. He answered, presumably from bed, in his deep throaty voice. He didn't get up until after eleven. Sometimes Scarlet would go round to the Campion Tower penthouse at midday and find him still in bed, warm and vigorous and inviting. Afterwards they would shower together beneath a generous blast of water and sometimes the sex would start all over again. Nopasaran's shower had been exceptionally fine in 1937, no doubt, but was down to a dribble now. The original shower head, advanced for its time, was, alas, in all the architectural records, and Louis became hysterical and threatened murder and suicide if Scarlet suggested it was replaced. Though she had to admit Nopasaran's bath was sumptuous, Carrera marble, rather like the ones you got in the old Savoy before the makeover. She had stayed there with a lover or two. Indeed, she had tried out many of the best hotels in London. The beds in the Ritz were best, but there was always building work going on somewhere, as in so many of the old hotels, and the sudden noise of pneumatic drills could be disturbing. New places, like Campion Tower, with its ten storeys and its glassy curved frontage, sensitive to Soho's planning requirements if not their spirit, needed little maintenance.

'I want to move in with you,' she'd said to Jackson, just like that. 'I want to come with my suitcases right now.'

There was only the briefest of pauses. 'That's fantastic,' he said. 'You're actually going to leave hubby?'

She wished he had not put it quite like that. What sort of world did he live in where people referred to their partners as hubby? Perhaps it was ironic? But Jackson, she had to admit, was not hot on irony.

'Yes I am,' she said, and the die was cast.

'You're not going to change your mind? I don't want my life shattered, not again.'

Jackson's life, shattered? He hadn't told her about that, whatever it was. So far all he had dwelt upon was the shallowness of relationships pre-Scarlet. Well, he would tell all, given time. Somehow she had assumed that Jackson, unlike Louis, had lived a charmed life, unafflicted by pain or trauma, that he had sprung into life fully formed in order to provide her with a bed to move into. But of course it was not like that.

'I won't do change it,' she said.

'Then I can't wait.'

He sounded as if he meant it. It wasn't a very good line, not an actor's line, a worked-on line: it was genuine. The only bad thing about Soho was the parking. But she could get a resident's parking space as soon as she moved in. And it was not some kind of major life decision, this was just a moving in, with not even a party to celebrate it.

Jackson told her he was on his way out now; he had one or two things to do, a meeting with the *Upstairs, Downstairs* movie people, which might drag on, but if she got to Costa's at lunchtime he would meet her there. She should park in the underground car park and he'd be down to help her with her suitcases. Everything was going to go right in her life from now on in. He admired her. She was so brave. He couldn't wait. Nor could she. He uttered a word or two of love, and she found parting, even just putting down the phone, to be such sweet sorrow it must be true love.

And that was that. Scarlet was off. You know how it is, reader, you know how it is, even though you so sensibly equate true love with neurotic dependency. Love has its charms, and wilful abandonment of common sense is one of them. Jackson actually had to go to his ex-wife's house in Battersea to collect his driving licence, and had been dropped from the *Upstairs, Downstairs* film that very week, and knew it. But he also knew what impressed women and what did not, and being banned from driving was one of the latter.

There were a few things Scarlet needed to clear up before Louis came back and found her gone. She must get the address book on a memory stick, answer a few e-mails which needed to be replied to that morning, take the box files marked 'family' and 'legal', and be off. If everything was in good order when Louis returned then he'd have nothing to complain about other than her actual absence.

Beverley! What about Beverley? Scarlet remembered she was meant to be stocking her grandmother's fridge that very morning. Beverley refused to have a live-in nurse while she convalesced, so it was left to her family to do it. 'Family' usually meant Scarlet, the others being so preoccupied with their own affairs. Her mother was skulking up in the North, Cynara was changing partners and her husband Jesper was now out of the picture, and Lola always looked blank if asked to help. Well, that was okay. Scarlet reckoned she could get round to Waitrose, buy and deliver at speed, try not to get into conversation, get back to pick up her bags and still be well on time to meet Jackson for lunch. She would ask Lola to pack for her. Lola would know what she needed. She shared Scarlet's taste in clothes. Cynara had done what she could to educate Lola out of excessive femininity but had failed. One of Lola's current complaints was that while she, Lola, wasn't even allowed to show her tummy, let alone navel pierce, and everything had to be machine washable at forty degrees, D'Dora had brought with her all kinds of frilly and velvety sensuous things that had to go to the dry cleaners, not to mention – as Lola was pleased to point out – chains, whips, black leather hoods and long red latex boots, which D'Dora claimed was a collection of Victorian erotica, more rare and valuable every year.

So that was how Scarlet, an unwilling listener to Beverley's life story, came that morning to be unloading ready-made meals from Waitrose into Beverley's fridge, while Jackson went off to see his ex-wife and Lola packed, and did the chambermaid's trick of stuffing a few of Scarlet's more delectable undies beneath a cushion to steal later.

Meanwhile the kehua hung unseen, folding and unfolding their shadowy wings like fruit bats, from the branches of the palm tree that exploded its fronds in Nopasaran's atrium, and chattered in excitement. Something was happening in the McLean hapu, for whom they had responsibility. Louis was at his office wondering if he should call Scarlet or let her stew, and the widower Gerry, Beverley's erstwhile sweetheart – whom we have yet to meet – was on the Faröe Islands, wondering whether a man would be wise to woo a woman who, however charming and wealthy, had already been widowed three times. Desire calls so often, yet practicalities and prudence intervene.

Back to the basement

Find your writer fresh and rational this Monday morning, after a good night's sleep and in charge of her material. Alas, it becomes apparent, those who hover around the brickwork, the old kitchen range, the wine cellar and the laundry tubs are also in fighting form, determined to make their presence felt.

Rex dismisses what I hear as 'auditory hallucinations' and I daresay he is right. There is nothing other-worldly to be seen, just rather a lot to be heard. I am not saying any of these sounds exist in actuality; it's just that I – defining 'I' as the sum of my senses, and how else can it be done? – hear things for which there is no obvious explanation. The laundress is back with a vengeance. I denied her existence last night and she is determined to make her point. I suspect that a hundred years ago or so she used to turn up on Monday mornings and has no intention of stopping, though a long time ago lost her corporeal form. I think she *liked* doing the laundry. I hear the sound of whooshing water and taps running – she is late enough in the house's history for there to be taps, though there will have been many visiting laundresses before and I daresay a few after – and hear the sound of bristle brush on fabric and the squeak of a wringer as the handle revolves and the rubber cylinders turn. There's also the fitful sound of what could be a woman singing. But then again it might be the plumbing of the house above or the central heating radiators down here – they are turned up high; it is very cold today – and it's true one interprets sound as one does sight, in accordance with what one expects.

I get up as smoothly as I can from my desk – I find I do not want to draw attention to myself, almost as if I am according her more right to be here than I have, which is absurd – scuttle to the wall, turn the knob of the central heating panel to off, and get back to my desk as quickly as possible. I don't want to disturb the status quo, lest I stir something up even more unsettling. The panel cools, its gurgling and hissing stops. But that leaves the other sounds, clearer than ever. What I'm hearing is what I heard vaguely last night, but now in detail: someone wetting the clean dried sheets, applying the iron – heated on the range – so the steam rises, hissing, and then the heavy hot weight smooths the damp, newly boiled white laundry: the sheets, the embroidered pillowslips and tablecloths, the aprons, and the master's shirts. The folding is being done to perfection, edge to exact edge. I reckon somebody who once worked here was so proud of their work they never quite wanted to go away. I prefer this comforting version of servant life, rather than the alternative – that past misery keeps their spirits trapped down here. Life may be hard but people have a great gift for enjoying it.

A house this size – substantial but not too grand – would have had a cook, a nanny when the children were small, a maid and perhaps a tweenie to assist; a manservant, a gardener's boy, and a groom. The cook would have slept down here near the kitchen, female servants would have slept up in the attics under the eaves, two or three to a bed if necessary – where now my husband has his office and plays his piano. The outdoor staff, the men, slept above the stables. No one was necessarily unhappy, and they certainly weren't lonely. At least they were safe, warm and fed, which was more than could be said for many.

The Yatt House staff would have a Saturday afternoon off once a month if it could be organised – looking after the gentry was a 24/7 affair – and a jaunt to Evensong every Sunday afternoon, when Sunday lunch was cleared away and a cold Sunday evening supper for upstairs had been prepared and laid. It isn't far to go; All Saints' Church, designed by Pugin, is just across the road. Once a year staff would have a weekend off to visit their families.

'There now, that be a good job, quist,' I hear a woman say, in my head or out of it. I also know I cannot believe the evidence of my own ears, since someone told me the other day that 'quist' in these parts was once used much as 'innit' is today. I have somehow got this notion of a wicker basket piled high with fresh, ironed, folded washing, and am all too likely to dredge my mind for convenient evidence.

The room is getting noticeably colder, but at least the sounds from the time-slipped world are diminishing, fading back to their proper place in, I imagine, somewhere around 1900. According to the local directory of that year a Mr and Mrs Bennett and their three sons Ernest, William and Thomas lived in this house. At any rate it feels safe enough for me to get up, turn the heating on again, listen to the gentle hissing and gurgling as hot water in the here-and-now world flows back into the pipes, and get back to my laptop.

Unfortunately it is now my characters' turn to take offence at my neglect of them; they will not come easily to mind, other than that Alice née McLean, daughter to Beverley McLean, is up in Chester on her knees praying for her daughters, christened Mary and Joan (now Cynara and Scarlet, the ingrates), and for funds for a new church building. I am tempted for some reason to make Alice a member of the Minnesota Light of the Divine Canyon Church, but this is what I mean by characters getting out of hand. She will be simply Church of England and devout. Someone brought up by Beverley will quite reasonably seek stability, faith and respectability in their middle age. I'm having trouble enough getting Scarlet out of Robinsdale and into Jackson's arms as it is, without involving an evangelical church in Minnesota.

In the kitchen at Robinsdale

'Are you running *to* someone,' asks Beverley, 'or just running away in general?'

'To someone,' says Scarlet, automatically, though she had meant to tell no one. 'Actually, it's Jackson Wright, you know, the film star?'

'No I don't, I'm sorry,' says Beverley. 'I don't go to the pictures very often. Films are so noisy nowadays.'

'He's rather like Russell Crowe.' Scarlet refrains from adding 'with vampire teeth', in case it gives Beverley the wrong impression. Jackson is the gentlest man.

'I'm afraid that doesn't help. Is he expecting you?'

'How do you mean?'

'I just remember the shock your poor Uncle Richie had when your Aunt Solange came knocking on his door with a suitcase in either hand, saying she had run away from her husband and children and was moving in with him. He wasn't expecting her at all. In fact he could hardly remember her name, but she had red hair, which he remembered from various art film festivals in the Rocky Mountains. It is so easy in these exotic locations for girls to get the wrong end of the stick. Your Uncle Richie thought he was passing the time every now and then, but she was a nice girl and assumed it was true love, just because he said it was. He let her stay – he had a film to finish and no time for domestic issues – and they are still together to this day and so far as I can see perfectly happy. I am sure it will work out okay for you too.'

Scarlet wonders why no one in her family takes her seriously. Perhaps if she could get out of fashion and into current affairs it would be better? As it is, in Cynara's eyes she is a traitor to the feminist cause, in Louis' eyes she is devoid of aesthetic understanding; in Lola's eyes out of touch and over the hill; and her own grandmother dismisses the very idea of a 'career' – saying there was no such thing, only a bunch of self-styled feminists fooled by capitalism in the name of divide and rule, lured on by the idea of promotion to keep them working harder and longer than one another to the point of exhaustion. And her mother Alice hadn't even cared enough about her to come to her wedding to Louis, saying 'she didn't have the time'. Which Cynara tactlessly reported to Scarlet as Alice thinking Louis and the whole fashion world was made up of homosexuals and druggies and she didn't approve.

Scarlet had reacted by throwing a hissy fit, saying, very well then, Louis and I will live in sin if that's what you prefer, calling off the wedding, and having the party without the ceremony, which few realised had not happened, they having gone straight to the reception in Nopasaran's concrete garden. A good compromise. A marriage is a piece of paper; a wedding party the real thing. Who cared about parental approval anyway? That had been years back. Scarlet had since made it up with Alice, who had even quite come round to Louis, and looked forward to grandchildren. Now Alice would have Jackson Wright to contend with.

'And you've known this film actor some time?' enquires Beverley.

'I went to his place three weeks ago to do an interview, and that was that,' says Scarlet. 'We've seen each other every day since then, except Sundays.'

'I can see explaining this to Louis could be quite difficult,' says Beverley. And she goes on to say that some warning before leaving home is customary, if only an e-mail or a fax, if anyone uses the latter any more, before saying goodbye. 'Your sister Cynara at least e-mailed her husband out jobhunting in Dubai to say he was out on his ear and D'Dora was moving in. I'm afraid the whole thing has rather upset Lola. How is poor Lola? Are you leaving her at home with Louis? Is that quite wise?'

Scarlet observes that this is the twenty-first century and a male and a female can be in a room together without actual sexual congress occurring, and besides, Lola is family.

'Not blood family to Louis,' says Beverley, and Scarlet goes off to text Jackson and says to make that tea, not lunch. She is obstructed by family matters.

'I hope you understand, Scarlet,' says Beverley, 'that Lola only came to stay with you in the first place to get back at her mother. And that you took her in to spite your sister, steal her toy. Children go to great lengths to be revenged on their parents, and siblings are almost as bad: they spend their time trying to drive the others out of the nest. Obviously Lola will now make as much trouble as she possibly can. Nature did not build happiness into the system, only the urge to survive.'

It occurs to Scarlet that Beverley is losing her marbles, retreating into some obscure Freudian fantasy about sibling rivalry. Is her brain going? Will she soon be sitting dribbling in a corner? Had not she, Scarlet, done everything she could not to take Lola in? If anyone had put pressure on her it was Louis.

'This running away habit can get compulsive,' says Beverley. 'I am the first to admit it. But you younger girls seem to do it for fun. You look for excuses to go, not reasons to stay. Alice uses Jesus,

Cynara uses D'Dora, you're using Lola. At least Cynara has the sense to stay in her own home and ease poor Jesper out. Louis is a perfectly nice man. If you want to have affairs, have them. But don't leave home.'

'He's dull,' says Scarlet.

'It's not a crime to be dull,' says Beverley. 'There are worse faults.'

'And anyway,' says Scarlet, 'we aren't legally married so he isn't my husband.'

'Another cop-out,' says Beverley. 'If you had married him you would be safer from Lola. That's how it works. Other women take a partnership as an invitation to mess things up, a marriage as a warning not to. Women without men are unhappy.'

Scarlet bites back the retort that Beverley was one to speak: she has married three men and buried three, and seems happy enough. Bad enough to have a sister who is a mad lesbian feminist, a mother who is a mad Jesus freak, and now a grandmother who, having started out as a mad Marxist, has ended up as a prim moralist. Why couldn't she, Scarlet, have come from a normal family? Perhaps she was switched at birth? The more she thinks about it the more likely it seems.

'Extremes, like murder, run in the family,' says Beverley. 'The whole lot of you have a talent for acting out. Cynara became a feminist to annoy Alice, Alice took to religion because I was a Marxist. You, Scarlet, have reacted by becoming the most non-aligned person I have ever met. Perhaps it's an advance. I dread the moment when Lola discovers the joys of alignment, joins animal rights and starts planting bombs.'

Murder in the family

'Extremes, like murder, run in the family.'

Scarlet had been startled when Beverley said this, but it came as no surprise to Lola, who already took pleasure in the fantasy that her great-grandmother was a serial husband killer. When asked by Scarlet to take over the mercy food-runs to Robinsdale, Lola had looked astonished and responded, 'On my own? No thanks. I'd be shit scared.'

Scarlet could point out as much as she liked that by the time any woman reached eighty the odds were that most of her husbands would have gone before to the grave, but reason cut no ice with Lola. The price Lola demanded if she was to fetch and carry for Beverley on her sickbed was to be allowed to drive Scarlet's little Toyota Prius, green as green can be. She was a good driver – Lola was good at most things, other than getting on with her family – the problem was that she was too young to have a licence. Scarlet reckoned it would be okay, Louis was determined that it was not. Louis won, Scarlet capitulated and Lola sulked. Scarcely a day had gone by since Lola had moved in that was not marked by some such emotional and unnecessary storm. Occasionally Louis won, as on this occasion, sometimes Scarlet, but mostly Lola.

The deaths of Beverley's husbands were certainly dramatic, though hardly suspicious. The first to die was Winter Max, in 1967.

He was a Marxist believer with private means, who disappeared on his way to join Che Guevara in the jungle and was presumed dead. The second was Harry Batcombe, the Architect Laureate, who took his own life after being involved in a homosexual scandal. The third was Marcus Fletzner, a right-wing journalist and notable drunk, who fell beneath an Underground train. Foul play was not suspected. The feeling in the family has always been that Beverley was pleased enough to see them go, but that Lola went too far in supposing murder. Beverley did not like being bored, that was all; the men she chose were at least seldom boring, and not likely to die peacefully in their beds in the first place.

'The dysfunctional fly to each other like iron filings to a magnet,' Louis once said to Scarlet. 'But better a family like yours than one like mine.'

He made the assumption that his own family was functional, which always rather puzzled Scarlet. Louis did a great deal to annoy his mother – taking up with Scarlet being one of his major departures from good form.

Or perhaps 'murder in the family' merely refers to Cynara's history of terminations? Is that how Beverley sees them? Cynara was always sexually active, while at the same time renouncing contraception as part of the male plot against women. Perhaps Lola is a single child because, of all her succession of pregnancies, Lola was the only female conception? The others being male and therefore not wanted in the world? Single-handed Cynara fought back against the beliefs of China, where the girls are aborted and the boys are treasured. She wanted to right the balance. She was a trained barrister, specialising in gender law. She liked justice.

'Tell me more about murder running in the family,' says Scarlet, and instantly wishes she hadn't.

The chutney, the coffee, the potato and tomato mash – just add water and stir – are now stacked in the cupboards. The mixed mushrooms with red wine polenta, which is to be Beverley's lunch, is gently heating in the slow oven of the Aga – which is a six-oven model. If Scarlet sits down and listens, who is to say whether she will get to Costa's even by teatime? She will need to check through what Lola's packed, and make sure she hasn't nicked the white transparent top she bought from Brown's in South Molton Street for £105 (it is Jackson's favourite) and confirm that Lola has actually taken her suitcase and left Nopasaran, as she promised. She can see that leaving Lola alone with Louis is not necessarily sensible, as Beverley points out, he not being a blood relative.

Moreover, Scarlet is seized by another anxiety. Supposing Jackson doesn't get the text, turns up at lunchtime, thinks she has decided to go back to Louis, and changes his mind? Supposing he's just another prize dangled before her by fate, only to be cruelly snatched away? Like the job on the *New York Times* op-ed pages that was once so nearly hers, that would have changed her life. Only someone else got the job, even younger and cheaper than she was. Like Eddie, the wealthy sports journalist, the one before Louis, who was so exciting and moved in with her and was an ex-alcoholic and ex-gambler, a frequenter of multiple-Anons, only it turned out he wasn't any kind of ex of anything after all. He broke the place up when she said she wasn't going to lend him any more money. He left shouting and screaming and stormed back to his previous girlfriend, a half-bottle of Scarlet's best whiskey under his arm. He said it was all Scarlet's fault for starting him off drinking again.

After Eddie, Louis had seemed a model of stability and genuine concern. It seemed so difficult to get everything into one person. She hadn't realised how trying 'dull' could be. Now, thinking of

Jackson, she has a strange airy feeling of exhilaration, fear, lust and anticipation mixed, that starts between her thighs and moves upwards to part her lips; it's a kind of psychic breathlessness.

But it is too late. The definitive question has been asked. Scarlet is going to have to hang around to listen to the answer and Beverley will make a meal of it. As she does.

'If you can bring yourself to sit down for a second, I will tell you. I swore I never would but circumstances require it. You're not the only one with secrets.'

So Scarlet sits and finally listens to Beverley's story, out of family courtesy, but she would much rather live in the here and now. She does not really want to know about the past.

A break for lunch

Come to think about it, your writer doesn't really want to think about the past either: she can see that her current view of the next pages is all too likely to suddenly shift and change; and so, moved by the thought of mixed mushrooms with red wine polenta, which she too happens to have in her freezer, she is now going to break for lunch. Writing makes you very hungry: it's a matter of the more you put out the more you need to take in. And food can steady you, whirled around as you so often are by a sudden flurry of possible alternatives. I am going to put on a lot of weight, I can see, between now and the end of the book, glued to my desk as I choose to be, instead of taking healthy exercise.

I go upstairs and wait for the microwave to do its work. It's bright up here too, and the trees in the front garden are heavy with snow: the noise of traffic is muffled. Technology would soon have done all those servants out of a job anyway. Hot water comes out of taps, warmth radiates from the central heating, the Hoover takes the place of the brush, the dishwasher washes the dishes, the washing and drying machines do the laundry. The world moves on, and we must do our best to keep up.

We still labour and toil but at less physically exhausting things. I can write novels in the basement while the household more or less looks after itself. Mind you, nothing ever runs quite smoothly. There have lately been signs of poltergeist activity upstairs too, not just auditory hallucinations, but disappearances. Just little annoying things.

The other day Rex said, 'Where's the key to the back door?' and I said, 'It's still in the lock, where you left it,' because I'd just seen it there a minute ago. He went to look. It wasn't there. We searched high and low and finally used the spare. The next day I found the missing key tucked away between two stacked cans of tomato purée on the shelf by the cooker. How could it possibly have got there other than by some agency wanting to make a minor nuisance of itself? Because we couldn't explain it – other than that I was deranged, which I was not prepared to accept – we forgot it. Just one of those things. Like the letter from the bank, which disappears from the kitchen table and is found later in a room where nobody's been – the Coronation mug which falls and breaks, and must have leapt by itself from the hook it hung upon, because neither hook nor handle seems to have broken – that kind of thing. Yet there the pieces of china lie, and if you catch your finger on a sharp edge it will bleed. Nothing like blood for proving a reality.

Okay. Overlook these random events. There are such things as joint delusion and who wants to doubt the immutable laws of physics? Lunch was fine. But the gas bill was in and a letter from Inland Revenue. It will be baked potatoes and cheese from now on, and from Lidl's at that. No more of this Waitrose frozen-food nonsense. My agent has gone to New York to see Wagner's *Götterdämmerung*. It feels fitting. I fear I will end up like Veronica Lake, my childhood idol, who died alone and in penury. Or the prolific Walter Scott, who died worrying about money, looking for another plot to the bitter end. He had his family to support.

It is thankfully that I return to Scarlet and her grandmother and the house in Highgate. I sit down on my typing chair and bring the laptop back to life. But escape into the alternative universe is not so easy today. I don't think this basement room can be described as technically or formally haunted, any more than is upstairs. Let me just say it seems rather more busy than usual down here; the air, which ought to be still, is overactive.

Where my typing table stands once stood a big solid pine table round which the staff would sit for meals. 'Mavis, Mavis, where be you too?' a voice calls, or perhaps it doesn't, how can I tell? Because you hear it in your head doesn't mean it has been said. Novelists have overactive imaginations: it's why they make bad drivers. They're always envisioning some scenario of disaster just over the brow of the hill.

I reckon Mavis is the tweeny, one down from the kitchen maid, two down from the cook. Life in the basement is strictly stratified. She's setting up for tea in the staff dining room and I can't see her but I can feel her. It's okay. She's just there, left over from the past when the generations got swept up. She's companionable. A flapping sound. That's her shaking out the tablecloth: she hasn't bothered to use the crumb tray, so the crumbs are scattered all over the floor. We'll get mice at this rate. Cook will be furious if she sees. Mavis doesn't want me to pay her any attention, she just wants to get on. Like Lola, she's sixteen, going on seventeen, but without the luxury of Lola's discontent, or Lola's postmodern anorexia. She has long, rather greasy dark hair – hot water is not easily come by, it is fifty years before the invention of detergent, and instead of each hair being coated with glossy conditioner it is coated with a soap scum which thickens it but makes it dull. Adding vinegar to the rinsing water helps but never enough. Mavis has a rounded figure, nice innocent brown eyes and a plump, still unformed face. I don't know how I know what she looks like, but I do. I see her as one would see an old photograph, mottled by age.

Like Mavis, I too must get on with my work. Is it cold in here? Yes, it is. But how can that be? The central heating is blasting away: the heating engineer who last worked on the house got his figures wrong so the large rooms are underheated and the small rooms too hot. I know that ghosts and cold chills are associated, but I reckon that warmth too is suffering a time slip at the moment. If Mavis shivers so do I, that's all. Or even more plausibly, since there are now a few inches of snow just the other side of a thin sheet of glass, it's not surprising that I am cold. I put on the mittens with the coloured-wool bobbles on the knuckles, which Lizzie gave me for Christmas, to keep my fingers thawed. Lizzie lives hereabouts; she is a friend, teaches the flute and keeps sheep, and I watch the bright bobbles fly as my fingers speed up. Lizzie has been down here to the basement to see my new office and assures me the house isn't haunted. It has a perfectly nice atmosphere. She speaks as one who has experience of these things.

The first murder: a set piece

'You never told me,' says Scarlet.

She can see the Alexandra Palace mast between the trees. She feels it is probably transmitting invisible rays of evil, jagged and ill-intentioned, cursing her designs for the future. Why did she have to find this out now? She feels wronged: and frightened that her resolution might drain away. In Japan, if a criminal act occurs in the family, the guilt and shame remain for generations. Even two hundred years later you sometimes can't get a job. Criminality ran in the blood, like Korean ancestry. She had researched an article on it, so she knew. Her great-grandfather had murdered her great-grandmother back in 1930-something-or-other, and no one had seen fit to mention it, but that didn't mean it hadn't happened.

'Well, no,' says Beverley. 'I wasn't going to tell you, not if you hadn't mentioned love at first sight. It's the kind of thing that's better forgotten. Then Walter my father went and shot himself. Well, men often do, in these circumstances. They've killed the thing they love. Though I don't suppose Louis has a gun. But do remember that murder, as well as victimhood, runs in your veins. I'd be more worried for this Jackson, if he ever runs out on you. But not to worry. I've managed to get through life without being accused of murder, as have all you young ones. Alice would be shocked at the very thought. Beryl Bainbridge had a near miss from your sister Cynara some years back, mind you. Asked for her definition of "woman", Beryl replied, "Why, a person who has babies," and Cynara ran on to the platform and attacked her. Mind you, if you count abortion as murder, Cynara is certainly a dab hand at it.'

'That's absurd,' says Scarlet, who has had two terminations herself.

'But we won't worry about that too much,' says Beverley. 'According to Maori mythology the ghosts of aborted or miscarried babies stay around to look after the family, so you two younger girls are well protected. They're probably a match for the kehua.'

'The kehua?'

'They flap around on the edges of one's vision if the proper rituals aren't carried out after death,' says Beverley. 'They can't get home. They live in trees. They attach themselves to the living, and do what they can to bring them back to the pa, the home village. Kehua can be a real drag. Mind you, we were only pakeha, white people, and I left New Zealand decades back. I can hardly have brought any with me. Me and mine are no use to them.'

Beverley is making it all up, thinks Scarlet. Her father wasn't even called Walter, he was a doctor called Arthur and there was a mother called Rita. This Kitchie has never been mentioned. And even if it is true, this is not Japan, and though it may be news to me, it is extremely old news. An event that happened seventy years ago can hardly be relevant today. As for kehua, ghostly flappings about the head, that way madness lies.

It was true that Scarlet herself occasionally suffered from zigzag flashes out of the corner of the eye, and had even complained about these visual disturbances to the doctor, but he had said it was a form of visual migraine and prescribed aspirin, which always worked.

All the same the ground seemed to have slightly shifted beneath her feet, as if she were getting out of bed after an earthquake she'd slept through, and found the floor was sloping. Last night she seemed to remember she'd picked up the bread knife and said to Louis, 'I'll kill you.' He had taken the knife from her hand because of course she had no intention of using it, and she had let it go easily enough before anyone hurt themselves. Though she had managed to nick his wrist and blood had flowed. Had she known then what she knew now, that murderous genes ran in the blood, would she have refrained from picking up the knife in the first place, or would it all have been worse? Apparently, when the knife goes in through living flesh it meets less resistance than one supposes, which is why knife wounds so often end up fatal.

'One-two, one-two, down the dusty road,' says Beverley. 'He who fights and runs away, lives to fight another day. Running away is so often the best answer, second best to doing nothing. But that's enough of that.'

'Running away' was all very well as a phrase, and Scarlet could see it was fine in theory, but then if you did there would be no home. It was like a piece of careful knitting, which you could undo by pulling a single thread and then suddenly it was just a pile of wool and no garment at all. She could change her mind now and no one would know a thing – except Lola, of course, waiting in the wings, packing Scarlet's runaway case even now, egging her on to leave, and if she, Scarlet, didn't follow through, Lola would despise her for her lack of purpose, her dithering and flapping, and rightly so. The coward's course was to do nothing, and that was the path Beverley was trying to make her follow. Well, she would not. She was young and brave: she would throw herself into the future as Lola was throwing herself into Haiti; would not run like Cynara from Jesper the frying pan into D'Dora the fire; or like her mother into the arms of Jesus. She was doing something far less drastic: holing up with Jackson for a little but still very definitely her own person. If she stayed with Louis she would end up a mother in Nopasaran and that would be the end of personhood, the end of her. She was already late with her life: she was nearly thirty and what had she achieved?

'Poor Cynara,' her grandmother was saying. 'She got all that feminist stuff so wrong. It was just a capitalist plot to lower male wages by getting women into the workforce. Which happened, and now look. We told them so but they dismissed us as male stooges. Now the rich are richer and the poor are poorer and no one can do anything about it. I don't suppose before you rush off to your lover you have time to wash my hair?'

'Oh Gran,' protests Scarlet, 'I really do have to rush. And it is such an important day for me. Doesn't your carer come this afternoon?'

'I've run out of shampoo,' says Beverley. 'And if she pops out to get some she'll bring back some kind of harsh stuff like oven cleaner because anything else is a wicked waste. You've no idea what these people are like.'

Scarlet compromises by staying to make her grandmother a cup of coffee. Beverley likes it hideously strong, with brandy in it. Scarlet does not mention that she has a couple of Alterna White Truffle shampoo sachets in her Chloé tote bag, being a wash-every-day person, and you never know quite where you'll end up. Scarlet bought the bag mostly to annoy her sister, who is affronted by needless extravagance. And she certainly doesn't want her grandmother asking how much the shampoo costs. As it is she has to peel the price labels from the Waitrose shopping before she brings it into the house, in case her grandmother demands she takes it all back and goes to Lidl's.

Jackson too is in a rush

Jackson Knight is an ex-child actor who starred in the 1980s remake of the children's film *Danny in the Orchard* and later as the teen hero of the *Vampire Rising* trilogy, and as a well-endowed young man in a number of unspectacular art movies. He hovers on the edges of B- and C-list celebrity and has made the columns of the *Daily Mail*, by virtue of appearing from time to time as an A-list squeeze. He has recently all but rescued his career by accepting the part of Hudson, the charming Scottish butler of admirable rectitude, in the big-budget film remake of the old TV show *Upstairs, Downstairs*. A drunken altercation in a pub with its director had left him without the part, or indeed an agent.

'Sorry, Jackson, you just don't get it.' Mike Bronstein had got through to him the next day. 'Sure, he's a TV director and never made a movie, but the Internet is the future, TV is the present and movies are maybe dead. And in my book – sorry mate – so are you. There is such a thing as *politesse*.'

Jackson then told Bronstein what he thought of him. Bronstein and his exploiting like were the scum of the earth. Twenty per cent in return for a few phone calls – what a shit way to earn a living. Bronstein told Jackson he was yesterday's man and had better get himself a job as a taxi driver. He wouldn't find another agent, unless he turned himself into a gay icon, which was a good idea. Heterosexuality was so last week, my dear. Hadn't Jackson realised? Probably not, being one sandwich short of a lunch box, one nostril short of a snort. He, Bronstein was shutting up shop, going home to look after his grandchildren. He was needed at home: he couldn't keep them in nannies any more. The film business was finished. So was he. He had busted a gut to get Jackson the part; as it turned out too many people had been looking for an excuse to get rid of him. Jackson had played right into their hands.

Jackson and Bronstein had ended up weeping on each other's shoulders in Groucho's, but that still didn't mean Jackson had an agent. Business would pick up again; it always did. An actor's life was full of ups and downs. It wasn't as if he was a girl and finished at thirty-seven. There was no point in telling Scarlet: he could scarcely tell himself. Losing the part meant he was in deep shit financially, which was astonishing, and for the first time in his life left him actually wondering how to pay the rent. He rented because he didn't want his ex-wife, or any future wife, to grab the home. Now he regretted it, though a man like him had to be careful; women flocked, but often for all the wrong reasons.

Scarlet earned good money and there was obviously more in the background – he had once filmed in Nopasaran – and the fact was not far from his mind when she called that morning and he said yes so promptly. But only of course one of the reasons. He liked her. He liked the way she had big breasts confined within a narrow frame. She made him feel he had a brain, that he was more than a sex toy. He wanted to move up the scale, intellectually and artistically. Of course she could move in. It would make the gossip columns. It would be easy enough to dump his latest, a small-time lingerie model of undoubted looks, serpentine body and sexual talent, with a gift for wrapping her long legs around a man's neck and practically knotting them. But she had no conversation, let his washing build up; he owed the dry cleaners money. That very morning some old biddy who didn't know who he was had all but refused to return his Diesel jeans from the other side of the counter. The jeans could be washed, apparently, but he didn't understand the instructions. What did a triangle with a line through it mean?

And that's the kind of person Jackson is, and if Scarlet wasn't so bored by Louis and fed up with Nopasaran she would not have been taken in by him for one minute. More, Jackson is both charming and needy, and has his sexual uncertainties. Bronstein is too old to understand. Since the world stopped seeing itself as being composed of two genders, but rather of a multiplicity of them – so far as desire if not procreation is concerned – the problem of who's good, who's bad; who's the hero and who's the villain, has become confused. And the sexually ambiguous, like the dysfunctional, cling together. You're confused, I'm confused – wow! You don't even have to touch if you're on the Internet – you're just in each other's company.

I the writer am not condemning Jackson. If a lingerie model slithers down from the tree of knowledge and twines her legs around his neck, why on earth should he resist? And if she brings a friend with her, why not? Who's talking about love round here? They may soon be talking about money because so far as they know and the world knows Jackson is loaded.

Now since Scarlet will be turning up with her suitcase, he quickly changes the sheets on the bed, tidies up a little, checks the sofa for stray panties – that happened to him once: one night's girl had found last night's scraps of torn lace, but had only laughed and asked what was the matter with the bed, though Jackson preferred the sofa; the bed smacked of permanence. And he would have to get down to his ex-wife's house in Battersea that morning to collect his driving licence, because if Scarlet was moving in it might be difficult for him to get out without her finding out where he was going, and he had to present the licence at the police station before the end of the week.

Beverley talks about her will

Beverley drinks her coffee; Scarlet, fearful always for her complexion, sips hot water.

'I really do appreciate your company, Scarlet,' says Beverley. 'Especially in the circumstances. I'd alter my will to give you even more money but I fear this new scoundrel actor of yours would only get his hands on it. It would end up with his first family. It always does.'

'He hasn't got a first family,' says Scarlet. 'And he isn't a scoundrel.'

'Of course he has a first family,' says Beverley. 'They always do. Sometimes it's in the past and sometimes it isn't. But it's always the way. And the brightest girls end up with the worst men. Look at me. Bright girls long to be absolved of their cleverness. Louis would run through your inheritance but at least he'd put it into bricks and mortar. That mad house of his. I'm assuming you have it in joint names? You're a fool if you haven't. Now Jesper's gone, anything I leave Cynara will end up with D'Dora and the Lesbian and Gay Sorority. But perhaps that's better than it all ending up with Lola, which would happen if Jesper was still around. Do be careful of Lola. She has endearing qualities, but many of the more undesirable family traits.'

'Like murdering people?' asks Scarlet, thinking she is joking, but

Beverley just shrugs her shoulders and says, 'More people do that than you would ever imagine.'

Beverley's knee is hurting. She thinks perhaps the wound, not yet quite healed, has been infected with MRSA after all. Everyone who has recently been in hospital has become a little nervous of these things. It's rather like the days of her youth back again – when people were reluctant to go to hospital in case they never came out: go in feet first, come out feet first. There was no MRSA then, she reflects, but there were no knee replacements either. Nothing is for nothing. Scarlet, as Beverley notices, in spite of her earlier ill-concealed longing to get away *now, now, now*, seems rather reluctant to do so. Perhaps some of the things Beverley has been saying are sinking in? It's unlikely, she knows. Wisdom has to be reborn with each generation.

'Gran,' Scarlet is saying, 'I have no choice. Last night Louis hit me. You must see that is unforgivable?'

'Who won't forgive it?' asks Beverley. Her mouth sets in a grim straight line, which it sometimes did, for no apparent reason, and which Scarlet, even as a small child, when the mouth was plumper and fuller than it is today, always wished it wouldn't. 'You? Or some mass consensus driven by your sister and her lesbian friends?'

'This is nothing to do with Cynara,' says Scarlet. 'And why do you have to say lesbian friends, why can't you just say friends? Men shouldn't hit women; I hope at least we agree on that. I have no intention of ending up a battered wife. If a man hits you it is practically your duty to leave.'

'I see no sign of injury,' says Beverley. 'Perhaps you had been drinking? Most domestic rows are fuelled by alcohol, and those involved regularly deny it. Too much champagne at MetaFashion for Louis? For you, perhaps too many vodka martinis – or whatever it is you drink these days – with your lover earlier on?'

MetaFashion is the business Louis runs and partly owns, designing and shipping sets for fashion shows the world over. A lot of accurate logistics and camp tension goes with the job. Everyone's gay except Louis.

'I was not drunk,' says Scarlet, glossing over the detail of the vodka martinis, which Beverley had not got exactly right. 'Louis had been drinking champagne with his partner D'Kath, because they'd finally got *Icehouse Vamp* out of the workshops and off to Paris.'

'I can't follow you,' says Beverley. 'But at least you take an interest in his work.'

'I don't just take an interest,' says Scarlet. 'I give him most of his ideas.'

'I know, I know,' says Beverley. 'And Louis makes you live in this dreadful house way out in the suburbs, that is to say, practically round the corner from me, which is falling to bits and on which he spends a fortune. Wealth trickles away. But it is not an awful house; people from all over come to admire it and you are a very, very lucky girl to have ended up in it.'

Scarlet acknowledges that she was glad enough to invite people to the party in Nopasaran's concrete garden after her and Louis' non-wedding, there being no other venue like it in all London. A great place for parties, and she knew at the time it would stand her in good stead if she ever wanted to move over into *Interiors* or *World of Design*.

'I've had six years of it,' says Scarlet. 'That's a long enough shift. And whose side are you on anyway?'

'Louis's,' says Beverley smartly.

Her knee is aching. Her hair feels horribly greasy. She thinks at any moment she is likely to die and she would at least like to lie in her coffin with her hair at its best. Or do undertakers do it for you anyway? As one gets older it is the kind of thing one wants to know.

'Just find me the painkillers before you leave, Scarlet. And do remember Louis is real, not a figment of your imagination. He can do real things, turn nasty, change locks, call lawyers, that kind of thing. An abandoned man feels you've upset the natural order of things and vengeance is in order. Failing that, he will certainly do what he can to replace you. He will have no trouble. Women prettier and younger than you will be queuing up at the faintest whiff of a free man.'

'They're welcome,' says Scarlet, and looks for the painkillers.

Beverley belonged to another age, in which man was the breadwinner and woman was the chattel, and the man used her jealousy as a weapon against her. 'If you don't oblige I'll soon find someone who does.' It was demeaning. Changing from one man to another was not the big deal it once was. The Walter and Kitchie story would hardly happen now, the human race evolved, got better, more self-aware. At any rate the middle classes did. Louis' anger at rejection could hardly make the heavens fall in, invoke hammer blows and lightning strikes from Thor, or whoever it was up there who punished you. All the same, she would be careful and not tell Louis about Campion Tower; he could have her solicitor's address. Partners switched all the time, everybody did it and everyone accepted it and tried to be civilised, and hearts got broken but soon mended. It wasn't as if she and Louis had children he could put in the back of the car and fix a pipe up from the exhaust with the engine running.

'I think you've got Louis all wrong,' says Scarlet.

'No one ever knows what a man is really like,' says Beverley. 'Did

Kitchie know what my father was like? I'd say probably not. All that red, sticky stuff when she annoyed him, tried to leave him. I wish I could remember the colour of my shoes, but I daresay I've blanked out the memory, and left only my knees going one-two, one-two, all the way to Rita. The blood probably didn't get up more than an inch or so: it depends what sort of thrashing around my poor mother did. I remember the blue and white checks of my dress, and the red streaks turning black as I ran. I've never been able to wear check gingham since. Odd.'

'You should get over that if you can,' says Scarlet, fighting back, cool as can be. 'Check gingham suits any age. It's lovely stuff. There was quite a fashion for it in the thirties, when most children's clothes were made at home. I wrote a piece about it once. I daresay Kitchie ran the dress up for you.'

'I daresay she did,' says Beverley. 'But one way and another it ended up quite spoiled. And do make sure Lola isn't there when Louis gets home. She's quite capable of saying one thing and doing another. She lives in so relative a universe she lacks even the concept of lie.'

'Gran,' says Scarlet. 'To Lola, Louis is Methuselah. To Louis, Lola is a cultureless baby. Let's stop fighting. If that story is true and not just you trying to frighten me into staying home, then it's terrible and I'm really sorry.'

'It is true,' says Beverley.

'And not just you wanting me to start having babies and add to the number of your descendants?'

'The way things are going,' says Beverley, dismally, 'certainly not. Better the line dies out.'

'I have no intention of breeding. There is more to life than passing it on.'

'You could have fooled me,' says her grandmother, so sadly Scarlet relents and says, 'Tell you what, I have some shampoo in my bag. I'll stay and do your hair if you like.'

'I thought you were meant to be running to your lover.'

'I've already texted him to say I'll be late,' says Scarlet.

Beverley's golden age, when you come to think of it, is probably as much now as it ever has been, enjoying the peace and tranquillity of Robinsdale, her family helping her out, elderly suitors thinking of visiting, private health insurance and behind her a life if not well spent, certainly lived to the full. The only thing Beverley lacks is youth, though some may see that as overwhelmingly important. We should not grudge her good fortune; she has had a hard time getting here. Three husbands down and possibly still one to go.

Night in the basement

It's cosy down here. Supper upstairs is over – a rerun of yesterday's, when we had people round. Couscous, minced beef and vegetables stirred together and reheated in the wok, and the remains of the fruit salad, by now slightly fermented and the better for it. Often I give up writing for the day at suppertime – but it's nine now and I'm still in writing mode so I thought I'd spend another couple of hours at the computer checking over that last conversation between Beverley and Scarlet and the description of Nopasaran. Years ago I stayed in a Wells Coates house in Yeoman's Row in Kensington and I've never forgotten it. Wells himself even once called by. Architects tend to live anywhere but in houses they have themselves designed. He was a very good-looking man. The house was so chic and so uncomfortable, and its inhabitants so truly good to me when I ran away from my own home that I still remember them with gratitude. I got a dreadful cold in the nose: 'Weeping with the nose, not with the eyes', a psychoanalyst later said, in the days when analysis was all the fashion. 'Not surprising. Always the shift downwards.'

I may have Nopasaran inhabited now by entirely fictional folk, but someone obsessive like Louis was bound to end up buying it, someone smart like Scarlet bound to share it with him. The flapping kehua are worldwide; the inheritance of trauma past, English version, follows me from generations back. The central heating is purring away. The boiler switches itself on and off. Too good to last.

There is a slight rustling noise from inside the storage cupboards that have been fitted sometime in the last fifty years, where once a kitchen grate used to be. A mouse? I open the cupboard. No movement. Just shelves and spare china and glasses put there for safety, but no apparent origin for the rustling, and now the sound of metal on metal, which might be there and might not. It's easy to imagine things. I shut the door again, quietly. I know what it is. It's the kitchen maid again. It's Mavis. She's clearing the grate of ashes and laying the fire – scraps of paper from Mrs Bennett's waste-paper basket upstairs, kindling chopped by Teaser the outside boy, and small coal. The chimney will still be warm, the kindling and coal will have dried out nicely, and the house is on a hill so this fire always draws nicely. She'll have no trouble lighting it.

I hear Mavis sigh: she must be tired but she likes to do things properly, even this late. The Bible tells her to be diligent. She is. I can't see her today, but I'm in her mind. She will be up at five to put a match to the fire, and lay for the staff breakfast at six. Cook will be down at five-thirty. Mr Bennett will breakfast at eight, before going off in the gig down the steep hill to Loddenham Station to catch the train to Salisbury, where he practises law. Cristobel Bennett likes her breakfast in bed. The three little boys, Ernest, William and Thomas, and their nanny, will have trays brought up to the nursery. Thomas is the one who survived the war to inherit the house. I don't know what Nanny's name is, for some reason. Perhaps she's never been granted one? Just generic 'Nanny'.

Silence now from the cupboard. Light, young footsteps across the floor in front of me, a puff of air as the lamp is extinguished and a slight smell of acrid oil smoke and its gone. All so quickly it might not have happened at all. I'm not frightened. Not a haunting, just a timeslip.

The Bennetts imposed their stamp upon Yatt House and it has not yet got out of the habit of following the routine it kept for so many years. We of the future are the ghosts, the shadowy people who will follow on. All the same I think I'll go upstairs now.

Now, about Louis

Another day, another chapter. Some novels, as I say, charge along like a river in flood; others spread sideways and lie calmly over neighbouring fields. This is one of the latter. I'll get Scarlet to Jackson eventually, but not yet.

Louis is very good-looking, in a peaceful, etiolated, fold-your-clothes-before-bed kind of way. He is lean and aesthetic-looking and a great relief to Scarlet after roaring, fleshy, ranting Eddie. Louis went to public school, feels at home in those clubs where the Princes go, has friends amongst the titled and can take you anywhere. Scarlet rather likes that.

Louis had worked with Scarlet as a colleague for a time, while she was doing PR for MetaFashion. Louis admired her for her energy, her determination, her general good cheer, her competence, her ability to make light of difficulties and later, her ability to make him feel good while making love. It came automatically to her and if she was usually thinking about something else he had no idea of it.

Louis' mother is called Annabel: she is a lone parent with genteel aspirations and family money. See him as the child an Anita Brookner heroine might have had, supposing an acceptable suitor had turned up to woo her and then she'd turned him away, although pregnant, on moral grounds. Perhaps he was already married and she didn't wish to upset his wife. However it happened, Annabel, being not short of family means, was able to send Louis to a good public school where he was only moderately unhappy. He was too arty and unfunny for general acceptance, but he was respected for putting on house plays. His nickname was 'Poofter', a soubriquet spoken matter-of-factly, without any particular animosity. He had a gift for piano playing, for maths, and theatrical skills. It was generally assumed that one day he would be an old boy of whom the school would be proud.

The male art teacher seduced him early, but by sixteen he had developed a crush on the Matron's daughter, fifteen-year-old Samantha, which was reciprocated, and they were caught by Matron *in flagrante* in the laundry room. His nickname changed overnight to 'Sexbomb', which Louis saw as progress, but too late to make him any happier; especially since, though not expelled, he was asked to leave at the end of term.

His mother was horrified. What would she tell her friends? Samantha was sent to a boarding school elsewhere. Stuart the art teacher, feeling betrayed by Louis, committed suicide, hanging himself from a pulley hook in the Art Block. Louis found him. Louis did not seek Samantha out after the fuss had died down.

Louis still occasionally has dreams so bad he wakes up making that choking sound people make when they are trying to scream but are asleep. And Scarlet will wake up too and try to comfort him.

'You have post-traumatic stress disorder,' says Scarlet. 'From that dreadful time at your toff school.'

'That's absurd,' he says. 'It's indigestion. You gave me mozzarella cheese for dinner.' He wants to be unmoved by emotion but is greatly prey to it. It affects him physically and his digestion is delicate. Her digestion is tough as old boots.

Louis wishes he had never told Scarlet about the art teacher, let alone about Samantha. He feels the shared knowledge gives her mastery over him. It's dangerous: sometimes he even fantasises she's a witch who steals fingernail clippings and uses them to cast a spell against their owner. However, the confidence was freely given, in the heat of his first love for Scarlet.

Scarlet washes Beverley's hair

Scarlet helps her grandmother to the bathroom. Beverley's hair has thinned against the scalp, rather horribly. But it will be the easier to wash and will dry quickly. Scarlet thinks of Jackson's fingers through her own luxuriant hair, and rejoices. He will grab it with a strong hand and force her mouth down on his cock and keep it there until she has to gasp for breath. She likes that. It is not how Louis behaves at all. Just the thought of it makes her falter and catch her breath.

'Are you not feeling well?' asks Beverley.

Beverley realises she won't be able to bend her head down into the basin. The blood rushes to her head these days and she gets a touch of visual migraine, lightning zigzags round the edges of the cornea. Scarlet, who is also sometimes affected, as is Cynara, but not Alice, swears aspirin cures it, but aspirin thins the blood, which means if you have a stroke you can get excessive bleeding in the brain, which can kill you even if the aneurysm doesn't, so thank you very much, Scarlet, but no thank-you.

So leaning over the basin is out, and letting the back of your head rest on the edge of the basin when sitting backwards can also cause a stroke, so she will just have to undress and stand in the bath while Scarlet uses the shower head. Beverley hates the feeling of her hair when it's greasy, when what's left of it lies flat and thinly against her head. When it's freshly washed it can fluff up and the thinness is not so apparent. She hates being old. You can tell yourself as much as you like that everyone takes shifts at being young, and the thought that all will come to it in the end – if they're lucky – is some consolation but not enough.

'I just felt a bit dizzy,' says Scarlet. 'But I'm okay.'

'Perhaps you're pregnant?'

'In your dreams,' says Scarlet. 'No, I expect I'm adjusting to having a murder in the family.'

'Don't worry about it,' says Beverley. 'It was a long time ago and you young people have so much to think about. Leaving home. Running away. Breaking up. Global warming. Credit Crunch. All these terms you throw around to make light work of complicated things. You all talk and think so fast, trying to pigeon-hole everything and get back to the next e-mail and make sure the bed of your choice is waiting.'

Scarlet helps Beverley take her clothes off. Beverley still has limited movement in the knee, and complains it is aching. There is the ongoing fear that she has contracted MRSA. But she hurts in her mind more than in her body. Once she had a body to be proud of. Now it takes an act of will not to mind being seen naked.

Scarlet feels an unaccustomed tenderness at the sight of her grandmother's body; it is so frail and yet so tough. The skin that wraps it is a couple of sizes too large, yet has to somehow fit, so it solves the problem by wrinkling. Yet the body still works well enough just to move the brain about from place to place, which is its only real purpose once the possibility of procreation is gone. Scarlet finds there are tears in her eyes. One day, she thinks, she will make her peace with her mother too, but not just yet.

'Bless you, Gran,' she says, without quite knowing why and Beverley looks surprised and touched. Sprays of water from the shower head bounce off her body; water streams down from her now wet head of hair and the sun breaks through a cloud and a shaft of sunlight illuminates Beverley in a golden cloak, which lasts a moment and then is gone again. And Scarlet thinks of the sequence in the old film *She*, when She Who Must Be Obeyed stands once too often in the path of the rolling, rumbling wheel of immortal flame, and withers into dust. If in the wavery translucence a minor kehua slips from Beverley to cling to Scarlet's T-shirt it would hardly be surprising; these creatures get about.

Beverley feels solid enough when Scarlet dabs her dry.

'Thank you for staying to do that,' she says when it is done and she is dried and dusted again. She feels unburdened and almost young again, as if with dirt and grease removed, her body and mind can get going again.

Louis thinks it over too

While Beverley is having her hair washed Louis is wondering whether he should call Scarlet and apologise. He said things the night before that he now regrets. He cannot remember the detail of what was said – which Scarlet can – but he remembers it as unpleasant and uncivilised. He had to take a knife from her, though she let it go easily enough.

His mother had murmured when she first met Scarlet, 'Isn't she rather hormonal for you, darling?' and a little later, 'She's not very good on classical music, darling, is she?' and then, 'Darling, she's a real sweetheart, but she's not going to feel very much at home amongst the architects, is she?' And once, 'If you set the dear girl down halfway between a kidney-shaped dressing table with frills and a William Morris chest, she'd gravitate towards the dressing table.'

But once she had accepted the permanence of the relationship, Annabel was sweetness personified – she just kept away. Louis has found Scarlet and lost a mother, and believes it is well worth it, but he wants Scarlet to acknowledge the fact. He wants her to admit that living in Nopasaran – he is not blind to its defects – is worth it. He wants her to assure him that her occasional disappearances – less and less occasional – are because something has indeed come up at the office. He wants her not to name-drop in company. He wants her to have his children. He wants her not to have asked Lola to stay, because although he is over it now, Lola went through a stage when he could not help noticing the sexy appeal of her upper lip and the body language she used when Scarlet was not looking. Lola would cross and uncross her legs like Sharon Stone in *Basic Instinct*, as she leant back on her chair wearing Scarlet's flimsiest tops with no bra and thrust her small tits at him. And that was when she was thirteen. Now she is three years older she behaves better, is almost plain, and more ruled by her brain than her body.

Student friends took Louis to a clairvoyante when he was young. 'A black cloud hangs over you. I can't go there, it is too frightening,' said the fat lady in the black curly wig, with bright rouged cheeks and scarlet lipstick spilling over into the lines around her mouth. 'No, it is clearing. I see many S's surrounding you. They protect you. One special S is destined for you but you are kept apart. You will marry someone whose name begins with S and have three children.'

Louis thought it was nonsense but somehow he knew it would come true. There was a signed letter from Princess Di on the wall so the fortune-teller had good credentials. The black cloud would clear, S would protect him. The three children existed in his mind – rather as Mavis and the laundress exist in mine – two girls and a boy. Sally, Susan and Simon.

Louis told Scarlet about that in the early days when he proposed, and she said she liked the names, and he thought that meant she wanted children, but as it turned out she didn't. Scarlet apparently did not forget what it was like when Lola was born, a creature spewing a strange yellow runny stuff from one end, and a milky fluid from the other. Scarlet was twelve at the time. Cynara had made a fuss during labour, insisting that the male midwife go away, swearing at him like someone with Tourette's, mixed with racial insults, so the whole staff had walked out and Scarlet was left alone with Cynara when the head showed. Scarlet had freaked and pressed the 'staff assault' button, so it was a vast black guy from Security who actually tugged Lola out while Cynara screamed, 'Get that black man off of me.' Scarlet had been well traumatised. And then a day later there was a midwife bending over Cynara, whose left breast was oozing pus, saying, 'Have you bonded yet, Mother?' as if nothing untoward had happened at all. So no, Scarlet was not actually into babies, though she didn't spread it around because she realised people thought it was selfish. Scarlet told Louis all this only when they had already been together for a couple of years, but Louis thought, well, she is young, she will change her mind, women mostly do.

What Scarlet was into was buzzing around in her Prius with its low carbon footprint, a perk from a Japanese car manufacturer. She had her own *Our Planet, Our Future* column in a monthly glossy, and lived amongst free gifts and samples not just from this source but from what came her way from her job as commissioning editor for *Lookz*, a not-so-glossy weekly. She'd started out as an idealistic graduate on *Prospect* but had drifted off to where the money was, as everyone did. Being with Louis, with his indeterminate 'private income', and his links with the art and fashion world, would help her get back on track. She was quite upfront with Louis about her motives, and he found her frankness entertaining and charming.

Presently Louis realised that Scarlet had a gift for looking you in the eye and appearing to see into your soul while actually her attention was altogether elsewhere. She'd have been thinking about something important, a deadline, perhaps, or how to get her silk blouse back from the cleaners. He had been going on boringly about names beginning with S and she had been nodding politely but hadn't heard a word. Her mother Alice, whom Louis had met so seldom, had the same gift – which, he concluded, could only make it the more difficult for them to get on with each other. Each knew only too well how little notice the other was taking of what was being said, no matter how impassioned.

In the basement

Spring has come so suddenly this year. I've been getting up really early to work, it being the best time for writing, and this morning when I opened the wooden shutters – they're the original ones; once Mavis would have had the task – a burst of sunlight struck across the lawn. I saw it was vivid green, and the Japanese cherries were in bud. I am really cheered. I can turn the central heating down to three instead of five, and take off the plain mittens a Norwegian fan knitted for me – less distracting than the ones with the bobbles – and unswaddle my knees from the pale mauve throw Vi our cleaner gave me for Christmas. She used to work in this house for Rex's mother and now she's gone and so we've taken over as Vi's employers. She comes in on Mondays.

It's just a coincidence that since we use the boiler room next door to this one for the washing machine and the dryer – and it's where Vi does the ironing – she passes through here on laundry day. At least once I thought it was coincidence; now I begin to realise it's the habit of the house asserting itself. The house drives me down here where the actual work is done, it's the house gets me up early, because work in this house is meant to start early. It can't stand its shutters being closed in daylight. I belong more down here than up there.

Vi says yes, it's a bit haunted down here but she doesn't mind, not as much as she minded seeing the rat run past the window in the snow, or the grass snake in the rhubarb down the end of the garden when she was pegging out the washing on the line. Forget the dryer – everything's so much fresher, she says, and smells so good, when it's been hung out. She goes upstairs with a basket of folded, beautifully ironed clothes, proud as the laundress of yesteryear.

Other than Vi pattering through the room it's quieter down here on Mondays than it is on other mornings. The others are used to me by now and take no notice: when Vi comes I get the feeling they welcome her. I listen out for the sounds that have become familiar, subdued noises from the kitchen, which I think can only be Cook panting and puffing away. She doesn't sound well. Cooks were an unhealthy lot, eating and drinking too much, leaning over hot stoves in a state of tension, famous for falling dead in the middle of dinner parties. Or had I just read that somewhere and now projected it on to the sounds of water in the pipes? Just as I might very well have interpreted the clanking of the old water system where it hadn't been renewed as Mavis clearing the grate, the sweep of ashes into the pan? I can think this easily on Mondays when the real living Vi is around, if only because I can hear her properly, not fuzzily. I hear the actual hiss of the water when she picks up the electric steam iron, and the other more shadowy sounds are still. The house is soothed by Vi.

Who's the snake? The one Vi saw last summer under the rhubarb? We know who the rat is – the one I saw in the winter, dragging its belly across the snow – it's Jackson. Probably the snake is Lola. I am not sure myself, but I have to get to know before she does. There is a kind of race going on between me and these characters. They are mine and they dance to my tune and I need to keep it like that.

They like to think they have control over their destinies and have free will but they can only dance so far on the end of my chain. If this is how I say it went, this is how it went. Those writers who claim their characters take off on their own are irresponsible. Their personages may escape, but they become lawless and inconsequential. Let them stick to their paths for their own good; rats and snakes though they may be, they need to be true to their natures.

Run, Lola, run

Lola Olsson, at sixteen, has as we know been fast-tracked through school under the gifted children scheme and before she dropped out of education had gained a provisional place studying law at Bristol University. Her mother Cynara is a barrister in the high-profile Human Rights' chambers of WVB (Wright, Varnes, Bovis). Her father is Jesper Olsson, a big wheel in the museum world and a specialist in Bronze Age artefacts. Lola complains he has Asperger's and lacks any capacity for human affection. Not that it matters much, she will add, since he has deserted her and gone to live in Dubai, leaving the matrimonial bed available for filling by D'Dora.

It was shortly after Jesper's departure that Lola failed to turn up to her A-level exams, and so lost her university place. She could have pleaded illness or stress, but chose not to. She had, she said, discovered that her mother was only waiting for her to go off to university before her lesbian lover moved in. So she would not go. She was as open about her motives to her family, teachers, counsellors, interested journalists, Facebook, Twitter and YouTube as Scarlet was in discussing with Louis her motives for marrying him.

'I see no reason to keep your affair with D'Dora secret,' she told her mother, when the latter pleaded for privacy. 'Why, are you ashamed of being a lesbian? Surely not.' To which of course there could be no answer. Other than: 'Why do you suddenly hate me?'

To which Lola, being Lola, replied, 'Because you are hateful to me.'

A year previously D'Dora Jones, founder of the Lesbian and Gay Sorority, or LGS, a person then unknown to Cynara, had sued her employers, Pinfold & Daughters, for unfair dismissal, alleging sexual harassment. WVB had taken on the case. P&D manufactured mountaineering equipment. Its CEO, Allegra Pinfold, alleged incompetence and deliberate absenteeism. D'Dora became headline news when she said she'd been fired, not for these two failings, which she freely admitted, but claimed they were the result of Allegra's sexual advances. Allegra Pinfold counter-claimed that she had been the seduced, not the seducer. D'Dora, thanks to Cynara's skilful defence, won, and was awarded half a million pounds in damages.

When the litigants left the Royal Courts of Justice after the verdict, Allegra physically attacked Cynara on the steps, shrieking that it was a dyke-ist set-up, and that Cynara and D'Dora were in a relationship, which was not initially the case, though during the four weeks of the court case it had become one. The attack had ended up on YouTube. The media furore had sent the hits on Cynara's blog off the scale, greatly increased the number of her WVB clients, firmed up Jesper's decision to take an offered Dubai job, and attracted journalists to Lola's school the week she was due to take her A-levels.

'Yes, and the dog ate her homework,' said D'Dora, cuddling Cynara to comfort her, when she brought home the news of her daughter's rebellion. 'More excuses. She spent too much time on computer games and not enough on revision; the reason she didn't sit her exams was because she knew she'd fail. Nothing to do with you and me.'

Lola spent a week with friends and came back with large black pupils and hollow eyes and the announcement that she had been taking hard drugs but what did her mother care?

'So what are you going to do with your life, Lola?' asked Cynara, distraught. 'What about your exams, law school, your future?'

'You should have thought of that,' said Lola, 'before getting rid of my father. I'm getting out of here and you can't stop me. I can use my own money.'

And it seemed that she had just handed it all over – some £2,000 accumulated in dribs and drabs since birth – to a charity called Help the Harmed, which dispatched young people to crisis points worldwide, where they could make a difference. The charity had booked her up for a three-month stint in Haiti at a Christian camp well away from any voodoo centres, and now she was waiting for the ticket to arrive. Cynara needn't worry to look out for it in the post, said Lola, she had given Nopasaran as a forwarding address. Aunt Scarlet, who might not be very bright but at least had style, not to mention contacts, and with whom she was going to stay, was less likely to lose letters out of malice than was D'Dora.

The latter had taken matters into her own hands and moved in to the home to comfort Cynara, who, what with press persecution and Lola's disappearance – once she had been gone three days the police had been alerted – had been beside herself with anxiety.

'Does Scarlet know of this plan?' asked Cynara, thin-lipped because she thinks perhaps Scarlet has been egging Lola on. Scarlet behaves towards Lola more like a flighty sister than a responsible aunt.

'No she doesn't,' said Lola. 'But she soon will.'

So that's how Lola comes to be staying with Scarlet and Louis. And, given even more strength by Lola's arrival, why the kehua are so madly and effectively fluttering their wings. *Run, run!* they are noisily beseeching Scarlet, descendant of Beverley, child of Kitchie McLean and her murderous husband, as once they urged little

Beverley. It seems to be working. When a child finds a mother murdered by the father it does not bode well for that child, or for the descendants of that child through the generations, especially if the purification rituals are not properly done. The kehua of the Maori, like the Furies of the Greek myths, will follow the straggler and his or her kin across the world if they have to. They are family, hapu, and that's enough for them.

The tohunga, priests, of the Ngai Tahu, in whose Southern lands the murder happened, were in no position to perform the cleansing ceremony. The two bodies, sullied, ended up in the morgue in Christchurch instead of in the local Maori standing place, the Takahanga Marae, and the pitiful remains were cursorily dealt with. So much so that some of the local kehua were obliged to follow little Beverley all the way up to Coromandel in the subtropical North, the land of the Ngati Whanaunga, to where she and her new, makeshift family, Rita and Arthur, had escaped. The kehua hoped to gather the child back into the fold; the adoptive parents to save the child from scandal and distress. All meant well.

But here in Coromandel the Ngai Tahu kehua were not at ease, though they stayed. They were used to rolling pastoral land, not this craggy watery beauty. Their presence stirred up rival taniwha, those disagreeable monsters that rise from time to time from the deep dark pools of the bush to protect the iwi, or tribe. Taniwha are clad in fur and feather, grand as any tribal chief, both protector and destroyer, with a row of cruel spikes along the hulking backbone, great creatures with birdlike heads, vengeful eyes and savage, toothy, curved beaks, there behind your eyelids when you go to sleep. Whatever frightens you, that's what they'll be.

The clustering, sheltering, rattling kehua are nothing compared to the taniwha when it comes to terror, but are lighter on their feet and clearly get about more. As little Tahuri suggests, the overhead locker of an aircraft will do just fine if they are obliged to travel, as once did the hold of an ocean liner when Beverley left her native land and came to England.

Lola's move to Nopasaran

It was on D'Dora's advice that Cynara did not put more obstacles in Lola's way when she announced that she was going to stay with Scarlet. D'Dora was a great advocate of tough love. 'Never show you care' was her motto. 'The one who shows most love loses.' And since D'Dora's tactics had worked so well on her, Cynara, leaving her a trembling, love-sick, sexually obsessed wreck, with her marriage finally ended, and rumblings from senior partners that she had brought in the wrong kind of clients, she could see such tactics might well work with Lola. If she told Lola to go, Lola would want to come back. And Cynara loved Lola, though it was sometimes hard to remember.

'Go,' she'd said. 'Go, if your Aunt Scarlet will have you, though I bet Louis kicks up a fuss. I don't suppose you can do her much damage; she thrives on media attention.'

Lola did not hang about. Within hours Scarlet was on the phone to Cynara saying Lola wanted to come and stay, and that was okay with her, but was it with Cynara? And Cynara was saying Scarlet should be aware that the letter from Help the Harmed might never turn up: why would a respectable charity take on a disturbed girl who wasn't yet seventeen? They might take her money but hardly her. At which Scarlet felt so strongly on Lola's side she quite forgot about Jackson and how she wanted Cynara to say no.

'I don't think you should call your own daughter disturbed,' she said. 'Frankly, Cynara, with all this D'Dora business I think we could fairly say you are the one who is disturbed.'

'I am not disturbed,' said Cynara. 'You are homophobic.'

They brought the phone call to a quick end. Alice had trained both girls to keep the family peace at all costs. Some families row all the time and are in a perpetual state of 'not speaking'. Alice found this vulgar, and un-Christian. 'If you can't find anything agreeable to say,' she would tell them, 'don't say anything at all.' The family solution, if things got tough, was just to stay out of each other's way for a while.

'It's not going to be more than a week or so, I suppose?' Scarlet asked Lola, all the same.

'Oh no,' said Lola. 'Days, I imagine.'

Though in truth Lola too suspected that Help the Harmed had found out that she was not yet seventeen, and were delaying her passage until her birthday in three months' time. There had been various text messages on her mobile from them which she failed to open. She was not really all that keen on going to Haiti.

Scarlet had been shocked to hear Lola's account of what was going on at home. Cynara seemed to have flipped her lid. Of course people should be free to choose the sexuality they wished, and Scarlet of all people understood the compulsion of sexual desire, but throwing out a husband and father against the daughter's wishes, and moving in a lesbian lover was surely extreme. She would of course, now it was a *fait accompli*, give Lola every help she could. Lola was 'difficult', everyone knew: but then Cynara was difficult too. Scarlet had always believed she could make a much better business of bringing up Lola than her sister ever had. And, even if Lola did find out about Jackson, the girl wouldn't tell Louis. She would surely be on Scarlet's side.

Lola would have to use the raw upper grey alcove for sleeping, Scarlet warned. The concrete here was unpainted and gloomily greasy and it was quite a climb. The more congenial lower alcove, cosier, painted grey and pink, with the original cushioned flooring, was currently being fitted with safety rails. English Heritage and Building Regulations between them had negotiated for months with Louis' lawyers over how best a compromise could be made between respect for the architect's Brutalist vision and the survival of the occupiers. They had come up with a stainless-steel option of slim, elegant rails, which horrified Louis, but which Scarlet actually rather liked. Louis had no option, such was the bureaucracy and the legal cost of arguing, but to seem to accept the compromise graciously. It was within the bounds of possibility that the health and safety authorities could condemn Nopasaran as unfit for human habitation, if such was their whim. They had power to do almost anything, so far as he could see. So he had best be polite.

Scarlet for her part could not see what the fuss was all about. The only real worry about the alcoves was the way sound travelled – you could practically hear the sound of clothes rustling as guests undressed, let alone anything else. Rails would make no difference.

'You're sure Louis won't mind?' Lola had asked. 'I don't want to be a nuisance.'

'Of course he won't mind,' said Scarlet. 'You're family. Just don't smoke.'

What is that fluttering in our ears? Is it a build-up of wax that requires a visit to the doctor's? It could be anything, anyone from anywhere: the distant flapping of the kehua, or the Furies, or the soft footfall of the grateful dead, or the faint trotting hooves of the watery Northern kelpies? Once the other side kept to their own centuries, their own lands. No longer. It is all globalisation now; the movement through time and space of the traditional emissaries of the dead becomes worldwide, *sans frontières*. Just a change of pressure in the head, there but barely there as they arrive, or depart satisfied if temporarily depleted. Take your choice: go off to the surgery to check symptoms, hide your head in the sand, or, if you're old-fashioned and wise like some of us, pray.

Would Louis mind?

Well of course, yes, Louis would mind. The tributaries of the narrative swell, the river banks can't hold the volume, the pressure of events past and present is too great, the flood waters of the narrative spread over the fields. Fish around down there in the mud and you come up with all sorts of extraordinary things, such as the detail of Louis minding.

Louis could put up with guests easily enough for a night or two, but much longer and they tended to get on his nerves. He liked silence at mealtimes, an end to the hysteria of the day. Scarlet, contrary to one's expectation, didn't mind the quiet at all; her days were busy and peopled enough and she could get on with her book, or *The Week*, or *Vogue*, and liked to read while she ate. Or, now she could just sit and dream about sex with Jackson until she trembled on the verge of orgasm and had to stop her breath coming so quickly in case Louis noticed. Louis for his part much appreciated Scarlet's capacity to be silent. Previous live-in companions had got offended and demanded attention and conversation, and had ended up moving out.

Scarlet acknowledged that life with Louis could be very companionable. Sometimes she thought how dreadful it would be if they had children, because she would never get to read the end of a page, let alone a chapter, without having to get up and *do* something. Louis on the other hand thought he would rather like to be distracted from the increasing melancholy of his thoughts by the cheerful prattle of children. If you brought them up properly and with a certain amount of kindly discipline, he was convinced, they would be quite quiet and not argue with him.

He could see Lola as a case in point: too clever for her own good, a victim of state education and wrongly handled by her family. But he liked her, and rather admired her. He saw her as a free spirit. The more Cynara tried to turn her into a boy, the more determined she was to be a girl. He liked the McLean family: he enjoyed their energy and eccentricity: he liked Beverley, and going round to Robinsdale for family teas and parties. He was sorry Jesper had been dismissed but no doubt he would be back in one form or another. D'Dora was a surprise but he, Louis, could cope better than most. D'Kath and she were both members of the LGS, a gay and lesbian subgroup whose members prefixed their given names with D for Dyke, the better to declare to the world their gender orientation, and he knew what it was wise to say and not to say.

Part of Scarlet's attraction for Louis, indeed, had been that she was a McLean. Now, asked by her whether he minded Lola coming to stay, he said without hesitation, no, I don't mind at all, and rather surprised himself. Lola had an annoyingly whiny voice, would be under his feet, interfere with his routine, and might even try to smoke, a habit he detested. On the other hand she had to be rescued from her mother, who was evidently going through a patch eccentric even for a McLean. Three years back he would have said instantly no; the girl was obviously in trouble with her oestrogen. But she had grown out of that now, and certainly so had he.

Even while she asked Louis whether he minded Lola coming to stay, Scarlet chafed. Fuck it, anyway, why did she need his permission? She invited who she wanted. This was her house as much as his, morally if not legally. Louis had said once, at the hectic time of the abandoned wedding, that he'd put Nopasaran in joint ownership, but Scarlet didn't think he'd ever got round to it as she'd never been asked to sign anything. And it would only have stirred up Annabel, who had put £50,000 towards the mortgage, and there would be no end to the lawyers and the explanations. Annabel loved consulting lawyers. It wasn't as if Lola would be any extra cost to Louis. She, Scarlet, paid the food and utility bills, and promptly, almost as though the sooner she got rid of her money the better.

Louis had difficulty parting with money. He wasn't exactly mean – he just viewed all bits of paper in a domestic context as suspect and dealing with them was a waste of talent and time. Yet at MetaFashion, it seemed, he was perfectly efficient. But that is so often the way of it, she supposed. People's neuroses surfaced at home, while at work they appeared perfectly reasonable people.

'Of course Louis won't mind,' Scarlet had said. She really wanted to help poor Lola. Sure, she needed to sit her exams, and get her degree and so on, but there was lots of time. Lola had been fast-tracked through the educational system much too young; do her good to catch up with a bit of real life. If you could cope with inner London as Lola did, you could cope with Haiti. For all her apparent street wisdom, Scarlet was just an innocent. Three weeks later there will Lola be, on the end of the phone to her mother, bad-mouthing poor Scarlet and demanding to come home.

At home with Cynara

Cynara is already worn out when Lola's phone call comes. Physically, because she's in the middle of shifting so much of D'Dora's 'stuff' out of her own bedroom, which until lately she has shared with Jesper, into the spare room. Until D'Dora's arrival, the spare room was designated as Lola's bedroom. But D'Dora has decided to use it to store her 'stuff', thus freeing up space in the marital bedroom as D'Dora likes to call it. The couple plan to have a civil ceremony as soon as Cynara's divorce goes through. D'Dora's 'stuff' is bulky, heavy and strange; it consists of odd-shaped exercise machines, S&M dungeon basics – stocks and shackles which she swears she doesn't use but doesn't want to throw away – mountain-climbing gear, and at least six pairs of muddy boots – albeit only a size three. D'Dora is very tiny and very pretty. All of which, plus craft equipment for a home business they mean to set up together, results in Cynara finding herself moving, with D'Dora's 'stuff,' into Lola's room while D'Dora stays conveniently out of sight. D'Dora works for Kids R Us, where she counsels deprived children, which is why she is a trained expert in 'tough love'.

Cynara is worn out emotionally because of the tough love imperative. She wants Lola back home again but then D'Dora will withdraw her love and Cynara can't bear that. The discovery that she's a lesbian seems to have rooted Cynara somehow in her physical body, so her intellectual being doesn't get a look-in, and that's shocking; she is so used to it being there, censoring her capacity for pleasure. She's taken to eating butter rather than margarine, simply because it tastes better, regardless of the fact that it's not good for you. She needs time and space to get used to her new self. And she doesn't think she's fit to look after Lola any more; look at the mess she's made of it so far.

It is unfortunate that Lola calls her mother in Parliam Road after three weeks' silence, just as these thoughts are going through Cynara's head.

No. 11 Parliam Road, NW2 is a small, mean but practical terraced house, its ground-floor front converted into a garage, a kitchen extension out the back with the bathroom on top of it, and a sooty plane tree all that is left of the front garden. Many a time Jesper has wanted to move to a more salubrious dwelling, and many a time Cynara has refused. She wanted to be where the 'real people' were. Also, it was easy to keep clean, convenient, near the Underground and Lola's school; and she could be at work in Holborn within twenty minutes.

Now she sees she was stupid. If Lola wants to come home, where can she be fitted in? Cynara should at her age be living in a bigger, grander house. She could easily have afforded it. She rode out the media storm Lola whipped up for her, and her relations with WVB have survived, just, but does she want to stay with them? She has lost interest in legal work. Once it seemed fascinating. Now it seems boring. She can hardly bear to answer the phone. Her mobile is switched off. She has abandoned ongoing cases to her assistants.

A young Muslim woman is claiming damages from her employer who runs a hair salon. She has been fired for turning up to work in full niqab. While she is working out her notice, fully veiled, the shop windows are broken on three occasions. Is it her brothers who object to her working, or Islamophobes who object to the niqab? The girl herself says she has grown a nasty wart on the side of her nose so she wears a veil not for religious reasons but aesthetic ones. Is the employer entitled to fire her or not? It had seemed so interesting and important, now it just seems depressing.

And Jesper quite understandably now says he wants half the value of the house. If she doesn't regain her interest in her job, how is she going to live? And support Lola? And support D'Dora, who hates to have financial matters discussed and makes her feel an uncreative fool if she does? And who so far has paid nothing towards her keep? The disadvantages of living with D'Dora are becoming more and more apparent.

When it came to moving furniture, for instance, Cynara missed the husband D'Dora had ousted. With Jesper's help, what she was doing would have taken her half the time. He was physically strong and as a male his spatial awareness was better than hers. Even D'Dora acknowledged this particular superiority of the male, it being useful up mountain peaks in adverse weather conditions when 'mental visual rotation' was required, though not enough, in D'Dora's opinion, to make up for the multiple other failings of the gender.

And if only D'Dora didn't travel so heavy. Jesper always travelled light. He would set out for foreign places with a change of underpants, a spare sweater and a memory stick in a backpack. What has she, Cynara, let herself in for?

And though Lola is giving D'Dora as an excuse for dropping out and leaving home, Cynara can see the advent of D'Dora hasn't exactly helped. Jesper is the one really at fault, in not showing strength and fighting back. But Cynara has to admit that D'Dora didn't just *happen*. Both she and Jesper had weakly bowed down to a force of nature; the marriage, growing in the wrong place, had simply cracked and fallen like a lone pine tree in a mountain gale. But then she couldn't be expected to go on suiting Lola's convenience for ever. Lola had become impossible.

Can a few hours of sexual exhilaration a few times a week really be worth all this trouble? Cynara is weighing all these things in the balance when the phone rings, and it is Lola.

In the battle to show the toughest love, who will win: Cynara or Lola? Lola, by wanting to move back in, has declared defeat. But if Cynara declares a truce and lets Lola back into the house, she will have to shift all D'Dora's stuff into the garage and henceforth join the battle for parking places in the street, where there is no residents' parking. This, for Cynara, is the tipping point. She decides. All you need is sex.

Beverley once told Cynara that nature had designed teenagers to become so difficult that when they left home the parent felt not grief but relief, and Cynara had dismissed the notion as ridiculous; now it seems a perfectly reasonable supposition.

Tough love wins. Cynara decides to say no to her daughter.

Understanding Louis better

Just a little more about Louis. Samantha the school matron's daughter used to wear shoes in which the two pieces of leather were cut and joined centrally, not down the sides, and Scarlet was wearing similar shoes when Louis first met her. Sometimes he thinks that the 'love at first sight' surge of attraction that overcame him when he met Scarlet at a media party was because of the way two pieces of shoe leather were stitched together. This, and the need to prove his heterosexual credentials.

Louis had hoped when he declared his intention of marrying Scarlet that his colleagues at MetaFashion would stop pressuring him to go with them to gay clubs. But then when the wedding was cancelled, and only the party remained, they giggled and assumed he and Scarlet had made a non-marriage of convenience. 'You closety old girl, you!' they cheered. Wasn't her sister the famous Cynara Olsson, the gender lawyer who was all over TV, and who kept both a husband and a lesbian blog in which she complained about him? That was style.

But these he knew to be unworthy motives, and when he and Scarlet were not living through the fall-out of a row, which lately had become a great deal of the time – more especially since she had met Jackson, though she would have vigorously denied that this was the case – Louis blanked out these thoughts, and remembered they had got together because he loved her, and because she and he balanced each other – she so outgoing, confident and sociable, he with the quiet inner seriousness she knew she lacked.

And while her family taught him about generosity and immediacy of response, he in his turn had been able to teach her many things to which her family seemed blind. How to choose a good bottle of wine, how to tell the difference between a Monet and a Manet, how not to apologise or explain, how not to let your social aspirations show – Scarlet sopped up his instruction like blotting paper; and in the end, he thought, displayed the quizzicality, sophistication and self-confidence that a good education brings. Anyone, meeting Scarlet casually, would assume she had been if not to Oxford, at least to Bristol or St Andrews.

For her part Scarlet could admit that his love of Nopasaran – before she realised how difficult and time-consuming a house it was to live in; minimalism meaning high maintenance, as she assured her friends – demonstrated something special and endearingly eccentric about Louis. It was a point of singularity, and of many gratifying conversations. Louis was not like other men.

Louis' mother Annabel, her expectations of a career for her son as a concert pianist or a latter-day Einstein dashed, let him drift out of her quiet life. She too assumed he was gay, and his proposed marriage to Scarlet took her by surprise. This bright, noisy, effective, undereducated girl – a BA in journalism from Kingston? Where was that? – this quiet, thoughtful man: what perversity could have attracted him to her?

When the wedding was cancelled Annabel was relieved, but went to the party along with everyone else, in a floaty grey outfit and a powerful white hat, curious about the girl's relatives, and finding them disconcerting, people of little background, goodish looks, some notoriety, forceful opinions, and not a title between them, she smiled sweetly at them all. Then, duty done, she allowed them to absent themselves from her life. She rather hoped Louis and Scarlet would split up before there were children. The world was overpopulated as it was, and she did not want to end up with grandchildren who took after their mother and not their father. They probably would; the genes, she could see, were strong.

That's enough of Louis, more than enough, other than that he makes love in the missionary position. That used to be no problem to Scarlet: she would be thinking of something else anyway; orgasms came easily, just a kind of shiver on the surface when she turned her attention to what was going on. If she wanted anything more profound or exciting she could look for it outside the home. Louis wouldn't notice, so it didn't count as infidelity or betrayal of trust. But now she has found Jackson, suddenly it is not so okay as it was. Indeed, it now constitutes a real grievance. If only they had ever got married she could argue that the constant missionary position amounted to mental cruelty, grounds for divorce.

She has tried talking about it to Louis, as the therapists advise, but if she starts any conversation during sex his thing shrivels and weakens at once, and if she tries at other times he looks so distressed and embarrassed she desists. She is fond of him, and would rather not distress and embarrass him. But she does feel this lack of imagination in him legitimises the unholy passion she feels for Jackson.

Another place, another time

The basement is quiet today, and has been for a couple of weeks, enough to make your writer feel all this vaguely paranormal disturbance has been wholly of her own creation. If she doesn't write about them it doesn't happen. So she's stopped.

All the same I have a premonition that they're all only biding their time; that if they've stopped chattering and Mavis has given up clearing her grates, it's only because the cold weather has rendered them somnolent. When the north wind changes to a south-westerly, and the hard winter ends, there may again be more general downstairs activity to be heard, more vibrancy in the warmer air. Mavis may be back scattering crumbs, and Cook and the laundress be back about their business. Next time round, is my fear, I may actually *see* someone walk between me and the window. I don't want that to happen, so I will get quickly on to another subject.

The weather sites tell me northerly winds have set in for quite a while, and I am relieved, safe for the moment to deal with the fictional kehua without stirring up too much other-worldliness down here.

I will transport you back to Coromandel, New Zealand, in the 1940s, placing time and distance between you and the flashy metropolitan people we have been discussing. Beverley spent most of her childhood in Coromandel, and the place is very relevant to what she has become today, as childhood landscapes are, and to the fortunes of her children, her grandchildren and now, indeed, her great-grandchildren.

Coromandel is the peninsula that sticks its little finger out into the sea at the top right of New Zealand's North Island. It is hot, sunny, romantic, craggy, wild and beautiful, and when Beverley was a child, and moved up here from Amberley in the South Island, with her adoptive parents, Arthur and Rita, it was still very much pioneering country. The nation is proud of its past, as well it might be. Its ghosts are plentiful and acknowledged. Even today reports of ghosts, presences, spirit orbs and so on are frequent, though there they seldom involve servants; Kiwis, as New Zealanders like to call themselves, never having been, like European forebears, in the habit of keeping others in servitude.

One hundred and seventy or so years ago, around the time Yatt House was built, emigrants were fleeing the country to escape oppression, poverty, dismal weather, agricultural depression, bad government, and indeed the servant culture, the better to build a new and better land. The indigenous people, the Maori, tried to reason with them, deal with them and share with them, but it ended with war and a good deal of bitterness, and it may well be that the paranormal, which features so much on today's TVNZ, does indeed still linger. If modern New Zealanders are in the habit of seeing or sensing what is not quite there, the outward manifestation of the inner distress of the past, it is not surprising.

More so even than around Glastonbury down the road from us, site of ancient Avalon, though there it's pretty bad. You can be sure a great deal of bloodshed, general mayhem and Dark Ages bitterness went on around there, even leaving aside what happened to the Abbot of Glastonbury a thousand years later. He thought he could appease Henry VIII by turning the other cheek, paying him the dues Thomas Cromwell demanded and more, not arguing. The only result was that the King, seeing there was no resistance, came in, seized all valuables, knocked down the Abbey, and beheaded the Abbot on the top of the Tor, so his head rolled down the hill to come to rest at the site of the school one of my children went to for a time. Spirits abound here too.

It is not surprising if when Beverley was a child, taniwha still lurked in the deep forest pools, tohunga flourished, kehua hovered above the hapless heads of the unabsolved, and nested in the bushes, and could emigrate if necessary to Robinsdale, and 11 Parliam Road, NW2, where Cynara and Lola (and D'Dora, but she has her own ghosts) have their homes, to Alice's home, Lakeside Chase in the North, to Nopasaran, and inevitably, should Scarlet ever get there, and I am beginning to think she will, to the Campion Tower penthouse.

Beverley was no Maori, just a pakeha, a white person. But Kitchie, dying, will have prayed in desperation to all available powers for the safety of her child, and a three-year-old in any culture is a three-year-old worthy of care, so such spiritual beings as were in the neighbourhood may well have felt obliged to take her on as one of their own, birthright or not. Christianity still lay lightly on the land at that time. The pretty Anglican church in Amberley, built in 1877 on Maori lands, with love and gratitude to God for bringing them to this fertile land, was torn down by a hurricane in 1899 so it had to be rebuilt, and a few years later fire destroyed the church school, so it may well be that the God of Israel was having a hard time laying down His rules and rituals in this Southern clime. Be that as it may, Amberley kehua will have been on major alert that night in 1937 when murder was committed, as they are whenever violent and sudden death occurs.

The trouble was compounded because the house in Amberley where this murder happened was never properly purified, nor, indeed, were the bodies of the dead. The Christian rituals were not adequate. The karakia, prayers of exorcism, were not spoken. The ritual spraying of water never happened. The local kehua could not escort the deceased home and, the way I see it, attached themselves instead to the desperate little morsel of life that was Beverley, and thereafter did their duty by her. Decades later they were still there, hoping to chivvy her back to join her hapu, to find her urupa, her beautiful place, to be eventually with the whanau. They would follow her to the ends of the earth until it happened, until one day she finally chose to up sticks and make for home, and then they could get home too. Half blessing to her, half curse, her kehua welcomed change, anything to hasten the day. *Run, Beverley, run!* It was in their interests that she did.

Aroha and Tahuri call by briefly and unexpectedly, on their way to stay with friends in the West Country, and I come up from the basement for air, and we have coffee in the kitchen. Tahuri goes downstairs to see if the dried-up daddy-long-legs is still there on the windowsill and to my shame comes back to report that it is. She says she doesn't like it down there and, when asked why, claims she has seen a kehua. Her mother assures her there are no such things. She loses interest. For her it is not so big a deal.

'But if there were,' I ask Aroha, 'and you could catch kehua like the measles, would your children and your children's children catch them too?'

Aroha says she supposes yes, since they too would be whanau. Family. Ghosts and spirits in many cultures, she points out, are used as metaphors for a hereditary dysfunction: curses last even unto the seventh generation: she cites *et ta grandmère!*, the mysterious French insult. Things come out of your family history to accost you. The present is always haunted by a past which needs to be acknowledged, purified. So I can see I am on the right track. And that the shower as Beverley washed her hair and stood naked under flowing water, together with Scarlet's inadvertent blessing, could indeed shift something in the scheme of things. Certainly even this partial purification stirred up the kehua, pulled them back from listless dormancy, gave them a whiff of the possibility of change. Surges of natural affection have great power in the unchancy spirit world. Beverley now finds herself able to face one or two facts about her past, which hitherto she had not.

When Beverley was seventeen and fled her adopted whanau to the Antipodes, she assumed, as the young do, that she would be able to start a new life fresh over, but no. See it like this: that kehua came after her, with their naggings and their dubious advice, and so it was never really a new life, just a variation of the old. The trauma when she was three, as Kitchie died in a welter of draining life blood, and the *run, run, run* instruction which made her daughter's stout little legs run one-two, one-two, white knees pumping, to safety, could never be quite forgotten either by Beverley or her kehua. Weakened and dispersed over decades as her kehua were, resigned to sitting it out a long way from home, they revived on occasion to parrot the phrase. Sometimes they were heard, sometimes not. Sometimes it could be misconstrued as *kill, kill, kill.* As Aroha pointed out that day on my basement stairs, when the subject of the kehua first came up, they are not all that bright, being dead.

But Beverley was lucky to hear them loud and clear on her seventeenth birthday, and did indeed respond to them, and just as well. That was in Coromandel, when her kehua were nourished by their native soil, and strong. On later occasions their advice was not necessarily good. This is the problem with 'the other side'. It is all too prone to error, misjudging what goes on in our real world. The connections are often faulty. The keys that Uri Geller twists are no good for opening doors, the spoons he bends won't scoop dessert, the watches he stops won't tell the time, the worst ghosts in the night can do to you is turn your hair white. What's the use of that? The Church of England provides 'deliverers', once called exorcists, to free buildings of lingering spirits but does so reluctantly and with as little publicity as possible. Take these things seriously and they become too serious. Write about them and they may become true. But I won't dwell on that.

But I will just mention that in 1987 I wrote about a three-year-old who escaped alive from an air crash: she was in the very back of the plane with the smokers – those were the days – and the tail broke off and circled down like a sycamore leaf and landed in mud. 'Oh come on now!' said my editors, but a couple of months later a four-year-old was sole survivor of the crash of Northwest flight 255 in Detroit, Michigan. 'It's where the toddler sat that allowed her to survive,' a spokesperson said. The child was seated in the tail of a plane which came down in mud. And even as I write this they've just picked out of the sea a six-year-old sole survivor of an aircraft flying into the Yemen.

The run, Beverley run advice is embedded in her consciousness – much as today's journalists are 'embedded' in a war, as if the army was conscious of itself as an entity with a single personality, rather than a muddle of dangerous activity. One way or another the kehua's admonitions are, years later, still fluttering round Beverley's head, beating her skull with their shadowy wings, though by now she is so old her legs will scarcely carry her anywhere. Immobility traps her. On occasion she may even have heard *Kill, Beverley, kill before you are killed.* If so perhaps the mother's kehua linked with the father's, he being the perp, to use the language of US cop fiction. The perpetrator. The perp and the taniwha are the same kind of creature, thrown up by the dark pools of any culture: destroyers and protectors both, villain and hero, like the Mafia boss. The thing that frightens you, and threatens you, yet keeps you in order, that's the taniwha.

It is conceivable that whenever Beverley gave birth the kehua split and multiplied and travelled, even in this strange new Antipodean land of piled-up concrete, mist and rain. A whole tribe of them by now, clustering round Beverley's female bloodline, embedded no doubt in the mitochondrial DNA, coming down through the female line, prodding and murmuring, *Run, Alice, Cynara, Scarlet, Lola, run, run, run,* so they all hear it and partly hear it. It's in their heads as they wake up.

Look at Scarlet this morning, with Lola egging her on. One long *Let's get out of here.* They run instead of turning and facing. Fair enough in a three-year-old – quite right not to turn and look: who else could have been in that slaughter room? – but scarcely appropriate in adult women. Even Alice in her turn has chosen to run; if she sings hymns loud enough she can blot out the voices. Richie, being Beverley's son, and male, will have been spared them.

Be that as it may, we can be satisfied that the ritual purification in the marae, the tribal meeting house, did not happen as it should. The burial in the Anglican church of Amberley did not suffice. Too few people attended; the vicar was too old to understand what was going on, having been told only by the Bishop in Christchurch that the young man was not to be buried in consecrated ground, but only the young woman. It seemed so odd and unkind an instruction that the vicar told the churchwarden who told the gravedigger to bury them both together. And the gravedigger chose outside the wall because the ground there was softer and easier to dig and he too was old and tired. Whatever the rites, from whatever religion, and however apparently unreasonable, they need to be properly observed.

It is possible, on the other hand, that when Scarlet played the shower over her grandmother's body, some part of the purification ceremony was completed, and the hovering kehua just left Beverley and went to Scarlet, because Beverley is old and tired, and Scarlet young and vigorous, in the same way a magnetic current leaps from what is weak to what is strong. We will see.

And again, the question of why the kehua claimed little Beverley as their own in the first place may need more explanation. Kehua do not usually bother the pakeha. Perhaps it was more than pity; perhaps the little blonde girl had just played in the yellow, sandy soil too much, and they claimed her only as she ran along the dusty road, one-two, one-two, in her little cotton blue and white check dress with the white collar, and then went back to claim Kitchie and Beverley's father too, chattering and clattering, summonsed by the sudden violence of their demise.

We find it as hard to understand the motivation of the restless undead as they find ours.

Down here writing

The weather's getting warmer. The wind has switched to the south-west. The basement ghosts are coming into their own again. Just as I had begun to be confident that the earlier phenomena were nothing but this old house adapting to the weather with creaking joists and contracting plumbing, and that all the new fictional characters I was bringing to life on the page just happened to be throwing up random Mavises and Cooks and Mr Bennetts, I am obliged to rethink. Even as I write this I see a pattern emerging on the old faded striped wallpaper I stare at when I raise my head from the keyboard. It looks like a face: round large eyes, a slash for a mouth, shaggy hair. A rather cruel face. I look again and it's just splodges of damp: of course. All the same, it wasn't nice.

It's a wet and windy March: the drains outside this window blocked last week and there was quite a flood; rainwater flowed down the concrete stairs from the garden to basement level, and under the back door into the corridor, and was only held back when it reached the stone step up to this room where I work. Like the major traumas of the past, these events are never quite over. Mop up as we will, now I have faces on damp wallpaper, alarming me. I'm going upstairs for some coffee. I turn off my laptop. I do not want anyone who does not understand it to see what's on the screen. The face does not look as if it belonged to anyone computer-literate.

Novels do not drop ready written from the skies. They have to be written in real time. Your couple of hours' reading is my half-year's work. Don't think I'm grudging you – get to roughly the halfway word-count and the process begins to be enjoyable. You know enough about your characters, and what they are going to do next, to stop feeling anxious and insecure and accept them, even taking pleasure in their company. Like Scarlet at the moment, I'd rather have Jackson, rat that he is, than uptight Louis – though I can un-uptight him at will, tilting the balance of choice in his favour. And I know pretty much by now how Lola is going to meet her come-uppance. At five o'clock this morning I was startled awake by the clear realisation of what was going to happen at the end of the book. I sat upright in bed like someone in a cartoon, hair sticking up.

There is a degree in which novels will write themselves if you allow them to, but the process of allowing them to do so is tiring, difficult, and registers with the writer as really hard work. You use bits of the brain which are not normally exercised; it's like taking a strange dog for a walk on the end of a lead: it either charges ahead in the wrong direction, or has to be tugged behind, or turns and snaps at your ankles, or worse, just sits down on its haunches and stares at you. When all you were doing in the first place, in taking the dog for a walk, was fulfilling some social obligation – a favour you owe the neighbour who looked after your cat, or your friend who is sick. It's bitter. But by the time you get the creature home again, you are normally on good terms, albeit exhausted. I am on good terms with this novel.

I wasn't sure at first about the kehua business but it becomes more and more convincing. It is as plausible a way of explaining the way some of us turn our lives into a mess as any therapist's notion of compulsive behaviour. The sins of the past, the traumas that our forebears endured, come back to haunt us, like stains through wallpaper. If you don't bother to strip the old wallpaper off, but cut corners, just putting up new over old, it looks fine at first, but give it a bit of damp and eventually the old pattern shows through and you are left with a mess and have to start all over again. I can see the troubles of my own life, forget Scarlet's, as being due in great part to the tragedies and traumas that afflicted my own family's past, though they did not include murder. Their restless ghosts are still with us; we try to forget them, but they speak to us in our sleep.

End of coffee break. Back to the laptop.

Today's New Zealand is no longer a country of embattled pioneers; it is regarded by the rest of the world as the most socially conscious and peace-loving nation in the world. The rich myth and legend of the Maori peoples feed into today's culture, though the battles on the way were fierce. If you go up to Coromandel these days, up to the subtropical North, where the pohutakawa trees line the rocky coast, and the dolphins sport in a warm sea, and in the deep dark kauri forests where the tui birds break the silence and the bellbirds chime, you could well believe that the spirit of the taniwha has been put to sleep. But it is too much to hope that, with Scarlet's inadvertent blessing and the purification of the shower, the kehua hanging around Beverley's head could finally have been satisfied and gone home. Resolution is not so easy.

The modern translation of all this being 'The tendency to dysfunction in a family is hereditary, until therapy undoes the traumas of the past.' Without therapy it may take several generations for the family to, as they say, 'move on'. And yet 'moving on' is such a giving up, such a disgustingly timid denial of the realities of the past, of rage and discontent and vigour, such a flaccid response to the savagery of those Maori wars – while Hone Heke's rebellion was being put down, this house was being built – such a welcoming of entropy, I am reluctant to embrace it.

I do not mean to be defeated. I've gone back down to take my seat in my spooky room, haunted both by the ghosts of my imagination and whoever once lived and worked here, and sure enough, the face on the wallpaper is gone. It has dried out. I left the central heating radiator on full blast.

'Then fancies flee away.' I sing to myself Bunyan's hymn, *To Be a Pilgrim*: 'I'll labour night and day...'

Hobgoblin and foul fiend, I'll have no more of you. Tap, tap, tap goes my keyboard. I shift in my typist's chair to ease the ache in my back. I expect you feel the same, Mavis, as you bend to sweep the grates. And you're younger than me in one way, but a hundred years older in another. I hope I'm not inadvertently discommoding you, by even thinking of it.

Everything is going to be fine. No moans from Mavis, no untoward noises. I tell myself I have set my own kehua to rest. Then I hear barking. But there are no dogs who live round here. I am instantly paranoiac. But it's not a whining, complaining irritating bark – rather that of an excited dog playing a game of catch in the garden with the Bennetts' children, Ernest, Thomas and William. A kindly-looking dog, a black-and-white Welsh border collie, walks by the window: not exactly walks, more like gliding, as if attached to a moving band. I take it to be Bonzo, which means our friend Martin his owner is upstairs having a cup of coffee. But I didn't hear his car drive up. And Bonzo usually walks by from the other direction – out the back door, in the front. This dog is walking in the opposite direction. His white patches are differently arranged. It's not Bonzo. Bonzo is older and has a limp. Then the dog on the moving band is past the window and gone. But it's not on a moving band, of course; what I saw was a dog walking from the knees up – the ground level will have risen since its original passed by this window. Oh my God, too much knowledge.

Only yesterday someone was talking about the ghosts of Roman soldiers seen marching along the old Roman road which runs from Badbury Rings to Bath. They march along as though amputated at the knee, on moving bands. My problem is I am the most suggestible, gullible person on earth.

I go out into the garden to look but there is no dog. I didn't really expect to see one. I project my own fantasies in rather too lively a way, that's all. I am a writer: I make things up. I am not going to flee upstairs again. It's pathetic. The dog will only follow me up there if I am in the wrong frame of mind. He was on the other side of glass. He's not threatening me. I don't suppose ghost dogs draw real blood, and anyway he seemed a friendly, relaxed and amiable creature. Had he looked in through the window I daresay he would have seen me, and I for him would have been a ghost and made his hair bristle.

But he didn't, and it didn't. I turn my computer back on. It takes its time and then there's the familiar sound of the 'welcome' chords of Microsoft materialising: real and not real, aetheric yet so very here and now. I suppose they are from this world, not the other, crossed over to delude us all? How could one tell? Do we understand the mechanism by which they are now heard in every house in the land?

Beverley feels better

Beverley thinks perhaps her knee hasn't been infected with MRSA after all. Now her hair is fluffed out she thinks she will Skype her friend Gerry, an oil engineer prospecting in the Faröes, and ask him what to do about Scarlet. Should she call Louis and tell him to get home quickly before Scarlet does something silly, or should she just do nothing and not get involved? Perhaps a lifetime's policy of not standing between her family and their follies, feeling it is always wiser to run than to stay, has been misguided. Better still, she decides, she will call Louis, before she calls Gerry, the minute Scarlet is out the door.

'I mustn't hold you up any longer,' she says to Scarlet. 'You'd better run along now. Where are you meeting your lover? Somewhere smart?'

'Costa's in Soho,' says Scarlet. 'You won't know it. No one important will recognise him there.'

Or he can't pay for anything better, thinks Beverley, and if he doesn't get recognised in Soho where will he be? But she doesn't say so and smiles sweetly at Scarlet, to hurry her out of the door.

'Why are you rubbing your eyes?' asks Beverley.

'I've got the beginnings of a migraine,' says Scarlet, and she takes an aspirin out of the pack in the little Marc Jacobs handbag (£205, Harvey Nichols sale, 30 per cent off) she keeps in the Chloé tote bag, and swallows it without even bothering to find water. She coughs a little as it dissolves in her throat.

'It's hereditary,' observes Beverley, and closes her own eyes to see how the flashes are getting on behind her lids and for once finds there are none. Thoughts of the kehua do not enter her mind, but they enter into mine, your writer's. The voices which say *run, run* are stronger in Scarlet's head than ever. The problem with dealing with ghosts is that they are so unpredictable. There today, gone tomorrow, undetectable by any technology so far discovered.

Scarlet takes her nice little Stella McCartney jacket (silk, striped black and white, £965 – Jackson loves it; Louis, for all he's in the fashion world, albeit on its edges, hasn't even noticed) and prepares to go. It is a pity the Prada top is navy but it's a dark shade and Jackson probably won't notice in the haste to get it off. If as she makes her way to her smart little ecologically sound Toyota Prius an unexpected gust of wind follows her so she shivers in the silk jacket and wishes she had worn wool, the thought lasts only a second or so and is forgotten, but lingers with your writer.

The souls of the dead in most cultures pass as breath in the wind but can do so with some force. The pain in the back, the flashes in the eyes – flail around and burn a witch! Perhaps some kehua forced themselves through the window seals to get into the Prius, perhaps others carried on to reinforce those already in Nopasaran down the road, where Lola was on the phone to Cynara. Beverley's shower may have simply made them disperse, not disappear. That's the trouble with the grateful dead: they are never convinced we are better off without their help.

Soon the Northern kelpies are going to enter on the scene, they too in search of their own. The living travel the world; nationalities no longer contain them. It's no different for the dead. They're all over the place, like the chords of Microsoft. No wonder the world is in a mess.

What Lola is doing in the meanwhile

Now yes, where were we with Lola? She is on the phone to her mother and her mother is dumping her in favour of her lesbian lover. I have neglected to tell you what Cynara looks like. She has the hard edges of the busy businesswoman, the accomplished and self-confident lawyer – though her confidence is currently under some threat. She is brisk and beautiful and has the plentiful frizzy hair and the wary, determined look cultivated by the committed feminist. (Though which comes first, the chicken or the egg, the hair or the nature, it is hard to say.) She is broader and dumpier than her young sister Scarlet, wears flats, and carries a rape alarm. Her grandmother, her mother, her sister, and indeed her daughter, would not deign to do either. It is not so much the set of the features but the lines into which the expression falls that mark them as belonging to the same stock. Male genes enter into the generations and cloud the mix. Cynara and Scarlet have the same mother but a different father, thus diffusing their genes still further, but Cynara and Scarlet are not aware of this, and Alice certainly has no intention of telling them.

Cynara's skin has seldom seen face cream. But she has fine eyes, a voluptuous mouth, likeability, high principles and a working mind. Sometimes she wonders how she and Jesper managed to beget this child, Lola, who seems to have so little to do with her. Her friends all seem to be wondering the same thing. It's as if you didn't beget your own daughters any more, but pulled them out of some central pool where they lie waiting to be claimed, ready formed. Some of them are better-looking than others but that's all there is to it. All have longer legs than their parents. They speak a strange language, have alien views, communicate to their friends and find their parents as weird as their parents find them. Lola is at least one of the better-looking, brighter ones.

Cynara tells herself it is her social and personal duty to follow the authenticity of her sexual orientation. In attempting to live her own life, go where her emotions direct and relate to women more than to men, she has done something admirable, not disgraceful. She, Cynara, would rather share her bed with D'Dora than with Jesper: that is the simple truth of it. If she is to create a different, better world for Lola to live in, and Lola chooses to take offence, too bad. She will live to thank her mother, so be it.

Jesper, who had a Swedish father and an English mother, was himself a declared feminist, and so when Cynara texted him to announce her decision that he was to live elsewhere, he took it nobly. He was away on business in Dubai anyway, employed in the construction and design of the new museum of Atlantis. Cynara was even a little hurt at the ease with which he emailed back 'OK'. Jesper put up with the present, because he had to live in it, but preferred the past. He did not actively reject the present, but it was not his main concern in life. The plan was that he would take some small convenient flat round the corner from where Cynara and Lola live, which Lola could see as a second home when he came back to England to present papers, see funding bodies, talk to colleagues about two-horned helmets, refute suggestions that Atlantis had been situated off the Danish coast and so forth, and everything would go on much as before.

And so far so good. Jesper has even put down a deposit on a suitable flat, only now Lola has taken it into her head to move out and go and stay with her Aunt Scarlet, who in Cynara's eyes is too young to be serious, and has no interest in the fate of nations, only in fashion. In her worst moments, angry at her daughter's desertion, Cynara sees Scarlet as having bribed her way into the child's affections from the beginning by buying her the in-present every Christmas, its only merit being that it was difficult to get hold of. And as D'Dora pointed out, it was Scarlet's habit of buying little Lola ostentatiously expensive clothes far too precocious for her age that Scarlet would claim were 'cute' and 'cool', words which Lola would pick up and use against her mother as ammunition in the daily battle to get her to school in decent clothes.

And now back for the detail of Lola on the phone only weeks after declaring she's gone for good. Cynara reflects that the better everyone else behaves, the worse Lola will and probably none of it is Scarlet's fault at all. Lola is a little cow, incapable of gratitude, and she, Cynara, chose the wrong father in Jesper; just because he looked like good breeding stock didn't mean he was.

'I want to come home,' Lola was saying. 'Scarlet's such a bitch. She treats me like a servant. She threw a vase of flowers at him last night and left me to pick up the pieces. I got a bit of china in my hand and it's bleeding and she doesn't care; she's just gone shopping at Waitrose. Shop, shop, shop. Now she's had the nerve to ask me to pack her things, because she's running off with Jackson Wright. She's been having it off with him for ages under poor Louis' nose. She has this white blouse thing from Brown's, which she's far too old and fat to wear. I asked her if I could have it and she said no, just to be mean.' Which was true; Scarlet had. 'Now it's got blood all over it and serve her right.'

'But darling,' says Cynara, 'you told me you were never coming home. You were staying with Auntie Scarlet until your flight was arranged. So I'm clearing your room out. It's hard work.'

'You mean you've given my room to your fat dyke friend?' screeches Lola in her nasal, druggie voice, or so her mother heard it.

'Dyke is not a word of opprobrium,' says her mother. 'On the contrary. I'm using your room to store my things, and as it happens D'Dora is sharing my bedroom.'

'You've thrown all Dad's things out too?' shrieks her daughter. 'To make way for her? You bloody cow!'

'No darling,' says her mother peaceably, ignoring the insult. Lola had got into the habit of flinging insults and Cynara of taking little notice. 'Daddy helped me take them up to the attic,' she lies. 'He was just here on a flying visit. He sent his love, said it was a good idea about staying with your Auntie Scarlet and wishes you well on the Haiti trip.'

'What have you done with all my things? Burned them?'

'They're all safe and sound in the attic too, darling, so you can come and take them away when you have a place of your own.'

'So what's happening in my room?'

'D'Dora and I are using it as a workshop. We're weaving wreaths and making felt flowers for the Mother Goddess festival. You should do more crafts, Lola. It would make you feel so much better about yourself.'

Lola makes sick noises down the phone.

'I feel just fine about myself, Mum,' says Lola. 'But how do you feel – about you? You never wanted me anyway. Why didn't you just abort me in the first place? The reason you don't want me around is D'Dora fancies me. She gives me the creeps. She's only with you to get at me. Like Humbert Humbert with Lolita.'

It has occurred to Cynara that this is a possibility, just as any mother of a fetching sixteen-year-old is wise to check a new partner out. Indeed, the police run a special service for worried single mothers to do exactly this for fear of possibly paedophile new stepfathers, and what is sauce for the gander is sauce for the goose. But Cynara has dismissed the thought with contempt. More reasonable to be worried that there was something slightly unhealthy about Jesper's interest in his daughter, or, rather, in Lola's interest in her father. Just as Cynara's more extreme friends spread the doctrine that all men are rapists, so do D'Dora's friends suppose that all fathers are child abusers, thus clouding any number of issues.

At the end of the phone call Lola slams down the phone then calls Help the Harmed, tells them she is cancelling her membership, they're a racket anyway, she's too young to go to Haiti, and she wants her money back.

She will stay and keep Louis company. She will find out if he is really gay. That will serve everyone right.

What happened next, in that other country long ago

Beverley grew up more or less believing herself to be the daughter of Dr Arthur and Mrs Rita Audley of Coromandel, North Island, New Zealand, the World, the Galaxy, the Universe, Space. Beyond the vision of her pumping knees on some desperate errand, and the bloodied dress above them, and playing in the yellow dust under the macrocarpa hedge, and a young woman turning cartwheels on the lawn – whom she assumes to be Rita – she has only the scantiest memories of her very early life. Usually between the ages of two and three years, the brain of a child switches from the tactile and olfactory to the verbal processing of memories. After that age we develop a self-image and can place other images within that main one – before that, all is amnesia.

Beverley was a bright child – as is Lola – and had developed her language skills, speaking, writing and reading early, so more memories were likely to be retained. Experiences deposit images, and though childhood trauma can have the effect of wiping out whole sections of memory altogether, Beverley was a tough and resilient little creature and the images remained. Which is why I say 'more or less believing herself to be the daughter', etc., and not a simple 'believed'. Ask little Beverley for the names of her parents and she'd pause for a second before replying Arthur and Rita, and she'd look at you with a slight air of doubt once she had done so.

When at the age of six her friend Evelyn Hammer confided that she, Evelyn, had been switched at birth, and was really a princess, Beverley said, 'I wasn't switched, I was adopted,' and knew it to be true, though how, she couldn't say. Nobody had ever told her, let alone suggested it. She thought she'd probably imagined it, just as Evelyn imagined herself to be a princess.

'What's adopted?' asked Evelyn, and Beverley explained. 'It's when your mother dies and you get put up for sale and somebody buys you.'

Rita was a young woman of twenty-seven when little Beverley, bloodied, came knocking for help at her farmhouse door. Rita phoned the operator who phoned the neighbours and all quickly congregated at Walter McLean's door, to find the horror of poor dead Kitchie, his wife, inside. Nobody had to break down doors; nobody locked doors then. A search party went looking for Walter, who was found in a nearby gully, lying dead, a blackened bullet hole in his temple. His dog Patch lay dead not far away, his own Webley revolver was lying beside him, and assumptions were easily made.

The unfortunate Walter McLean had taken a knife to his faithless wife, fled the scene of the crime, and then turned his gun first on Patch, then on himself. The child had woken from her afternoon rest to find the mother's body and, brave little thing, had run to the neighbour, local farmer's daughter Rita Hardy, for help. Police from Christchurch, thirty-four miles away, were called in, and both bodies were wrapped and transported quickly to the morgue in that city. The weather was hot. There had been no real evidence of a lover, but the general supposition from the first was that there must have been. Kitchie, a flirtatious lass from England who put on airs and was no kind of wife for a hard-working Canterbury sheep farmer, must have driven the poor man to it. The name of Arthur

Audley, the newly qualified doctor, was bandied about as a possible lover – mainly because he was young and handsome and the only local man anyone could envisage Kitchie taking an interest in – but the rumour soon died. Walter was known to have a temper, and Patch was not the only dog he had shot. Dogs suspected of worrying his sheep got short shrift, sometimes off his own land, and this had caused some local feeling. The inquests had been brief and to the point. Marital murder/suicide was always unpleasant, but not a rarity in rural parts.

Rita, unusual in her generosity and kindness, had done her neighbourly best to befriend Kitchie in the early days of her marriage, one of the few who did, and now extended that kindness to little Bev. Rita was lonely, plain, valiant and unmarried in a town where most were married by the age of twenty. She had inherited the farm from her parents; it was going to rack and ruin but she had property, so she had suitors. She also had her pride and her principles, and was almost thirty and still unmarried when Bev turned up on the step. Rita thought that put paid to any chance of marriage – who would ever want to take on another man's child, let alone Bev, with her history – but she took her in nonetheless. Then young Dr Audley had come courting, and been prepared to take Bev on. They would adopt her formally, sell the farm, and move north for the child's sake, to be distanced from scandal and memory.

So that is what happened. Rita sold the farm and with the proceeds Arthur bought a practice in the town of Coromandel, on the rugged, mysterious peninsula of the same name south-east of Auckland. Fifty years before, with New Zealand's own gold rush, the place had grown and swelled from sleepy fishing village to rough and raucous gold-mining town, complete with saloon, banks and whorehouses, but as the gold veins ran out and the population melted away, it had sunk again into a quiet, benevolent, satisfied sleep, as might some respectable matron with a wild past.

It was assumed in Coromandel that Beverley was the Audleys' child. Rita would have liked more children but Arthur had said Beverley was enough and pointed out that a doctor's wife always had a great deal to get on with. She had to keep the appointments, run the surgery, offer medical advice when he was on his rounds, help at the hospital in an emergency and act as the neighbourhood's unpaid social worker. There was status, more so than in being a farmer's wife, but there was work too.

There's a nice solid patch of conventional prose to be getting on with. It works. No more faces now appearing in the wallpaper and fading out again, no more mysterious footfalls, just the steady pitter-pat of the rain falling the other side of the window, and a firm reality.

'Ve haf vays of making you write,' the Great Cultural Gauleiter in the Sky is saying to me, in no uncertain terms. For your information, the GCGITS is the one in charge of all cultural events in the Western world, big and small. He it is who creates bizarre coincidences and accidents when any creative work is under way. It is his doing when the composer of the unknown music 'just happens' to be sitting next to the film director in the pub when he goes for a drink. Why John Stuart Mill's maid just happens to burn Carlyle's manuscript, so an improved version has to be written. Burroughs' *Naked Lunch* is a well-known case in point – had his pistol not happened to miss the apple on his wife's head and get her temple instead, would post-modern fiction have got under way, would Kerouac's paper-roll manuscript of *On the Road* have survived rejection by forty publishers intact? Was this why Kerouac told people the book had been dictated by the Holy Ghost? The GCGITS (whose acronym is as unpronounceable as the Tetragrammaton, the Hebrew name of God) looks after, or destroys, the tiniest sparrow too, and is now producing ghosts out of the wall to dictate what happens next in this book.

He and the GSWITS – the Great Screen Writer in the Sky who is composing the script for world events, and who alas is a rotten writer, a B-movie writer, what with his fall of Troy, his *Marie Celeste*, his grassy knoll, his global warming, his Credit Crunch, his Bernie Madoff, his Underpants Bomber – is making fictional events come so thick and fast I fear he's building up to a really bizarre end – like a child's story I just received. Written for a competition by an eight-year-old boy, it finishes, as he gets bored, thus: '– and then suddenly there was a great explosion and that was the end of everything – a-a-a-a-argh!' The GSWITS and the GCGITS are down at the pub most of the time, I fear, egging each other on. And there's no one, absolutely no one, in charge of anything.

But this is just me putting off the moment of decision: I could now go and follow Jackson as he visits his supremely uninteresting ex-wife and children in Battersea, and tries to down-scale her monthly maintenance cheque, I could stay with the young Beverley, or I could give you a further update on Cynara, D'Dora and Lola. Or I could give you an update on me. Guess what, it's going to be me. Me, me, me, that's all you get these days. But it is relevant, and for once I'm not in the basement.

A friend from Glastonbury drops by

Janice Barrington is an old friend; I knew her well when we were both young things in advertising and lived around the corner from each other. I hadn't seen her for some twenty years, and she hadn't been to Yatt House before. I was pleased to see her when I emerged from the basement and stopped work for the day. She was looking okay, if a bit shaggy-haired and startled, and rather older than her years, with the unkempt look of people who live in the country, see no point in getting up to town, and would weave their own clothes if they could. I don't suppose I looked much better: a rabbit startled in the dark by sudden headlights. The sunlight seemed very bright when I opened the door to her.

She had once been as bright, smart, rational and self-possessed as, say, Scarlet, but had married a mean kind of man, who had left her with two small babies and no means of support other than state benefits. She had moved to Glastonbury, thinking she might as well be poor in Glastonbury, home of the Festival, astrologers, crystal shops and King Arthur, as anywhere else, and soon discovered everyone who lives there is, by rationalist standards, and indeed mine, nuts. The further south-west you go in England, the more spiritual, poetic and poor everyone becomes. Janice's children are grown now and one of them – as his horoscope predicted, you may be sure – ended up rich and sufficiently unlike his father to house his mother in a nice little new bungalow just outside the town. I was glad for her.

She came in through the front door to our house and the first thing she said (instead of what most people did: 'What a lovely house, aren't you lucky, just look at that view') was: 'Oh dear, I don't know how you can live in an old house like this.' Which I took to mean she was jealous and wanted to make me feel bad.

I said, but the English like to live in old houses, and she said houses sop up the vibes of whoever lived in them, reflected them back, and were pretty much bound in the end to infect anyone who lived there with bad karma. The older the house was, the worse the effect. She personally had felt so much better since she started living in her new bungalow. More energy, no more depression.

It was not a good start to a reunion. But old friends are old friends and I excused her inwardly on the grounds that she had had a difficult life, and I made her coffee and we chatted about the children and so forth, but actually I wanted to get back to Beverley, Scarlet, Cynara, Lola, friends and family. We were sitting in the kitchen when she suddenly shivered and said, didn't I feel a cold draught, so I closed the window I had just opened. I had offered her hot milk in her coffee, and left the pan on the Aga, and it had boiled over. Not much, I'd got it in time, just a drop or two – but she'd raised her eyebrows and said, from the look of me I'd been working too hard. Thanks.

'Here it comes,' she said, triumphantly. 'I knew it. The poltergeist smell.'

I asked her what kind of smell poltergeists had and she said it was very distinctive. Acrid, like electrical wires overheating and a slight metallic whiff of opium poppy. Had I noticed any activity? I said I had not, and to me it smelled like burned milk. She then said she had been studying as a medium and could tell from my body language I was in denial. I ignored this and said I didn't know people could study to be mediums, I thought it was a gift which you either had or didn't have, and personally I was pleased not to have it. Here and now were quite enough to be getting on with. She said there was more to life than getting through it, and I had a sense of déjà vu, and realised it was Scarlet saying, 'There is more to life than passing it on.' So I replied, like Beverley, 'You could have fooled me,' and then thought really it was pretty pathetic to be mimicking your own fictional characters.

Janice looked around the house without much interest and asked me how I coped with so many stairs. She looked in my pretty living room and shuddered, saying something very unhappy had happened here. She poked her face around the door to the basement stairs and said, 'Ugh, I'm not going down there, darling. Bright red smudges on little blue shoes. Terribly like blood.'

I thought, 'That's okay, she's only picking up on little Beverley, and at least now we know her shoes were blue,' and then thought it was really wise to stay away from the occult, it could so easily drive you mad.

'I'd try to stay above ground, if I were you,' she advised, 'there are so many walk-ins about. It's the war, you know.'

Walk-ins, it seems, are spirit refugees from the Twin Dog Star Sirius, where a war is going on between the organic and the inorganic life forms. Yes, we are on the side of the organic. Mostly they're a high form of life, angel incarnations of an elevated kind, but there are one or two baddies amongst them, who tend to hover at ground level or below. They can move into your body at will, and can make you steal, cheat and even murder someone without you knowing anything about it.

'How convenient,' I said, and she looked hurt, and I was sorry. But I was feeling thoroughly foolish for having succumbed to my own other-world fantasies. I could see them all of a sudden for what they were, nourishment for saddos and weirdos with not enough to do. It would have been polite to offer Janice lunch but I didn't. I just wanted her to go.

She gave me her card, saying that if I wanted any advice she was there for me.

Janice Barrington, clairvoyant and medium extraordinaire. Karma cleared, houses delivered, walk-ins contacted. Don't trust your luck, trust me! Terms and conditions – and an e-mail address. Well, it was one way of making a living, and did explain her rather odd behaviour. I excused her. She was drumming up business as I daresay she had to. The son had lost his job in the City. The more ghosts she saw the more she would earn, and a house like mine was a godsend; and I was a sitting duck. She was off to the School of Occult Studies in Salisbury where she was studying for a diploma in Rosicrucian approaches to ageless living, with presumably extra modules on body language.

'Well, I must run,' she said, as she got into her valiant little banger. And I thought, it's all women do, really, isn't it, run. Tuck the children under the arm and try and find somewhere better, safer. You get into the habit when they're small and then just carry on.

I went down to the basement and travelled swiftly north, from whence the Borean wind blows. Better a cold wind than warm deceiving Livas, who blows in God knows what from the southwest. I've seen Boreas on Greek vases, a massively strong, winged old man with shaggy hair and beard, and a violent temper to match. But I can cope with him, better than I can Livas' sneaky demons. I bet Livas looks like a male version of Janice.

What Beverley does when Scarlet leaves

When Beverley heard the front door click behind Scarlet and was convinced that she had indeed left the house, she put down her book, took her laptop and Skyped her friend Gerry Askell in the Faröe Islands. Modern technology is wonderful.

At sixty-seven Gerry was eleven years Beverley's junior. Not that eleven years, at this stage of the game, made much difference. She switched the camera on: now that she'd had her hair done she looked okay, and webcams, showing a moving, talking image, have the knack of transmitting the spirit of the person, not just their looks. Gerry, responding, clicked his camera on. He had very little hair to worry about these days, anyway, and besides, was confident enough that women usually liked the look of him. His general appearance was of someone halfway between a man of action and an academic: he had a good strong build, a square face, bright eyes and a stubbly chin, which with a day or two of neglect would burst into a shaggy beard. He felt himself, not without reason, to be a veritable Harrison Ford of a man.

Beverley could see beyond Gerry to the gabled, grassy roofs and red wooden buildings of Tórshavn, and the North Sea beyond. There was no way she would ever move there, but it was pretty to look at. And perhaps it would be wiser to have Gerry stay where he was, all promise and no fruition. She liked having him at the end of a phone. It had been too long. But whether she actually wanted the exhaustion of having him in her bed was another matter. Beverley could see his gold fillings and the ridges along the top of his mouth. His deceased wife Fiona, Beverley's rival, had not ensured that he looked after his teeth properly.

Gerry for his part could see the daffodils of an English garden behind the clump of Beverley's expensively shampooed hair, and the arms of her expensively upholstered sofa, and the various lineaments of a contented old age which he would rather like for himself. He was in the Faröes, and had been for ten years or so, studying the second of the three plates of volcanic basalt which composed the island, one of which had lately proved to be oil bearing. But oil prospecting was a young man's job. His employers were thinking of pensioning him off. It was a good enough pension but even oil companies went bust, and he needed security, company and comfort. Gardens, a warm sun and daffodils beckoned, and Beverley still looked in pretty good nick and might even see him out.

And Beverley, seeing her ex-lover again, remembering the good times not the bad, and feeling a real pang of affection for him, could see she might do worse than to encourage him. She did not want a quiet life, to go peacefully to her grave. This could only be why she had Skyped him.

'I'm in a muddle, Gerry,' she said. 'I'm quite upset.' She had become good at playing helpless over the decades, and was of a generation who saw no need to be anything else. She was a lapsed Marxist, not a feminist.

'What's gone wrong?' he asked. 'I can come over if you need me.'

'No thank you, Gerry.' The tune from *The Beggar's Opera* ran through her mind. *By keeping men off you keep them on.* Tra-la-la. All the old tricks, still there.

'It's Scarlet. You know Scarlet?'

'My dear, how can I not? I know all your family like the back of my hand. You are the Marxist, Cynara the feminist, Scarlet the non-aligned and Alice is the born-again Christian.'

'Not exactly born-again. Kind of refound. I believe she's a Methodist, not a charismatic; anyway, she's certainly very much in love with Jesus at the moment. It may change, it has before. Cynara has decided she's a lesbian.'

'These girls will do anything to annoy. I don't suppose it will last long. And Scarlet? I hear she has Lola living in an alcove halfway up a wall with no safety rail, Cynara is hopping mad with her, and Scarlet is about to run off with Jackson Wright the vampire.'

'How can you possibly know this?' Beverley was startled. 'You're in the middle of the North Sea.'

'Because I've just clicked off from Cynara.'

'Why on earth? What has Cynara got to do with you?'

'In the old days, Bev, I spent time in your bed. We all but lived together. Did I make so little impression on you? Cynara was around. I was her father figure. But I see you have forgotten. No wonder I fled to Fiona's arms...'

Back in the mists of time Gerry had left Beverley's bed as the sun rose and by the time it set had married a fellow geologist called Fiona. Fiona had finally met her come-uppance, dying suddenly of leukaemia. That had been two years ago. She had forgiven Gerry, though he had caused her grief. Death is the final victory over sexual rivals; animosity weakens and disappears.

'...Cynara and I always got on. We kept in touch. I hated women and she hated men. We'd sound off together.'

'Cynara never told me this.'

'Why would she? She liked me and you hated me.'

'That was only when poor dear Fiona was alive.'

'Don't you poor dear me,' said Gerry. 'At least I'm only one wife down, you're three husbands. Wouldn't that make any man rather nervous?'

'Men have no staying power,' she said. 'Poor dear Winter got himself shot, your friend poor dear Harry died by his own hand, and poor dear Marcus fell under a train. No common cause.'

'Only exhaustion,' he said. 'Shall I come over? Just for a week or two?'

'I'll think about it,' she said, and heard the fall away of the Skype connection as she clicked the red button. She'll think about it but perhaps leave it at that. Why bother with flesh and blood since the picture on the screen provides so agreeable, intense and temporary an association?

She did not like the idea of Cynara keeping in touch with Gerry. It was going behind her back. It was bad enough when daughters defied you, hardly worse, it seemed, than when granddaughters did. She had failed her children. They resented her. They had interpreted her 'so long as you're happy' approach as idleness and lack of concern. Perhaps it had been. Alice was still acting out – Cynara maintained that her mother's flirtation with Jesus was a response to Beverley's long love affair with Marx; that Richie's flight to Hollywood and his homophobia were precipitated by Beverley's marriage to the bisexual Harry; that her own childhood had been so marred by her grandmother's disastrous heterosexual affairs it was no wonder she had turned to women for safety and comfort. But then, Beverley comforted herself, Cynara was a born blamer – her mother, the law, men, her assistants, anyone. The hell with it.

Beverley, Gerry and Fiona

There's this novel laid out like flood water over fields, quite calm and serene. And then all of a sudden Janice the trainee medium from Glastonbury comes tearing over the surface of the water like a speedboat, churning things up, sending waves slapping to the shore and making a terrible noise. She has shocked me back into some kind of sense. I have to forget all this ghostliness and get this story moving. The past has been clinging on to me: holding me back: making the present spread wide instead of moving on into the future. Somehow I have to get all this massive weight of water draining away from the fields and rushing through its proper channels again, and I promise I will. Even if it means moving out of here and shifting my laptop to some new bungalow in an urban estate. Free, as Janice would say, from the vibes coming out of these walls.

I should have been more understanding of Janice and asked her to lunch. One needs to be on good terms with witches, mediums and sorcerers. They can strike you down with writer's block in a mere flutter of kehua around the head, forget the Furies.

But back to the story and I will try and keep out of it for a while. I am doing myself no good by engaging with the real ghosts that live in these walls around me, while inventing these characters of mine. I am really disconcerted by the way Janice picked up on little Beverley while ignoring Mavis and the weekly laundress, both of whom at least once had a real existence in time. Novel is novel, I am I, ghosts are ghosts, fictional characters are fictional. It is surely not too difficult to keep them apart in one's mind. If I continue the novel in a more orthodox manner and keep clear of the diary form things should go more smoothly. To move upstairs and write in a more conventional space would seem a dereliction of a writer's duty, which is not to shy away from experience. Nor is it their nature. I am not surprised that Scarlet is a writer, as yet only of fashion journalism, but given time who knows what she will blossom into.

Onwards. But first allow me a little discursion now into the history of Beverley, Gerry and Fiona.

Gerry had been a good friend of Beverley's second husband Harry, architect to the Queen. Harry had died – by his own hand – exposed as gay by the *News of the World* – 'Queen's architect found in bed with male Palace employee' – at a time when homosexuality was still scandalous and certainly not admitted to be close to the monarchy. Gerry had courted Beverley assiduously for a whole three years after Harry's death, while she held him off. He got tired of waiting and one day ran off without warning with a fellow geologist. Love amongst the rocks and sediments.

Fiona, plainer and more academic than Beverley by far, had tiny hands and feet and noticeably short little fingers, which had made Beverley, who had strong broad colonial pioneering hands, dismiss her at first as any kind of rival. Effective rivals often come in deceptively callow forms. Better to be ousted by someone younger and prettier than by someone plainer and thicker. It's less painful, being explicable. Beverley had failed to notice the impressive string of degrees after Fiona's name, let alone her willingness to follow Gerry to the ends of the earth, which she did. Norway, the Orkneys, Iceland, the Faröes – where Gerry went Fiona gladly went.

Gerry thus snatched away, Beverley married Marcus Fletzner the journalist, who had been researching a book on the scandal around Harry's death. That had lasted four years, before he too died, stumbling under a train in the wrong company.

Gerry had lived and worked contentedly enough with Fiona in various places in the Borean far North, until she died of leukaemia. Beverley felt it was not surprising. Fiona had been a bloodless sort of person. And there is always a little *Schadenfreude* when a person responsible for discomfiture or embarrassment is removed from the world. It is a kind of victory. You have survived to give your version of the tale. They have not.

Gerry and Fiona had gone up from Tórshavn in the Faröes to the far island of Kalsoy for Christmas. It is not as cold up there as you might suppose as the Gulf Stream brushes around the islands. On Twelfth Night they'd been to the little fishing village of Mikladalur; it has pitch-black wooden houses with green turf roofs, and a pretty, white, red-roofed church in which model ships are strung from the ceiling, offerings from those grateful to God for preserving them in dangerous seas.

People keep a traditional watch for the seals here – folklore has it that they congregate in a cavern in these parts every Twelfth Night, throw off their skins and dance as the people they once were, before the sea took them. Fiona had wanted to go: she was born on Skye and loved the folklore of the sea creatures and the kelpies of the rivers and lakes.

'But how do you know which twelfth night?' said Gerry.

'The Christian one will do,' said Fiona, 'and besides, we have the time.'

So in that strange lonely holiday time after Christmas, Gerry and Fiona turned up on the dawn of Twelfth Night to stand where the tussock met the sand beneath a reddy-grey sky and to gaze out over a flat sea.

'Red in the morning, shepherds' warning,' said Gerry, 'there's going to be a storm.' They were the only people there. They were wrapped up well against the cold. Nothing happened except a shaggy horse came wandering down by the shore, stood still as if in a painting, and then wandered off again.

'That was no horse,' said Fiona. 'That was a kelpie. A water spirit.'

They were in a light-hearted mood. They went back to the boarding house to have breakfast, walked and bird-watched through the short day, and came again to the church and the shore at dusk, and stood there to wait and watch with a few other seal-sighting hopefuls. Someone played the fiddle, a cheerful ring dance about the selkie wife who shed her seal skin and married a farmer, and sure enough as Gerry and Fiona watched, presently a single seal did come ashore. Clouds were racing past the full moon: it was hard to be sure what was happening: everything gleamed so, and then yes, it was really a seal, and then another, and another, shiny sea creatures, so elegant in the water, so clumsy on land, flopping forward amongst the rounded rocks and driftwood, driven by God knows what – some say they respond to impending earthquakes on the seabed, hundreds of miles away, and Fiona collapsed.

She'd been complaining of tiredness, which was why she and Gerry had taken the holiday. A helicopter took her to the hospital at Tórshavn, where they did a white blood cell count, then whisked her off to Copenhagen. There they changed every drop of her blood, and watched her turn from pale to pink, but diagnosed acute lymphatic leukaemia and by the end of January she was dead.

Poor Fiona, who was rambling towards the end, kept assuring the nurses the seals had claimed her red blood cells for their own –

the phocids needed extra haemoglobin for diving, the seas being so polluted they must dive ever deeper – and left her only the white ones. It wasn't the nurses' fault they could do nothing. It was hers. What was the point of Gerry explaining to her that she'd been working with benzene: a series of experiments on the emulsification of oil and brine, and the varying levels of pH toxicity in sea water, and just hadn't been careful enough. Benzene kills, but not phocids.

Women can pass out of male lives with surprising ease. When Beverley wrote to Gerry with her condolences she had a letter back within the week, suggesting they get together again. He saw himself as a practical man, a man of decision and action. She had said no but they could, eventually, resume their friendship. Since then he had become an on-and-off semi-suitor. She supposed he coveted her house as much as he did her. He had lived a wandering life and had no fixed abode, and hers would do very nicely to retire into in his old age. But if you waited for a man without self-interest you would wait for ever.

She should not have Skyped him when she was feeling bored, as one should not go shopping when one is hungry. He might indeed take it into his head to come over and rescue her. Men were forever rescuing you and landing you in worse trouble than when you began. She should not have stirred him up. But she was fed up with the way the young had it so easy: how confident they were, how they dreaded so little and expected so much. She wanted a companion to tell things to, true – but surely she could employ a ghost-writer just to get it all down? Suddenly her past needed a proper airing. She had had to wait many decades to feel able to face it.

She went back to her book. It was only a dog-eared copy of an old Tom Clancy thriller, which she could reach from her sofa without having to get up. The book was both too familiar and boring, so she put it down and got through to Louis on his mobile.

The trouble with Beverley, as she would be the first to admit, is that she will do anything for a bit of excitement. The conversation with Gerry has merely whetted her appetite.

Down here writing

It's not working. Yet here I have been behaving properly as a writer, have I not? Uninvolved, temperate, superior, rational, in command of my material, but good practice has not been as I hoped; it has not been enough to hold back the meta-real. The sounds are beginning again. It may be nothing to do with the wind direction, just something to do with too-abrupt changes in the temperature – or am I looking for excuses? We had five days of really hot sunny weather, during which time I was pleased to be down here in the cool, but now suddenly overnight it's a normal English June, which means hail is battering the roses, and I am seeing as well as hearing things I had rather not. I really can't blame the weather any longer. For a writer to brush too close to the other side is a dangerous business: to talk of ghosts is to create them. 'Talk of the Devil' – and all that. Janice was the final straw. I can hardly believe that writing about the seal creatures of the North, the shape-shifting selkies, let alone Maori kehua, is going to summon a whole batch of Victorian domestic ghosts to the here and now, yet it seems to be so. It's not just some harmless timeslip but something more disconcerting and even threatening.

Today my senses seem rather too acute for comfort. From time to time there's another sound in the room, a raspy asthmatic breathing. I once lived with my mother in a converted barn, where horses had been stabled, and she swore that on quiet evenings she could hear them breathing.

I look around; there's no one there, of course, just the old sheet which keeps the dust out, draped over the portable midi keyboard that's kept down here in case of gigs. Just an old sheet, I say, but actually it's quite special to me, so worn from use and many washings that its original red and green French swirls have faded to something beautiful. It's seen me through many beds and many marriages. I bought it at enormous expense from a linen store in Sloane Street back in the seventies; it cost £120 even then, king-size. Those were the days.

It's not moving or swaying or anything, just this kind of ticking sound and a sniffling from beneath it. Perhaps the midi piano has virtual air in virtual organ pipes, if that's what they have. Perhaps, probably, not. I would think a wall heater behind it had been turned on, and the plumbing was coming to life, but there's no wall heater there. Not quite ticking now, more the sound of chopping on a wooden board, and then it slows, stops, starts again. I realise what it is. My eyes are watering slightly. It is the cook chopping onions a hundred or so years ago. I can swear it's that. And if that's all it is it's not so bad at all. But I had a nasty fright.

It's raining hard outside. Perhaps whenever it rains hard she chops onions. Perhaps Cook, whose name is Mrs Avis – the Mrs is a courtesy: she is really a Miss – was chopping onions, with tears streaming out of her eyes and said one day back then, 'My tears are going as hard as they raindrops,' and somehow the moment has lingered, and whenever it rains really hard the moment re-creates itself. I hope it's onion tears, not tears of grief: I hope it doesn't presage something awful; no, it's surely more like the fluttering of the kehua above Scarlet's head, with their bad advice heard or not heard.

I'm pretty sure the kehua have left Beverley alone; surely Beverley has been cleansed and is liberated: why otherwise did I make her stand beneath the shower, and set off in pursuit of Gerry? How else can I know as much as I do about her childhood, other than now she is letting me in to look at her memories?

No, these are onion tears, not funeral tears. They don't mean I'm going to pop my clogs any moment now, even before I finish this book. Do they?

What a wet day it is; the wheelbarrow Maureen has left outside my window is six inches full of water. Maureen is our gardener – this house still requires its servants, it seems. She makes wickerwork cradles and coffins and when she has time she hews and digs for us. Not today. No one with any sense goes out on days like this unless they have to. The daisies on the lawn, the other side of the window, at my eye level, haven't even bothered opening. The buttercups seem defeated and the remaining apple-blossom pink is dulled and sodden. The washing machine is churning away in the room next door – on the hot wash with the towels so there's a warm sudsy smell.

I am going upstairs to have a cup of coffee. If this room is haunted how am I going to finish this novel? Mavis and Mr Bennett were a kind of conceit; this feels a bit too real. How do I know about Mrs Avis? Did I simply make it up?

Then fortunately upstairs the doorbell goes, and I hear Bonzo bouncing in to be dog-sat by Rex my husband, who comes down from his attic fastness to offer him affection, concern and lamb bones. Bonzo comes galloping down the cellar stairs to make sure I'm here, bringing a healthy wet-dog smell with him; he stares puzzled at the draped piano and then decides it's okay whatever it is, circles me, nuzzles me, lollops upstairs again to slurp water and crunch lamb bones. He's a Welsh collie; they're really smart. If he thinks it checks out, it does. I will postpone my coffee, agree with Bonzo that it's just one of those things, stay where I am and get on.

Louis at work when Beverley's call is put through

MetaFashion is in Maddox Street, in that rather dim, elderly section of London between Bond Street and Regent Street where property speculators have not yet got a foothold, and things look pretty much as they did in the fifties. Small family businesses continue to operate. Tailors sit cross-legged under first-floor windows and sew by hand, the law of 'ancient lights' still in force, so no new building can stand between them and their right to light. MetaFashion employs a regular staff of sixteen when things are quiet, rising to as many as fifty when they're busy – designers, carpenters, sexually ambiguous electricians, butch builders, and a clutch of eight regulars, girls (more or less) too anorexic to be sexually active, but good with needle and thread. There's a showroom in front, offices above, and extensive workshops behind. *Icehouse Vamp* was finally shipped out the day before; approved designs for *Caribbean Mayday* are not yet in from Moscow, so today, thank God, they are quiet.

MetaFashion is a family company owned and controlled by Louis, who is also its business manager, his mother Annabel (a sleeping partner, who likes to be kept informed) and his cousin D'Kath, who inherited it from her mother Amanda Stapleton, the society beauty and heiress. Fortunately D'Kath and Louis get on very well, and she is one of the few people at MetaFashion who does not assume, to Louis' chagrin, that he is a closet gay. D'Kath is the acknowledged driving force of MetaFashion; she it is who selects the staff, barks at the men, hisses in a sibylline way at women, and has a pool of coffee-making interns at her fingertips, pretty girls who turn up to learn the trade, earn no money and wear lipstick well. Those with less than well-defined lips apply for jobs in vain.

Where other similar companies struggle in a recession, Meta-Fashion – in its noisy, panicky, excitable way – prospers. It reads the minds of top designers, tempers fantasy with practicality, meets its deadlines, produces themed sets and catwalks that do not crumble, or bend, or trip the models, and most importantly knows how to pack safely and transport efficiently. Thanks to Louis, it also makes a profit. Louis is much appreciated for his sensitivity, his tact, his reliability and his business acumen. Unlike Scarlet, he operates on a you-win/I-win basis and has no truck with head-games.

But this is not how Louis wants to be known. He wants his creativity to be understood and appreciated. He wants to write his novel: it is all in his head; he watches and observes, a still centre, while those around him whizz and snap like sparklers and fizzle out. He has forgotten all about the row with Scarlet when he gets the call from Beverley. He has been on the phone to the Moscow fashion house, trying to explain that to combine a concept of May-day as an English spring ritual, a call for help for aircraft in distress, and the Caribbean as a pirates' playground may prove difficult. Mind you, MetaFashion had had a thematic difficulty with *Icehouse Vamp*, just shipped off to Paris in numbered parts ready for reconstruction the other end – a fantasy of blue-and-silver trees in which models rose from coffins on to a gold-leaf-covered catwalk. Gold leaf always impressed clients but was actually cheaper than you'd think. That phone call was made and successfully concluded and now here was Beverley on the phone suggesting he drop everything and go to Costa's in Soho because Scarlet had taken his suitcases and was running off with a film star called Jackson Wright.

Had Beverley been able to say 'running off with your wife' it might have made more impact – the impulse would be to run off and get the property back, and beat up the thief. But the impulse is not so strong when it comes to partners; the other is a person, not property, and this has both advantages and drawbacks. Louis felt he had one or two things around the office he had to see to before he made his way to Costa's. Scarlet was a free agent. He had hoped she was not 'seeing someone else', but found he had no trouble imagining that she was.

Scarlet did not share his enthusiasm for Nopasaran; the offence she took when her mother declined to come to the projected wedding had always seemed disingenuous – she had simply decided to keep her options open in case someone better came along. Now she had made it clear that she did not want children, so really it would be sensible of him just to stay where he was and not pursue her. It would certainly please his mother if he did not.

Yet Scarlet and he were accustomed to one another, and he half loved her, and it was not common sense that was of prime importance here; rather it was sensibility. He did not like to think of her with another man. He assumed she had never brought whoever it was home to Nopasaran: she surely would not go as far as that. He would in time go after her. But not at once. Let her not think he would come running: he had an independent life outside Meta-Fashion, outside Nopasaran, outside Scarlet. She was bluffing: trying to get him to sell the house. Well, he wouldn't.

Instead he made a call to Samantha, the Matron's daughter from long ago. He had traced her through Facebook, one morning after a particularly savage row with Scarlet, and acquired her number through a mutual friend. He had not called her until now, but merely kept her phone number in his wallet, which he knew Scarlet was not interested enough to search. Samantha had many, many friends. Her favourite film was ET, which Louis and she had seen together, in the school days before disaster, before Stuart had hanged himself and thus made everything thereafter impossible. There was one particular Facebook snapshot with her husband, standing on a sand dune on a family holiday: her husband was shorter than she was, and it looked as if her sandals were cut with the leather seam in the centre. It was a camping holiday: the tent was in the background. It was so different a world from the one Louis inhabited that he had ventured no further. Now he did.

How Jackson is getting on

Jackson is running late. Cleaning up for Scarlet took more time than he thought and then the traffic was bad. It is possible, he can see, that he may soon lose his licence. The night the police stopped him his drinking companions ought to have taken his keys away before he set off for home, instead of plying him with yet more booze. Full of arseholes, the Hampstead pub where that fuck of a second-rate TV director hangs out and holds court. Jackson is normally careful about his alcohol intake. Drugs are one thing, can even brighten the eye and speed the mind, but alcohol blurs a man's looks, and he is honest enough on a good day to face the fact that he earns his living as much by his looks as by his acting ability.

Now, stuck in gridlock at Waterloo, he can foresee a future in which he has to travel by public transport and he does not look forward to it. At least Scarlet will be able to drive him around. The Prius is trendy enough, though more of a woman's car than a man's. He tries not to let himself be depressed, tells himself the fates are on his side, one door opens and the other closes. *Upstairs, Downstairs* today, *Hamlet* tomorrow. The life of an actor is all uncertainty. He does not want to actually see his ex-wife Briony, and hopes he will not have to. With any luck she will be at work, teaching.

These days Briony is polite to him but affects to despise him; women are so good at that. Briony makes like a sniffy wet blanket wherever she goes. He prefers the company of girls who know they are bad and like money and a good time, who despise themselves more than they despise him. Scarlet marvels, rather than despises, and is at ease in all company, which Jackson is not. He prefers circles where nobody has a university degree, though this is a problem in the film business, which has become poncified and over-educated, while still riddled with public-school wankers who never seem to go away.

Scarlet, he can take her anywhere; and she can open doors for him usefully in high circles. He might even marry her. If she splits with Louis there will be a property settlement of some kind, and her house should fetch a lot. And if not, she has a good job and a steady salary, and an accountant has explained to him that when it comes to paying off debts, 'regularity of income' is the key.

Jackson finds a parking place in the once dreary, now posh street where he and Briony had bought a house together when they married. He was twenty and she was thirty-six. He was making the first of the vampire films; she was the make-up girl; she seduced him and got pregnant. She said no, she wasn't going to have a termination, this was her last chance to settle down: Jackson – he had only just become Jackson Wright: in the beginning he had answered to Colin Wince – had better marry her. If his fans thought their youthful angel had fathered a baby by an older woman and then dumped her it would be bad for his career. So he married her. He could scarcely remember the ceremony he was so high at the time. But it was only weed; those gentle days of soft drugs, not hard, natural not chemical. He'd then made a series of bad script and life choices, mostly because he followed Briony's advice.

His agent Mike Bronstein had advised him to pull out after the first two vampires but Briony said why pay an agent 15 per cent when all you had to do was to bother to read the contracts yourself, and the scripts were brilliant. So he'd signed up for the series and ended up without the residuals that would have made him really rich. He'd been robbed. But Briony had what she wanted, namely, a house and a baby, and soon she was pregnant with the next. And once she had what she wanted she lost interest in Jackson; treated him like a tomcat who might eat the kittens if he came near, despised and reviled him as a useless thesp with his brain in his dick, wouldn't share the bed, revealed she was a Catholic and wouldn't use contraceptives, turned the children against him, divorced him, and having persuaded him he didn't need a lawyer, took the house and vast sums in maintenance as well.

That was Briony. But oddly the South London house still felt like home. He guessed if you hoped for affection from someone and they didn't give it you would go on battering yourself against that person for ever in the vain hope that they eventually would. He wanted some sign of recognition and acceptance from her. But she was like his mother, and cold.

After the divorce he wouldn't come and take away his belongings so she'd piled them all into one room and put a notice up for the boys: DO NOT ENTER: TOMCAT'S LITTER BOX. All because she resented some poor girl called Flora he used to meet in a trans-sexual bar, and then visit in hospital where she was to die of Aids. 'Oh good,' Briony said when he told her. 'One more piece of human crap out of the way.'

Though after Flora died Briony gradually became more friendly and when he called round to collect something or other from the cat-litter room as she still called it, she'd give him a cup of coffee and an update on the boys' progress. They were good-looking boys and had both gone to university, one studying philosophy, the other theoretical physics.

'At least they have your looks and my brains,' their mother had once said by way of acknowledgement. 'Supposing it had been the other way round!'

He'd tried to keep in touch when the boys were small, but now they were out of his intellectual reach and seldom contacted him. They didn't even remember Father's Day. 'Our dad the film star' didn't have the cachet for them it did in circles which were more vampire oriented. His boys didn't even go to the cinema. Perhaps Scarlet would change; she might want babies with him and he could get it right next time around. He'd met Louis, a pallid kind of bloke and a closet gay, and what Scarlet saw in him he couldn't understand. He would have thought more of Scarlet if he had thought better of Louis.

What Jackson did next

Jackson opened the door with the key his ex-wife kept in a false rock just by the dustbins, where only a few brave plants and shrubs survived the onslaught of toxic traffic fumes from nearby Clapham High Street. He was glad to find the key there, though he had warned Briony time and time again about the absurdity of using a plastic box as a hiding place.

'It doesn't even look like a rock,' he had complained. 'Far more like the turd of a big dog.'

'All the more reason for people not to look inside it,' she'd said. She was sharp and shrewd and unpleasant but couldn't help it.

As soon as the boys left home she had had the builders in, divided the house into four and let it out to what Jackson was convinced were illegal immigrants, and then trained as a teacher. She spent nothing and must have accumulated a fortune in unspent alimony and undeclared rents. She was as mean as a ferret. Even her coffee came from Lidl.

'Anyway you don't live here any more, so what's it got to do with you, what kind of coffee I choose?'

The dustbins had increased in number since last he visited: two weeks back there were only four, now there were six, differently coloured and labelled, with days of the week painted on them. Wandsworth Council had been busy with its drive to save the planet. All were overdue for collection, judging by the sweet sickly smell of fermentation that rose from them. The number of doorbells had increased too. That meant even more tenants.

Even as he put the key to the lock the door opened and Briony pushed past him towards the bins, strong workaday hands carrying two full plastic sacks, one flung over each shoulder. He had it in his head that she'd be off teaching and was taken aback to see her. The Briony he had married had been lithe and lissome, a red-headed, freckled Doris Day with a smiley face, an artist at home amongst the pots and paints and creams and all the wizardry of the studio make-up room. It had been a disguise. The real Briony had always been lurking underneath, a stocky, blunt-looking woman in her mid-fifties, with a grey pudding-basin haircut, decent but hardly erotic in a pair of striped flannel pyjamas. Jackson thought of Scarlet and her little white hands, elegant heels and languorous waist.

'What are you doing here?' Briony asked. Her South London accent seemed stronger than ever. 'What do you want? Did you think I'd be out?'

'I just needed a couple of things from the house,' he said.

'Oh, what?'

'Just my driving licence,' he said.

'Just, just,' she said. 'Always just. Never ever head-on or definite. I don't know how she stands it. I don't suppose she will for long.'

'Who?' Jackson asked, startled.

'This girl you're seeing, the journalist. I read her column sometimes. I thought she was meant to be happily married.'

How did she know about Scarlet? He'd said nothing. There had been a fairly constant flow of girls to the penthouse, in and out, all found wanting; they had the looks or sparkle to make you interested, but in the morning all you wanted was for them to go away.

Scarlet was different; he wanted her for the night, for breakfast, and now for lunch, dinner and bed in between. But how was Briony to know that? He realised she was jealous. She hadn't been like this about any of the others. Women seemed to have an unholy instinct for when anything fundamentally changed.

'You'd better come in now you're here,' she said. 'I can't stand around in my pyjamas. So what's she really like?'

He followed her inside. She put on the kettle and measured out a meagre tablespoon of coffee for the cafetière, and even that she levelled off with a knife. Inside, the house seemed the same as when he'd left it, the same style of practical untidiness, just the right side of squalor. She didn't like change.

'She's going to move in with me,' he said.

'And you had to come and tell Mummy,' she said. 'Do what you like. It's nothing to do with me.'

'We could get together again,' he said. 'You and me. I'm thinking of giving up the film business.'

That quietened the tongue for a second or so. But then she was back.

'You mean the film business is giving you up? No longer the boy wonder? The drink and the drugs and the girls have rather taken their toll. I always told you they would.'

'We were together in the beginning,' was all he could say.

'In your dreams,' she said. He felt angry now.

'You must be doing all right here,' he said. 'I'm going to stop the maintenance. It was meant to stop when Howell was eighteen. I'm entitled.'

'You never even send him a birthday card,' Briony said. 'You never cared about either of them. I wish you'd take your things away and not keep turning up where you're not wanted. I could let the room.'

He found the driving licence where he hoped he would, in the drawer of his desk, and left. She watched him go, unsmiling. He hoped he wouldn't be late for Scarlet. There was always a gap between saying you were leaving, and actually leaving. He needed to be there when he said he would be. It would be difficult explaining to Scarlet about Briony.

Look, he would say to her, try and understand. She's more like my mother than an ex-wife. If I go near Briony she spits and bites like a female cat to keep me off. It was all too like incest. We thought we could get away with it. But then the boys came along and they felt more like brothers than sons. We didn't know what to do. No, actually, he wouldn't say that. He hardly understood it himself. Why would Scarlet?

Coming back across Waterloo Bridge he saw that *Oedipus Rex* was on at the National. Now there was a part! He would try and make things up with Bronstein. His original ambition had been stage, not film. Vampires had waylaid him, turned him into the living dead.

Things are not working out in the basement

I have tried, I really have. I've kept myself out of the story. I've tried not to comment. I have even taken to putting a string of garlic above my desk to keep out vampires, kehua, breathing laundresses, chopping cooks, fidgety kitchenmaids, revenant collies, whatever. I have tried to keep characters and ghosts separate, and under control, while acknowledging that none has any reality, but are all projections of my own fancy transmitted through Microsoft. They have no true existence until translated on to the screen via a keyboard.

The trouble is, I get less real, these characters get more real. I hardly go out of the house now: I feel I have to get on. Another thousand words, another; before whatever magic it is dries up and I have to rely on rational thought and an acquired and practised past to get it on to the page. I have written thirty-four novels in my life, and God knows how many short stories: it is more than most writers manage and with good reason. The brain can barely contain them. They fizzle and snap and laugh and cry and complain in there, and ease what is left of me out. They *reject* me.

Willy-nilly, *volens, nolens,* I find myself turning into what the New Agers call a channeller, which Janice claims to be: someone who picks up and communicates with the spirits, only for me it is with fictional characters. The ghosts of the past are reluctant to come forward, but these personages from alternative universes have no shame. 'Me, me, me, what about me!' they cry. I have been fighting back – determined to keep myself in here with them, but I think perhaps I have been misguided, worn too easy a passage for them. I must change tactics.

A couple of things happened recently to bring me to this conclusion. I was shaken, I must say, when Jackson turned out to be more worthy of sympathy than I thought. He was not going to be just the rat that ran across the purity of new snow and soiled it and was a threat to our Scarlet; he was going to have to be taken seriously as a person, he was not going to be just a shagpile penthouse villain. Though I have met them and they exist. And then his past turns out to involve vampires. I hadn't expected that at all. I could just as well have had him star in the first place in a series of college comedies, I nearly did; really I didn't give the matter two thoughts, and that was before I had even realised about the kehua as metaphor for generational family dysfunction.

It's why I tell my MA students – I teach creative writing in a university, one day a week – not to delete passages apparently irrelevant to what you are trying to do – but to keep an off-cut file and save them there in case you realise later why it was you wrote that: it wasn't irrelevant at all, but key to the whole thing. The sensation is that you don't exactly write novels – you simply unfold them, or fish them up from a well, or hook them down from the sky. But you're still the one in charge – the appointee, without particular merit, just there to do the job – and you have your responsibilities. If I'm not careful Lola is going to end up striking Jackson dead with a silver paperknife, equivalent to a silver bullet or a stake through the heart.

Because really if Gerry the heartless is to sit amid gravestones (which he is) and mourn the loss of the wife he seemed to take so lightly, Cynara the powerhouse of moral authority is to be in thrall to Dyke Dora, the pretty little mountain climber, and Louis is to want to write a novel – where indeed will it end? Things are getting out of control, and I suspect it's because these creatures of my invention are tapping into the energies that already reside in these stone walls. Two sets of ghosts might yet combine to make one wandering dybbuk, to waylay me on the way to the supermarket. I am trying to be light and facetious but it is difficult. I am spooked, spooked, spooked.

I am going to move upstairs to my regular office. That's not really giving in. It is common sense. Things happened, and not just Jackson and the vampires, which led me to conclude that garlic alone was not enough. I even tried burning sage and circling my desk with the ash, but Vi came and vacuumed it up.

What I suffered was a hallucination that was, finally, visual as well as auditory. The face which appeared in the wallpaper was, I am sure, only damp. True, I had been working hard and I was tired, and too much coffee to keep one awake may make one over-prone to imagine things. It was a Sunday and over the road in All Saints' Church (I am talking the reality of here and now), Evensong was in full swing. The only trouble, on reflection, is that the church here and now across the road is deconsecrated and no services are held there, yet I had heard the church bells clearly enough and paid them no attention, and strains of organ music likewise. So the staff were all over the road attending to their souls, and only Mavis was left behind. The fire had been playing up and needed relighting and Mavis had been delegated to be the one to do it. And I could actually see Mavis for once, with her beskirted little bum in the air as she bent over to feed paper spills and kindling into its reluctant heart.

Then I watched as Mr Bennett came down into the basement,

and as he brushed by me the breath of his violent passing actually ruffled the papers on my desk. That was too much overlapping for comfort. He was breathing heavily – and I realised I had heard that sound quite often. He was a big man, dark and flushed, very handsome in a portly kind of way, with a moustache, and a beard that ran from his ears to under his chin, which was clean shaven. Quite fancy for a small-town country solicitor. I knew it was Mr Bennett and I knew he was angry with Mrs Bennett, who wouldn't let him into her bed since she had three children already and had no intention of having any more; he was a man in his mid-fifties who was accustomed to getting what he wanted whenever he wanted it. The rest of the Bennett family had gone out to tea in the gig, so Mr Bennett was down here, naturally enough, to see if Mavis would oblige. I don't know how I knew this any more than I knew how Jackson came to be in *Vampire Rising* all those years back, or forwards, depending on your perspective.

Mavis didn't hear him coming, and when his long strong fingers pinched her rump she uttered a little gasping squeal of surprise which would really have turned him on, so when she wheeled to see who it was and he pulled her to him and pressed her small body to him she'd have felt the hard determined lump beneath the skin-tight trousers. I'd heard that little gasp many a time but not known until now what it was about. Mavis being pinched. I'm not saying it really happened, just that I remembered it happening, in much the same way as I remembered Briony using the blade of a knife to even off the measured tablespoon of coffee, or indeed Rex this Sunday suppertime, checking over mussels for the *moules marinière*, making sure all the shells were safely closed, so we weren't poisoned.

'Mr Bennett, sir, you should be ashamed of yourself,' I heard her say. 'Poor Mrs Bennett being out and all.'

'Don't be hard on me, Mavis,' he said, 'I'll pay you double.'

I caught a glimpse of Mavis' face, pale but pretty, with brown button eyes and a naughty mouth, and then the pair of them faded out, and a sound-only background track started again; Mr Bennett's heavy breathing as he lunged downstairs, Mavis's little squeal: but no words, no pictures. The GCGITS was editing the tape as it looped, messing around; he will sometimes allow a glimpse, no more. Well, I could cope with that. Nothing terrible was happening. Mavis was obviously in command of the situation. Little girls can be quite competent when it comes to dealing with big men. I felt quite privileged to be allowed this vision of the past; it was like having one's screenplay performed, one's own invention, until now confined to words on paper, coming to life as actors seize the words and voice them. There is nothing more gratifying.

But then something more disturbing happened. Janice looked in on her way back from the Rosicrucian course in Salisbury. The doorbell rang and I saved the text, and went upstairs to answer it. Rex usually does but it was a Thursday and I knew he was out at the market. Janice looked even odder than she had on the outward journey: her eyes even more poppy and her hair flatter and straighter and thinner, as if all of her was being consumed from within, leaving her even less substantial amongst her voluminous hand-crafted garments. The passage of the spirits through the body as you channel them from one world to the next can quite wear one away, it seems. (Not so, alas, with fictional characters, or perhaps I just take care to pad myself well with flesh to stop it happening; though come to think of it writing in the basement had mysteriously left me thinner, though I eat as well as usual.) Janice wouldn't take tea or coffee or fruit juice, but only hot water. Rex came back from the market and put the fish in the fridge, and then excused himself and fled upstairs to the attic. Janice's spiritual absurdities disturb him; he is a good Christian, as am I. Faux religions tend to bring the real ones into disrepute and it distresses him to witness it.

I asked Janice politely if it had been a successful course, and she said yes, it had, it had sharpened her channelling powers. Humanity was learning a great lesson at this time.

'We must learn to realise our Godhood, that we are intertwined with the Prime Creator and all that exists,' she said. 'Over the weekend that understanding became part of me.'

I said I was glad for her. She said her over-self was stronger than ever; her connections with superior alien intelligences firmer; this was a crucial transition time in helping earth bring in an era of peace. The old ones were with us to guide us to the light. She had been especially chosen to play her part.

I asked if she had met anyone interesting and she smiled and looked almost pretty and said a Master had come amongst them, a superior being, who had chosen her to share an intimate encounter. Well, I was pleased for her, though the encounter didn't seem to have returned her to sanity; on the contrary. The 'good shag' that men so often believe is 'all she needs' can be counter-productive. Mind you, one didn't know how good or otherwise it had actually been, and 'Master' sounded a bit exploitative. But I didn't delve any further.

She had a proposition to put to me, she said, which was really why she had come by. The vibes in my house had been so strong she wanted to bring round a party of ghost hunters from Glastonbury to stay in the house overnight. She would charge £100 per person; she could probably get a group of twenty people and we would share the profit. I said no, my home and its past were not up for commercial exploitation and anyway Rex would never hear of such a thing. Husbands, like mothers, are very useful for citing as reasons why one cannot do as one is asked.

She said it was a pity and hoped I would change my mind. She was sure I would. I was something of a medium myself, she told me, though I was in denial. She had been to a very enlightening session on the development of psychic powers and could now see my white aura, which meant spirits were part of me. The automatic writing was part of it all, surely I realised that? It was often used by spirits to communicate; did I astral travel? Sometimes she felt when she read my work that I had been in my dreams to these places I wrote about. I was pleased to hear that she read my work, though she probably didn't buy – she was not the sort – she'd use the library.

Janice asked if she could go down into the cellar and just sit a while, and having disappointed her about the ghost hunters I said yes and she disappeared down the worn stone steps. I trusted she wouldn't meet Mr Bennett on the way. I left her to it. I realised too late she would see the garlic and would now never let me alone. Within five minutes she was upstairs again. She was fluttering her hands and looked upset, though it was always a bit difficult to tell what was upset in Janice, and what was enthusiasm. It turned out to be enthusiasm.

She asked me who Alice was. She had met such a nice woman down there, with a high forehead, called Alice – who was singing hymns and praying for someone. I asked her what she was singing. Janice replied, 'A hymn. *Glad that I Live am I.* And what a beautiful, golden, positive hymn it was. I had no need to be frightened. The spirits in the basement were plentiful but all were well intentioned: I could get rid of the garlic, it didn't work anyway.

The trouble with the mad is that they often sound so convincingly sane one can begin to think as they do. I did not want to believe that she had picked up on my Alice, who was pretty much a subsidiary character anyway. Perhaps the Bennetts' cook had been called Alice? Though a nice woman praying did sound rather more like my Alice up in the North than the basement cook in the past, from whom I had mostly got rather irritated and possibly drunken vibes. It was no use asking Janice what Alice looked like because I did not know either. I had not turned my attention to a description because she hadn't actually appeared on the scene, just been someone in the background who disapproved of gays sufficiently not to come to her own daughter's wedding in case she was marrying one. So I asked her who this Alice had been praying for, which was rather brave of me, considering. Janice said she couldn't be sure, someone whose name started with a C: Clara? Cynara?

And that did it. I moved my laptop back up to my regular office on the first floor, where I have a pleasant view of the Pugin church and pink roses growing up the old rowan tree. My mother-in-law, aged ninety-three, died in this room – it was once the master bedroom, where the Bennetts would have slept or tried to sleep, but it was peaceful and bright, and sunlight chased away ghosts and fancies. And I am in the real rational world again, and ready to carry on.

I am now going to move to Part Two, where I will give an account of Beverley's growing up and the various adventures which brought her to Robinsdale. Just remember to keep in mind the story so far, please, while I get on with the *mater familias*.

Remember that Scarlet is about to meet Jackson at Costa's.

Jackson is on his way back from visiting his ex-wife Briony.

Gerry is on his way to rescue Beverley, who by virtue of Scarlet's good deed has been set free, released from kehua, Furies, grateful dead, kelpies, whatever, or however the dysfunctional genes which plague this family are registered.

Lola is on her mission to seduce her uncle Louis, who, reluctant to save Scarlet from herself, is calling up his lost love Samantha.

Cynara is heaving D'Dora's possessions about and feeling guilty about Lola.

And Alice, one can only suppose on Janice's evidence, is praying for Cynara.

It is possible for you to simply move on to Part Three and get back to how the family resolved their problems, by one simple murder, and be done with Beverley. It depends on how interested you are in how life experience, over time, makes one what one is. But if you've got this far, you might as well just read on.

The 'one simple murder', by the way, was spur of the moment, but I'll try and make it work.

PART TWO

Beverley, pre-pubertal

By the age of seven Beverley regarded both her parents as crass usurpers, and had decided with her friend Evelyn that she too had been switched at birth and was a princess by rights. But by twelve she had quite fallen in love with the man she knew as her father, and was proud to claim him as her own. He had, she thought, the looks of Leslie Howard in *The Scarlet Pimpernel*, screened at the Coromandel Town Hall in 1942, to that small town's great excitement. Dr Arthur Audley was well fitted to play romantic leads. He was long-nosed, high-browed, short-jawed and sensitive, with haunted and haunting eyes and full, sensuous lips. His women patients adored him, though by now he was noticeably ageing and his hair was receding, making his tall brow taller still. Rita had grown tougher and more gauntly horse-like as the years went by; she was kind, busy and practical, but lacked eroticism. Beverley liked her but dismissed her as of no account, disparaging her as she grew into her disdainful teenage years with just a raised eyebrow here, a quizzical eyebrow there. It drove Rita mad.

'Do you think she knows?' she asked Arthur once.

'There's nothing for her to know,' Arthur said. 'She was too small.'

'We'll have to tell her one day,' said Rita. 'Supposing someone from Amberley comes up here and puts two and two together and she finds out?'

'We'll tell her when she's seventeen,' said Arthur. 'She's growing up to be quite a looker. She'll be more than old enough by then to know who she wants as a father and who she doesn't.'

Which Rita thought was a slightly odd way of putting it, but didn't say so. She was glad enough that Arthur had agreed that Beverley needed to be told eventually. A lot of families thought family secrets should be just that. Arthur went on to talk about incest and how rare it was in the Maori tribes and how common amongst the white pakeha in isolated areas, and the conversation moved on, to Rita's relief.

Arthur had a new Ford Mercury with a mighty V8 engine, of which he was inordinately proud. It was a great black monster, which had survived Axis submarines to get to New Zealand. It climbed the hills with impressive alacrity –some were so steep in Coromandel that the old Model Ts could only get up them in reverse gear. Little Beverley would sit in the front passenger seat beside him in the Merc when he went on house calls, sharing his pride. She was the Doctor's daughter, and the title gave her a sense of prestige and status which stayed with her for the rest of her life, and which even in direst circumstances would come to her aid. If some strange man bent over her naked body taking his pleasure at her expense, breathing fish and chips vinegar over her (only once, that), or she was reduced to cleaning toilets for a living, she could still say to herself ,'Yes, but I'm still the Doctor's daughter.'

Rita wouldn't go with Arthur on these excursions, too terrified of the hairpin bends, the rough surface of unmade-up roads, the precipitate drop down the mountainside if anything went wrong. Beverley was without fear. One day, halfway over the hill road to Kennedy Bay, the engine began to steam and they had to stop and get out and wait for it to cool. Arthur opened the bonnet and showed her how engines worked.

'Lie down beside me here,' he said, so she lay beside him in the yellow dust and he pointed out the brake cable and said this was the way to get rid of enemies. You weakened the cable by slicing it almost through with a Stanley knife. On these steep hills, with these hairpin bends, brake cables were a matter of life and death. Beverley thought that was a strange thing to say. He could be quite a frightening man, as well as a charming one. They lay there in the dust until the engine cooled; then they got up and brushed themselves down and continued on their way.

She'd waited three hours in the car that day while he delivered a baby. It was a difficult birth: a Maori family, and they had no money to pay. She wondered if there was anyone he wanted to kill? He was so good to his patients, but not always nice to Rita.

'Quite the little figure you're getting there,' he observed, on the way home.

She was wearing a summer dress with a pattern in blue and white oyster-shape whirls and she quite liked it, except she had noticed that instead of falling straight down it poked out a little on either side of her chest. It hadn't quite occurred to her that she was going to turn into a woman. She preferred herself as an eternal child. She blushed, and he laughed, and brushed his finger up against her cheek, affectionately, and through the cotton dress to feel the nipple, which stood up the way it did when she was swimming and the water was cold. That made her tingle and there was a sudden sort of plunging feeling between her legs. She supposed it was all right but wasn't quite sure. Then he added, 'Every day in every way, more and more like your mother.'

It didn't make sense. She didn't look in the least like Rita. Rita these days was flat all the way down and getting flatter. Did he see nothing? She stopped going out with her father on house calls, saying she had too much homework to do. She had, too. She was doing English, Maths, Latin, History, French, Chemistry, Physics and Biology for her school certificate. Beverley lost her admiration for Arthur and padded around after Rita instead, grateful for her attention, helping her with the surgery, looking after the livestock grateful patients left in lieu of payments – chickens, ducks, rabbits, once a sheep. She asked Rita if she could get a bra like the other girls, and Rita found her a strange garment with circular stitching, which made her small breasts stick forward like beacons. The men who stood around outside the Star and Garter waited for her to go by with the milk pail after school, and at home she would catch Arthur looking, so she stopped wearing the bra: instead she wore a too-tight vest, one she'd grown out of, to flatten herself, and got on with her lessons.

Her periods started, and the news that this was going to happen to her once a month, five whole days of that month, was shocking. She worked it out. That was a sixth of your life until you were fifty when you might as well be dead anyway.

Rita must have told Arthur because he looked at her in the odd way men had begun to and said, 'I hear you're quite the little woman, Bev.' She would have to change her name. Bev was intolerable: Cynara, perhaps, after Dowson. 'I have been faithful to thee, Cynara, in my fashion.' And she quite went off Rita, too. They'd talked about her behind her back.

Lola, pre-pubertal

Just a short break from my account of Beverley, because I was thinking of Lola at the same age, and wondering whether heredity showed through as far as a great-grandchild. It didn't. Lola became for a time so ethereally lovely that people of all genders, all ages, looked after her in the street. The sudden burst of oestrogen, running so near the surface of a tender, still childlike skin, was almost shocking in its impact. But Lola didn't mind: she liked it: she knew everything: she watched porn. It became her habit to sit on her father's knee while they watched TV, her firm peaky breasts pressed into his chest, her chin nuzzling into his neck. Jesper would shift uncomfortably and say, 'You're too old for this, Lola,' and once Lola replied 'Why call me Lola then? It's a bad-girl's name. What did you have in mind for me?'

Her mother Cynara had caught the daughter's eye and knew that she was being teased and not very pleasantly, and that what Lola felt for her mother was not so much love, as competition and anger. Cynara had had to subdue the impulse to slap. The stage passed quickly, thank God, the transparent quality went, so that by sixteen she was just another pretty, too-thin girl in a too-short skirt. She still had her virginity, so far as Cynara knew. As D'Dora remarked, 'Lola sees herself as Paris Hilton and probably has plans to wait until it's legal and then surrender it on YouTube.'

Beverley lived in a culture where children were seen and not heard, schoolgirls didn't date, nudity was shocking, porn unobtainable, and at the approach of puberty the sexes were segregated. Even in the primary schools there were separate entrances for boys and girls. You did not answer back, and you respected your elders and betters.

There, I should not have left Beverley. It is eleven o'clock on a hot Sunday morning and I can hear the church bells ringing, though there are no services over the road. The sound must be blowing up from St John's in the High Street. The window is wide open. And something flies in. It looks like a baby hummingbird, tiny, darting, brightly coloured, wings beating so fast they're just a blur. It rests for a moment on the top of my computer and stares at me with tiny glassy eyes, and is off again, and I am worrying for it almost as much as for me that it will blunder into something and hurt itself. Then, as suddenly as it has appeared, it is out of the window and is gone. Rex comes in – I must have cried out – and I describe this apparition and he laughs and says it was a hawk moth, and closes the window. But I take it as a lesson not to deviate from my account of Beverley, without straying into Lola territory, and then the untoward is less likely to happen. Sorry, folks.

Beverley at Fifteen

Beverley was a weekly boarder at Thames High School for Girls (founded 1880: motto, *Ut Prosim Patriae* – That I may be worthy of my country). The bus journey from Coromandel took a couple of hours along the coast road, and landslips or sudden torrential floods often made it impassable for days at a time so it was more sensible for her to board. The school uniform consisted of a blazer with the school crest, a white shirt, a pleated gymslip which disguised the figure, lisle stockings and lace-up shoes, a felt hat in winter and a panama in summer. In high summer a blue and white checked summer dress in cotton with a white collar was optional. Beverley chose never to wear it, which others found a little strange, but she was otherwise a gregarious, biddable, clever child among clever children, youngest in her class, serious but popular, with a gift for entertaining her friends, a way with words and no trouble at all to her teachers, other than the slight lift of the eyebrows, surprise at others' total crassness, that had irked Rita. She was even made Head Girl, in spite of a few doubts expressed in the staff room.

'She's laughing at us,' said Miss Butt, who taught Latin. 'She runs rings around us and pities us.'

'It's true,' said Miss Ferguson, the gym teacher. 'When she's working on the vaulting horse she gets this expression of, what – incredulity? Otherwise she's too good to be true.'

But Miss Crossly who taught maths said just because she was too good to be true didn't mean she wasn't. Mrs Barker the headmistress, who had been sent papers on the child's background, was the only one to know the girl's history, and said nothing.

Beverley as Head Girl proved to be fair, just and reliable. She knew no boys of her own age. While you wore school uniform you were out of bounds to men, and you could easily be in school uniform until you were eighteen. She had a vague theoretical notion of what went on in marriage between men and women, but had scarcely seen a naked body either in the flesh or in photographs – though there was a Fuseli in the Auckland Art Gallery, *The Serpent Tempting Eve*, which was instructive, and the Dowson poem, *Vitae Summa Brevis*, which haunted her, and made her long to be older and better able to understand it.

They are not long, the weeping and the laughter,
Love and desire and hate:
I think they have no portion in us after
We pass the gate.

They are not long, the days of wine and roses:
Out of a misty dream
Our path emerges for a while, then closes
Within a dream.

And then of course Cynara:

All night upon mine heart I felt her warm heart beat,
Night-long within mine arms in love and sleep she lay;
Surely the kisses of her bought red mouth were sweet;

But I was desolate and sick of an old passion,
When I awoke and found the dawn was grey:
I have been faithful to thee, Cynara! in my fashion.

I have forgot much, Cynara! gone with the wind,
Flung roses, roses riotously with the throng,
Dancing, to put thy pale, lost lilies out of mind;
But I was desolate and sick of an old passion,
Yea, all the time, because the dance was long:
I have been faithful to thee, Cynara! in my fashion.

I cried for madder music and for stronger wine,
But when the feast is finish'd and the lamps expire,
Then falls thy shadow, Cynara! the night is thine;
And I am desolate and sick of an old passion,
Yea, hungry for the lips of my desire:
I have been faithful to thee, Cynara! in my fashion.

She found it almost unbearable. She wanted to cry, but couldn't be sure what about. It was so strange, so unlike any passion anyone could admit to in this practical landscape; no one flung roses here. They drank too much beer; but no one called for wilder music or for stronger wine. She was not sure she fancied being Cynara, she of the pale lost lilies. The one of the bought red mouth probably got a better deal of it from Dowson. Then she found from books – teachers never told you this kind of thing – that Dowson had been unhappily in love with a girl of twelve, who was probably Cynara, and died of alcoholism at the age of thirty-two, and Beverley didn't know what to think.

Beverley at sixteen

Every now and then Arthur would talk about her looking more and more like her mother, and the more she looked less and less like Rita the more puzzled she became. She waited until her parents were out and looked through the drawers marked 'Private – keep out – that means you'. She found adoption papers in Rita's drawer that referred to the Canterbury Girls' Receiving Society. She escaped for long enough on a school trip to the Auckland Library to look up records in the Christchurch Press from the mid-thirties. She came across headlines:

Amberley Tragedy: local farmer and father kills young wife and dog

Walter McLean's body found by cousin: locum Doctor James (Arthur to his friends) McLean finds slain farmer in ditch

Balance of mind disturbed…financial crash claims new victim

Party-goer Kitchie McLean, 23, new migrant from England, slain in 'crime passionnel'

'She never settled', claim neighbours

Friends say farmer Walter McLean had become recluse

Orphaned three-year-old to be cared for by family friend: local beauty and heiress Rita Davies.

Local beauty and heiress? Rita? It depended on your standards. Beverley went back into the obituaries. Rita's parents had been killed in a farming accident and she had inherited the farm when she was twenty. That would have made her attractive to Arthur, Beverley could see. Arthur would often talk about the depression and how so many doctors had been out of work, how the war had brought prosperity as well as hardship. Beverley felt fond enough of Rita to be glad she had once been seen as a beauty, even though now she was just another of the tightly permed and kindly, effective matrons, who in practice ran the country while the men ran it in name.

Rita was a good sort, Beverley decided, but not a patch on Kitchie, a snapshot of whom, turning a cartwheel on the lawn, had been published in the *Christchurch Press*. Beverley felt quite calm and cool about her discoveries, almost numb. Or perhaps she had been numb until now. She thought perhaps she had always known the broad strokes; it was just the detail she was missing. Beverley turned the paper upside down to study her mother's face. Pretty, short wavy hair, big eyes, and a wide-lipped mouth. She could see she looked like her mother. She would be her real mother, then, but she would always run away before worse befell, as her mother had not. *Party-goer Kitchie*, shorthand for 'no better than she should be'. Good wives did not go to parties.

The most satisfactory narrative Beverley could come up with, there in Auckland Public Library, in the free Reading Rooms beneath the Victorian clock and tower that seemed to give the whole city such a feel of permanency, significance and purpose, was that that her father Walter McLean had killed her mother Kitchie, because she was about to run off with someone – could it possibly be popular Dr Arthur Audley? Who had discovered the body and married Rita on the rebound and had adopted her, Beverley, because she was *there*? Or perhaps because she, Beverley, had on the parents' death inherited the McLean farm? A matter which was never mentioned.

Now there was a thought.

When Beverley rejoined her school party she had been missing for three hours, and the library was ringing to the call of 'Beverley! Beverley Audley!' She was glad they cared, though her real name was Beverley McLean. It was probably wiser not to mention it, at least for the time being. She was given a detention, the first in her school life. Nobody seemed to notice that she was now a different person. So perhaps she wasn't. That was the trouble: how did you define what you were? How much of her was Kitchie of the pale, lost lilies, and how much was Walter, desolate and sick of an old passion? And how much had she become Beverley Audley the Doctor's daughter, creature of habit, who brushed her teeth in the mirror and passed exams and helped her mother about the house and didn't want to upset the apple-cart.

All she knew was that now, on the rare occasions she got to Auckland and passed the Library, she looked away, and hated and despised the tower and clock as small and provincial and dull, where once it had seemed impressive.

She matriculated early and was accepted by Auckland University for the following autumn.

Beverley's seventeenth birthday party

On her seventeenth birthday Rita and Arthur told Beverley there were things she needed to know and the time had come to tell her. But by the time they got round to telling her everyone was a little drunk.

Arthur her father had given her a violin for her birthday – she was good at music – and her mother a pair of brown court shoes, with one-and-a-half-inch heels, to celebrate her growing up, and a scarlet lipstick which looked horrible to Beverley so she said she'd keep it for a special occasion.

'This is a special occasion,' said Rita, hurt. 'But have it your own way.'

They had had a special birthday meal when Beverley came back from her holiday job as a ward orderly at the cottage hospital across the road. Roast chicken and kumera and peas from the back garden, and peaches and nectarines with cream for pudding, and Beverley had been allowed a glass of sherry. The parents got through many bottles of beer that evening and Beverley wished they wouldn't. It made them noisy and excited and they were usually so quiet.

She asked for more sherry, because now they'd given up beer and started on the sherry the more she had the more quickly they'd finish the bottle. They were feeling generous, and they gave her glass after glass of the thick, sweet, brownish liquid.

‘Let us have some music,’ cried Arthur, and Rita put on her favourite 78, The Wedding of the Painted Doll, with the blunt thorn needle that needed replacing. ‘More sherry,’ he cried, and Rita told him to calm down, what was the matter with him? He seemed almost to be crying, but telling her she was adopted, and she bet they weren’t going to tell her all the truth, just a bit of it. What was going on? Arthur was Dowson, calling for madder music and for stronger wine: the shadow was Kitchie’s. If he was Dowson, Cynara was Kitchie.

I cried for madder music and for stronger wine,
But when the feast is finish’d and the lamps expire,
Then falls thy shadow, Cynara! the night is thine;
And I am desolate and sick of an old passion,
Yea, hungry for the lips of my desire:
I have been faithful to thee, Cynara! in my fashion.

Rita scarcely had the ‘bought red mouth’ of Dowson’s description: it didn’t make sense. Beverley went into the bathroom where she smeared her lips with the scarlet lipstick, and found the bra pushed into the back of her drawer, and the dress with the oyster-shell design now much too short and tight for her, and went back into the living room wearing them. She thought there’d be some sort of row about it, but there wasn’t. Rita stared at her with a kind of hostility and said, ‘You’d best break into your savings, and get something decent that fits.’ But she could hardly complain, since she was the one who had given Beverley the lipstick. As for Arthur he put his hands over his crotch and said nothing.

There were flapping noises in Beverley’s head and flashings before her eyes. She was not used to alcohol. But she noticed well enough where Arthur's hands were and arched her back and thrust out her chest and flung back her head and ran her fingers through her hair to provoke him. She somehow couldn't help it. She had seen the Coromandel bad girls parade down the high street 'flaunting themselves' as Rita described it: now she was doing it and she liked it. Cynara was Kitchie, her mother, of the pale lost lilies, white with loss of blood; she, Beverley, would be the bought red mouth and survive.

'Stop that,' said Rita sharply, so Beverley did.

'Go on,' said Arthur, 'tell the girl what you need to tell her and be done with it.'

He crossed one leg over the other and bent sideways to switch on the lamp and his domed forehead gleamed. Then a moth got under the shade and fizzled up, and the smell of scorched insect was everywhere.

Rita told Beverley that she was adopted and that they loved her very much and had been in two minds about telling her, but on balance thought they should. The speech had been prepared and Beverley had already seen it in Rita's Keep Out drawer. Beverley asked about the circumstances of her birth.

Rita said she would tell her, but Beverley must be careful what she said to other people about it. Better to keep it secret. Others tended to think misfortune was catching, like the measles. There was no way – as there was not, at the time – that her birth parents could be traced. Arthur and Rita had been unable to have children of their own and had decided they wanted to adopt, and had chosen her from among dozens at the Girls' Receiving Society in Christchurch. Beverley asked if they knew anything at all about her real parents.

'We are your real parents,' said Rita.

Beverley said politely, of course, but could they tell her anything at all about her genetic parents? They said they had found out that her mother had been a young university student from Canterbury College in the South Island who had got herself pregnant by a soldier – an officer – so she had been offered up for adoption.

'Says you!' said Beverley, rather rudely, and then composed herself. 'It's a nice story, and I'm sure you tell it to make me feel good, so thank you. Especially the officer bit. But my mother was a farmer's wife in Amberley called Kitchie McLean and my father Walter allegedly cut her throat because she was running off with another man and then shot himself, and you took me in, which was nice of you, Rita, and probably quite advantageous to you, Arthur, but it doesn't change the facts of the matter. I am the daughter of a whore and a murderer.'

On balance, she had decided, she was probably Walter's child. It could be that she was Arthur's, and Walter had found out. If she pushed her hair back from her face her forehead was domed, but then lots of foreheads were. It could even be that Arthur had murdered both Kitchie and Walter, because she, Beverley, was his child, and he wanted both his child and the farm, and had faked the suicide, in which case she was still the daughter of a whore and a murderer.

Holding brief

I worry, reader, that as I get further into this you'll forget about the others milling about in the basement and you do need to keep them in mind. I will go down and sort them out presently, when I'm a bit stronger, but in the meantime life for them has moved on only an hour.

Scarlet is currently in her Prius on her way to Soho with two suitcases. She decided to use a car instead of a taxi in case Lola chose to borrow it in her absence. She could take the keys but it was not beyond the bounds of possibility that Lola knew how to hot-wire.

Lola is indeed currently looking for the keys.

Jackson is caught up in a tremendous jam in the Strand and is panicking in case Scarlet changes her mind.

Louis is waiting for Samantha to visit him in his office. She just happened to be round the corner in Liberty's, her favourite shop, when he got through to her.

D'Dora is looking up Facebook to find more details about the pretty girl she met at The Dungeonette last night, and forgetting that she is meant to be standing in for a colleague who has gone home with flu.

Cynara is wondering how much she really wants to earn her living working with felt flowers.

Beverley has almost fallen asleep over the Tom Clancy book,

which is so heavy it tires her wrist, and is still worrying in case she has brought up her children all wrong.

Gerry has his flight booked back to London and Beverley.

And now I am in the middle of a thunderstorm. *Sturm und Drang*. Really black clouds racing behind the church tower: I can't see a lightning conductor but I expect there is one, we're on such a high point. The interval between lighting bolts and thunder claps is shorter every time, it is coming this way: I have displeased the basement folk. I am meant to be writing about Beverley. A crash shakes me and the room, even as the space flashes brilliant electric white; there's the smell of sizzling moth. I'm not usually frightened by storms but this time I am. It's gross. Odin is out to get me.

'Where are you?' I cry to Rex.

He comes down from his attic, says there's a wonderful view from up there, better shut down the computer, it's protected against surges but you never know. Save. Shut down. I do.

A drunken scene in Coromandel

The storm has passed, but it was right overhead; the lightning hit the old rowan tree, the one with the pink roses over it. They are no more, withered and gone, once flung so riotously with Dawson's wild living throng. Quickly back to the Coromandel of long ago, before worse befalls.

Where were we? Yes.

'Daughter of a murderer and a whore,' Beverley was saying to her adoptive parents. She knows she is overstating her case but she has reason to be aggrieved. She is at an age when honesty seems to be of great importance, and instead of being grateful to Rita and Arthur, especially Rita, for taking her in in the first place, and trying to preserve the child's good opinion of her birth parents in the second, Beverley chooses to see only hypocrisy and deceit. She could say more. She could say Arthur fathered her, and murdered her father Walter, she could accuse Arthur of marrying Rita for her money and ask what happened to the farm she, Beverley, presumably inherited, but she does not. She is wise. And whore and murderer is enough to be getting on with.

After she says this there is silence. Then Rita says:

'Your mother was a sweet, lovely girl married to the wrong man. She was looking for love, and deserved it.'

'She deserved what she got,' says Arthur.

And Beverley thought, well then, no, probably not her father; Arthur was not the mystery lover. Otherwise their lines would have been the other way round. And only then did they want to know how she had found out.

'I know because I was there,' said Beverley, 'and I remember stamping about in the blood.' She doesn't quite remember that bit but, as I say, she is aggrieved. 'Can we stop having this conversation now before things get worse?'

'You can't possibly remember,' said Arthur. 'You were too young.'

'It was in all the newspapers,' said Beverley. 'With really big headlines.'

'You were too young to read,' said Arthur.

'I could read when I was three,' said Beverley. 'And anyway I read all about it in the Auckland Library. It was like an epiphany.'

'Whatever that means when it's at home,' said Rita, suppressing the urge to slap her daughter. 'Real mother', indeed, after all that. If she hadn't taken Beverley in she could have had two children or more of her own. They'd have been bright enough, Arthur being a doctor, and she could at least have read their minds, as ordinary mothers of ordinary children did. And Beverley was quite right, as she all too often was: Kitchie had a whore's temperament and Beverley had inherited it, look at her strutting around just now in a dress three sizes too small for her, and she, Rita, had always rather fancied Walter herself except he had a vile temper.

But the McLeans were the liveliest couple around, and Kitchie had a gift for wearing clothes just so, which she, Rita, had copied for a while but had given up when she married Arthur. She didn't know what Arthur did for sex these days, but he had to be really angry with her for it to happen, and he was slow to anger, as was she.

'My guess is you read about it but you didn't see it,' said Arthur.

'You weren't there when it happened. You were upstairs asleep.'

How did Arthur know that? Had he been in the room too?

'And then my father went and shot the dog, or someone did,' said Beverley. 'He was a nice dog. His name was Patch. I remember him. There was no need for that. Dogs can't talk.' She poured herself some more sherry and no one tried to stop her.

She had £230 12s 6d saved in her Post Office Savings Book, the accumulation of wages from holiday jobs at the hospital, school prizes, Christmas gifts from family friends and relatives who lived serenely in that other world parallel to this one, a world not tainted with murder, fear, flight, where the yellow-brick roads weren't sprinkled with pools of blood but were fit for dancing along.

'The only thing I don't know,' said Beverley, quite clearly and firmly to her father, 'is the name of the man she was running off with. I suppose it wasn't you, Daddy?'

Rita advanced and this time did slap her, quite hard across the face with the back of her hand.

'It was a cursed day for all of us,' said Rita, 'when your slut of a mother moved in down the road. I was mad to take you in. Everyone said so. Bad blood will out.'

Dido and Aeneas

Beverley had quite forgotten, in her preoccupation with her own drama, that Arthur and Rita had their passions too. That so far as she was concerned she was a bit-part player in their drama. It is easy for children to forget this and for all her scarlet lipstick, new strutting breasts and bold words she was still a child, and playing with fire.

'That's enough,' Arthur said. 'Women shouldn't hit, they can't hit hard enough.' Rita started to cry and Beverley was amazed. She had never seen Rita cry. Once when she was trying to make a mayonnaise and it curdled twice, but that was different.

'I was the locum,' said Arthur to Beverley. 'Your mother came to me with a split eardrum. Her husband had hit her.'

'Why did he hit her?' asked Beverley. She was already looking for excuses for her father, though she could not see quite where she would find them.

'That's a funny sort of question,' said Rita. 'Well, if you insist on knowing, because she was a bothersome slut and taunted him. Everyone knew he couldn't get it up and keep it up for longer than two minutes. When you came along, my, was everyone surprised. So don't you go thinking of yourself as anything grand.' She spoke to Beverley but looked at her husband. The tears had gone: her eyes were hard and glittering.

'I felt sorry for her. That was the idea, why she came to me, the sweet little thing, pale and small, little lost girl from a foreign land. Little Kitchie. She thought she could twist me around her little finger but she soon found otherwise.'

He was speaking now to Beverley, relaxing in his armchair, more beer in his hand; she had her arms crossed over her chest. She wished she hadn't put on this ridiculous dress. It was archetypal, elemental, it had set the wrong things off.

'She was the foreigner, not us,' said Rita. Arthur took no notice of her. It occurred to Beverley how very little notice Arthur ever took of Rita.

'And you know how it is, things develop,' said Arthur. 'I was a young man, a bachelor, the girls round there weren't up to much. Since you ask so many questions you might as well know. Okay, I was the fellow she wanted to run off with, because she'd had my baby, and she was fool enough to tell him, so he did her in with the bread knife with which she was making her special fancy cucumber sandwiches. She even peeled the cucumbers, nice thin slices and all. I had her bum in the air, skirt up over her head while she went on working. I must say, we used to have some fun, Kitchie and me. Then he was in the room and we had words, and before I could stop him, he had the knife and the serrated edge, very sharp, along the neck, through the carotid artery. Not much you can do about that.'

'Bullshitter,' said Rita, astonishingly. Arthur ignored her.

'And the dog leaping and barking its head off. Then he ran out of the house, and the dog followed. I did what I could for her, but there was no stopping the bleeding. I looked in on you but you were still asleep, so I went after him, heard the gunshot and found your father dead. Hard to miss with a gun to the head, otherwise he would have. He even got the dog quite cleanly, though it took three bullets. By the time I got back you were up at Rita's. Little bloody footsteps up the road. I felt it was all my fault.'

'So you were in the room when she died?' said Rita. 'I didn't know that.'

'I'd hardly be fool enough to tell you,' said Arthur.

'He should have killed you, not her,' said Rita. Her hands were clawed, looking like talons.

'You know how it is,' said Arthur. 'We fellows stick together. Pack behaviour, all that. I'd got the bitch, I was top dog, he recognised that. She went, I didn't.'

What have I done? thought Beverley. What have I unleashed? These two respectable people, he with his leather elbow patches, she in her best cardigan, revealed as warring Olympians with the passions of Aeneas and Dido, Jason and Medea, they are overwhelmed by loss, they are transfigured by hate. I have to get out of here, I have to run, before I do more damage. I will leave bloody footsteps until the end of time. That was the curse my father laid on me when he took the knife to my mother's throat. If he was my father, and not this man here.

'Was that the reason you married me? To own the child? It was never anything to do with me?'

Rita was pale and gaunt and carved in stone and yet softly massy and greasy grey like a whale. Even the pink cardy did not help; she had turned into something huge and elemental.

'You had the farm, I could do with that,' he said. 'I wasn't going to marry you for your looks, was I? But you were a good enough lay and you'd look after the child. A man's got to seize his opportunities.'

The good Doctor Jekyll had turned into Mr Hyde, and grown grotesque and vast as his wife: the parents who weren't parents.

Hyde blending into werewolf under the moon, the friend by day but Dracula by night: *Brief Encounter* on a monster screen with Trevor Howard played by King Kong. You didn't know who you were or where you are. King Kong picked up the knife, Kitchie struggled and kicked in the monstrous hands. Perhaps Arthur had done the knifing, run after the fleeing Walter, killed him with his own gun, faked a suicide.

'I've said too much, have I then, Rita? Got you all hot and bothered?'

He got to his feet and lurched into the kitchen. Was he looking for a knife? Would there be another pool of blood, for Beverley to splash through in her smart new shiny brown court shoes?

Life would always be the same – the premonition came so hard and fast and clear it made her tremble – or was it the gust of rage and hate shaking the ground beneath her? This was to be the future, dancing down the Yellow Brick Road in a nightmarish Land of Oz, where the faster your footwork the better you dodged the pools of blood. You could get quite skilled at it. But they would always be there. As it had been in the past, so would it be in the future. It was what you were born to.

The dusty yellow road to Rita's: she was past that now, she must go on and on, further, faster. She could not afford to stop. She would take the morning bus to Auckland. It left at six-thirty – another terrible part of her said this was a godsend: they could not object to her going. Her conscience would be clear. She was the innocent one, they the villains: she could run now to the ends of the earth, to England, to Home, without reproach or blame. Her mother, by dying, had set her free. Her heart soared, she licked her lips and wondered why, and thought my soul is trying to escape, and set her lips tightly so it didn't get out.

'You did it, didn't you,' screeched the whale monster at the shadowy Trevor Howard man, following him out of the room. Smoke from his pipe curled around him like fog blanketing the land of Mordor. 'It was you. That cucumber bit is just your vile fantasy. I know you. You loved her. She wouldn't leave Walter for you, and you were so angry you took a knife to that sluttish throat and then went out after that poor man, and shot him and poor Patch. You had no business killing Patch.'

'Just a dog,' said Arthur.

Beverley fled the room and didn't think they even noticed her going. They weren't her parents anyway: they'd only ever pretended they were. She would wait until morning and then she would flee. The kehua were flapping their wings and hissing *run, run, run now,* but sherry had dulled her ears.

The night before she ran

That night the man who was probably her father came in and sat on the end of her bed. He had never done this before. Beverley slept naked beneath a sheet – the nights were warm. The section of the verandah where she slept was glassed in, and in the evenings she would let down a curtain of mosquito netting to keep the insects out. She was lying awake, and saw him approach: he was wearing his red silk Noël Coward dressing gown and the slippers she had given him on his last birthday. He was smoking. The netting made his outline wavery until he pushed it aside, but at least he was back to human size. Whatever had possessed him, and possessed Rita too, had passed.

There was no doubt Arthur was a handsome man. She had always thought so, especially since her visit to the Auckland Library had stripped him of the father role and reclothed him in the glamour she had granted him when she was small. He seemed sober enough now. She had heard him and Rita having sex on the old sofa in the kitchen: at least she assumed that was what it was. She was surprised. It had not seemed part of what went on between them. She had seen a bull covering a cow: an old farmer had almost forced her to watch and watched her while she watched. She was around thirteen and had been out with her father on a house call. He'd been in the house with the wife. When her father came out it was still going on; she'd hoped he would take her away but he stayed to watch too. That just made her cross with him. He should have protected her but he didn't. He seemed on the farmer's side. The cow hadn't seemed to like it, but what could it do? The bull was just determined, and twice her size and massive. Beverley had tried to look superior and uninvolved, and had just shrugged when they asked if she had enjoyed it.

Now there were cries of protest, pleasure, pain from the kitchen – at the end his gaspings, and little mews of contentment from Rita. It was hard to know what she, Beverley, felt about this: mostly she felt stupid because of her ploy with the lipstick and the breasts, and infantile because the revelations were surely just part of some fantasy game they played, only this time they'd involved her, and she was nowhere nearer the truth. What she mainly felt now was left out, excluded when she'd heard Rita and Arthur pad off, and giggles and murmurs as the bedroom door closed behind them. She'd thought that would be all for the night.

But it wasn't...

When he came out to the verandah a couple of hours later she thought Arthur looked like a film star stepped out of the screen, finely sculpted but very male: the kind, understanding blue eyes, the slightly cruel mouth, the fair arched eyebrows; even the balding domed forehead suited him. He looked distinguished and intellectual: Leslie Howard playing a university professor. She had always recognised his good looks, even while she avoided him, especially since her visit to the Auckland Library when his status as father had somehow changed. It was not going to be incest: he was not her father.

She'd been lying there staring out at her friend the Southern Cross, and thinking about its distant stillness and how unimportant the affairs of mankind were, and how she must not fall asleep, and planning to get up really early so as to get her few things together and secretly get the six-thirty ferry to Auckland where she would stay with her friend Babs, and get to Sydney and thence a cheap fare to London. Migrant ships were flooding into Oz carrying tens of thousands of £10 poms outwards, almost empty on the return journey, except for ballast like her: runaway girls, anxious to start a new life, or girls out of college wanting to be where the action was, to put parental disapproval for once and all far, far behind them in the Antipodes. She wished Arthur had not come in. She did not want anything to change her mind. She wanted his behaviour, and Rita's, to be inexcusable.

'Sorry about all that,' he said. 'Sorry to involve you. Things got out of hand. You'll be headachy in the morning. I brought you in an aspirin.'

He was holding out a couple of pills. She leant on her elbow, took one from his familiar hand and swallowed it, without water. She was good at that: her specialty. Her friends admired her for it. He was handing her another one.

'Doctor's pills,' he said.

She took that one too. She realised he could see a patch of her breast when the sheet fell away as she supported herself on her elbow. She took her time and let it fall away a little more as he looked, then lay virtuously on her back with the sheet up to her chin.

'Out of hand. You can say that again,' she said. 'It's my life you're playing with.'

'Mine too,' he said. 'It's hard for Rita and me: all the rumours still going the rounds, even up here. I was the mystery lover, I did the murder, I was your father. Rita was in on it, that sort of thing.'

He moved closer to her, and now sat at waist level. She could feel his body against hers. She should sit up and say she wanted to be left alone; he would go then. She stayed where she was: an agreeable feeling of sulk and passivity mixed came over her: exhaustion from emotional shock, the sense of her own slight smooth body so close to his: the flattery of his interest in her. He was not her father, he was just someone who had married a friend of her mother's the better to set himself up in the world. She would go along with fate, see what happened next. Seventeen was too old to be a virgin, never to have been with a boy, not even kissed a man. And in the morning she would be gone. In the meantime she wanted his hand on her breast.

'What really happened?' she asked. She doubted that she'd get a true answer.

'No idea,' he said. 'No one will ever know. I called by with her medication, found her in a pool of blood, none left in her. A pile of fancy sandwiches half made – that bit was true, so were your little footprints outside – the bread knife on the floor. I got the police out from Christchurch, a search party went out after him and found him and the dog in the old quarry. Rita and I were already courting.'

He was smiling. 'You and that dress,' he said, 'and that lipstick. That was really something. Turns you on, doesn't it, talk of blood and death. It does me. But then I had to look after Rita, calm her down, the best way I knew.'

'You made me drunk,' she said.

'You made yourself drunk,' he said. 'You're not the little innocent you pretend. You're too much like your mother. She fancied me. Near as dammit had me. Would have, but the bugger knifed her.'

Beverley closed her eyes. She felt him move her head so it faced him. She smelled his breath. It was hot and warm and slightly sour.

'Open your eyes,' he said. When she did she could see the pores of his face and the new hair sprouting where he had shaved.

'All sorts of things are best forgotten,' he said. 'This too.'

The eyes were familiar, but strange, narrower and deeper: greener than the blue she'd thought they were. Perhaps they were the devil's eyes and the devil and the man were the same thing.

'What kind of eyes did my father have?' she asked.

'I've no idea,' he said, taking the hand away. 'I told you to forget all that.'

'Sorry,' she said. The hand returned. She could see if you did what was asked of you, you got what you wanted.

'So like little Kitchie,' he said. 'I've watched you grow into her. I've respected you. No one can say I haven't. But you want it too, don't you? You and that dress, oh my. Really shook our Rita, that did. She thought she'd better get in there first. But she doesn't know men. Women never do. Lie flat on your back, little Bev, and look at me.'

She did. He was the doctor, he was her father, she wanted to do as she was told. She lay flat but left the sheet up to her neck. She liked her body. She could make it do handstands, had won the gymnastic prize at school. She could bend over backwards and walk on her hands and then bring her legs up over her back and keep the position. No other girl at school could do that. She wanted him to see it, the neat little navel, the swell of her breasts, and yet she didn't.

'Take away the sheet,' he said.

'No, you do it,' she said. 'Then it's what you've done, not what I've done.'

'Kitchie said that to me once,' he said, and laughed. Ah yes, he was bringing the medication round. A likely story.

'I don't think you're little Beverley at all,' he said. 'I think you're Kitchie come back a few years younger, and you're still begging for it. Even though you're a ghost. That's okay by me.'

A bank of clouds had hidden the moon but now it shone brightly through the verandah windows. If anyone was passing by, the other side of the garden, past the picket fence and the brass Doctor's plate she polished every day, they could see right in. But there was nobody to pass, all decent people were abed, there was only this moment, and the moon, and the man who was not her father sitting on her bed, his hand feeling for her nipples beneath the sheet. She realised if they could see in she would not mind. She wanted everyone to see what was happening. His dressing gown fell open as he moved, and she averted her eyes from the hairy, strong, erect phallus, reddish and rough, as her friends had whispered about it to her, like a third person in the room, with a will of its own. It was scarcely owned by anyone: it did what it wanted.

'Ever heard of parthenogenesis?'

'We did it in biology,' she said. 'It's asexual reproduction. When the mother gives birth on her own, without a father. It doesn't happen in humans.'

'Yes it does. Very occasionally, but it does. The egg is self-fertilised and the mother gives birth to a daughter identical to herself. A clone. So you don't have to be her ghost, you can be her clone. How's that?'

He took the sheet down to her waist and she raised her arms above her head, she was not sure why, but it gave her small breasts more prominence and she liked the feeling of stretch. He ran his hands down her sides and flanks and pinched her nipples a little and then rubbed his finger around first one, then the other, so they stood up.

'Everything works,' he said. 'Doctor says so. You're ripe so you can carry on where Kitchie left off. Do you like that?'

She nodded. She should have screamed but she didn't: the night was too warm and the moon was too bright and what had begun would have to continue. She wondered what had been in the pills he gave her. Probably not aspirin. She had taken them without argument. She could see she had a liking for all things drastic. She remembered reading something about the White Slave Traffic. Bad oriental men drugged innocent white girls and carried them off as easy, willing victims to harems in foreign parts, and then kept them there by force. It was better than ending up teaching like Miss Butt, Miss Crossly, Miss Ferguson or Mrs Barker, which seemed the only opportunity open to her in life.

He slipped a tentative finger between her legs and she instinctively tightened up to stop him but he pushed her legs further apart and abruptly and roughly put in two fingers instead of one, then widened them inside her. Now her legs fell apart of their own volition.

'You're a natural,' he said and she felt flattered. He said, 'I'll only put it in a little way,' and she let him. It seemed too good to be true, on a par with being dead one moment alive the next. He was right. She was bringing her mother back to life, but the detail escaped her. Then she remembered and said, 'What if I get pregnant,' and he said, 'You won't, I'll see to that,' and put it in all the way. Then everything seemed vague, other than the weight of his body on hers was heavy, and the wiriness of the practised muscles as they stood out on his bare shoulders and forearms. It seemed what his body was made for. He should not be thwarted, it was dangerous to thwart men, she had picked that up from somewhere.

'You're not even a virgin, you naughty little bitch,' he said at one stage and she said she was so, child gymnasts often broke their hymens, and he said, 'Tell that to the marines.' Then he said, 'Next time I clone you we'll do without the gymnastics,' so perhaps he did believe her. He said the price of virgins the world over was high. He liked to talk, to keep up a running commentary. She wished he wouldn't. He might wake Rita and for all she was trying to keep quiet herself she couldn't. Her mouth kept uttering mews, grunts and squeals as if she was an animal, which she hated, and he put his hand over her mouth as he rutted away like the bull; and then a screeching fiend, Grendel's mother, suddenly upon them, bursting into their secret place, tearing them apart, pulling Beverley by her hair out of the bed, Arthur sent reeling into the verandah window and the glass broken, the dogs from the farm next door woken, barking, rattling their chains, Rita shouting that Arthur was nothing but a pervert or ever had been – what was he doing to the poor stupid child –

'Now you've been and done it, you silly cunt,' Arthur said. 'I was going to withdraw.'

Beverley at nineteen

By the time she was nineteen Beverley had a one-year-old daughter called Alice and was living in Earls Court in London. She had made an Australian friend, Dionne, on the boat over. Dionne was six foot two, blonde, luscious, big-haired and long-legged and went to drama school. She wanted to be taken seriously and play Lady Macbeth, and was doing a classical acting course, though the tutors hinted that perhaps singing-and-dancing was more suitable. Beverley paid for her tuition; Dionne helped Beverley with Alice. It seemed fair dos.

Beverley had embarked on a three-year course at Royal Holloway, an all-woman college, studying semantics and moral philosophy. It was 1952. Only 5 per cent of women went to university, but she had passed the entrance exam easily enough. She told no one about Alice's existence. Rita had warned her not to. Such girls as did graduate were expected to do a further secretarial course, leaving work when they got married and had children. A few women went on to have jobs in the civil service or teaching but then were expected to stay unmarried and give up their personal life.

Beverley preferred not to give the future too much attention. She had too much to think about what with Alice who, though she was a pretty, charming, easy baby, expected more time and attention than Beverley had reckoned on. Beverley had rather gone off sex, or if not sex, the kind of loaded emotional sex men seemed to demand, and sex itself was too overwhelming, and led to babies, an inbuilt sort of punishment. But she liked parties, and dressing up: she liked to lead men on and then turn them down and soon got the reputation of a pricktease, and on several occasions only escaped rape by the skin of her teeth. Men assumed that no meant yes, and it was reasonable to get violent if you kept insisting it didn't. Good girls didn't get themselves into these situations, bad girls did, and bad girls were fair game.

She liked older men; boys her own age were callow, pimply and weak and, though more likely to take no for an answer, never seemed to have sufficient weight on her body. Dionne, on the other hand, really liked pretty boys. Men's eyes followed Dionne wherever she went. Beverley felt quite jealous but Dionne comforted her by saying that even if they looked down her, Dionne's, cleavage, there was nothing to see, whereas Beverley had lots. The fashion was for full skirts with layers of petticoats beneath so they billowed out, a cinched-in belted waist and black V-necked tops which you could push right down over your shoulders to show as much cleavage as you dared. Beverley dared a lot and the feeling of going out without knickers was stirring. She got to see a lot of thick rough red penises, or penes, but the art was to never let them get inside you. None ever seemed as impressive as Arthur's but she pushed her mind away from that whenever she could. They both went to elocution lessons to get rid of their New Zealand accents. Both decided, whatever the future, it had better be posh.

When it became apparent to Beverley that she was pregnant, she had been in England for two months and was running out of money – so she wrote to Rita and asked her what she should do now. She didn't know who else to ask. She and Dionne were waitressing, earning £5 a week and sharing a room at £3 a week rental. Beverley was not entirely certain that Arthur was the father of the baby, having met an attractive and lively young naval officer on the way over, who also practised the withdrawal method so favoured at the time, though Arthur was the most likely.

Rita's reply was prompt and brisk. Beverley felt a wave of affection towards her. She knew enough by now that sex could send you mad: Rita had been mad: she, Beverley, had not been Arthur's helpless victim, she had wronged Rita, who had to live with a man who might be a murderer and might not be; just as she, Beverley, had put up with a father so ambiguous it didn't bear thinking about, and in all likelihood was grandfather to his own daughter. Alice had Arthur's high domed forehead but that didn't mean she was definitely Arthur's. She could still be the naval officer's child and the domed forehead come down from Beverley herself.

A cheque for a £1,000 fell out of the envelope. You could buy half a house for that, and a good one too.

Dear Beverley, wrote Rita, *this is a fine kettle of fish. I am glad to hear from you all the same, we were worried about you. But you are grown up now and it is natural for young people to make their own lives. I am enclosing a cheque for the amount left over from the sale of your father's farm, after your board and lodging for all those years is taken care of. I think this is fair. We always did our very best for you and I am sorry things turned out the way they did. About the baby. Abortion is a criminal offence so don't do that or you'll end up dead or in prison. Some people I know try drinking gin and taking very hot baths but I've never known it to work. Buy yourself a wedding ring from Woolworth's and always tell people you are a widow, or they won't talk to you. Go to an adoption society and see if they'll take you on. Tell them the father is a good-looking young medical student you met on holiday and he gave you a false name. If they think there might be anything wrong with Baby they won't have you on their books. Or a French or Belgian soldier, an officer, is another favourite I don't know why. So long as you don't make him a German. The money I've sent you will help if you want to keep Baby, but it won't last for ever, and you are a pretty girl so your best bet is to find someone to marry you and give you and the baby a roof over your heads. Not many men will take on a girl who has a bastard, but sometimes an older man will, though he won't be the pick of the crop. Arthur took me on, and you as well, so it sometimes works out, and Mr Right does come along, so don't be too sorry for yourself. At least you were born to respectable married folk and weren't sullied before you were even born, which happens to some. Best not to keep in touch, dear. Things got very complicated round here and I don't suppose they'll get much better. I told Arthur your news and all he said was how do I know it's mine. You know how men are. Well, we all make our beds and have to lie on them. I wish you all the best in the world. Love from your mother Rita.*

Beverley folded the letter up many times until it was just a small wedge and put it at the back of her drawer and kept it through her many travels, and has it today at Robinsdale, in the drawer where she keeps her valuables. She has never reread it since that one time. It contains all the confusions of her early days. Arthur ruined her, money saved her. Rita was just not very bright.

Beverley was entitled to a small grant to get her through university – not much because she was from abroad – and was able to pay for Dionne's drama school course and their elocution lessons out of Rita's money. The rest she put in Post Office Savings, and that, and the money she earned cleaning, one shilling and sixpence the hour, kept her going until Alice was five. Dionne did nude modelling for a men's photographic club three evenings a week at five shillings the hour. She stood on a stand with no clothes on striking poses while old men took photographs of her. It was quite harmless, though she worried that when she was famous someone could use the pictures to blackmail her. Sometimes Beverley joined her but never without black bra and panties. They were risqué enough; the norm was white or pink. But the girls got by. They even had a good time.

They shared a flat on the fourth floor of a large Victorian house in Earls Court. They lived rent free. The landlord was an amiable young Maltese called Jesus who ran a thriving whoring business elsewhere, liked the girls and required nothing of them but that they both spent a couple of hours with him on Friday evenings between ten and twelve. When they pointed out that that would leave Alice without a babysitter he changed his requirements to one hour each on Wednesday and Friday nights, and threw in the electricity bill. He was very protective of Alice.

Beverley and Dionne were more than satisfied with this arrangement. His first suggestion had been problematic: it would have been embarrassing to face one another on Saturday mornings after performing whatever intimate lesbian antics Jesus would have expected of them on Friday nights. As it turned out, their obligations were not onerous, even rather sweet. All that was required in the new arrangement was one or other of them kept him company, whilst sitting decorously at the kitchen table, albeit naked, embroidering prayer kneeling cushions, cross-stitching tapestry cushions in the Berlin pattern, as his mother and aunts did back home, occasionally getting up to stir the soup he was making. Sometimes there was full sex, but it was perfectly conventional and soon done: he had a fiancée at home and missed her.

Afterwards he would call either Dionne, if it was Wednesday night with Beverley, or Beverley, if it was Wednesday night with Dionne, to come down with baby Alice and join him, decently clothed to eat the meal he had made. He liked to cook for them: his specialty was kawlata soup, made of cabbage and pork. Jesus loved London, where he could grow rich modernising its antiquated sex industry, but found the food execrable.

He liked to feel he was playing a part in helping the girls get an education: it was an investment: with his help they would end up as high-class call-girls, bound for the top escort agencies, rather than lapsing into the hard-eyed hookerdom which was the fate of so many lost girls with no family.

'But why? Why?' Beverley would ask. She found men strange. 'Why? Why?' was a refrain that echoed through her life. It was more in Dionne's nature to answer questions than to ask them. She was forever offering unlikely solutions to imponderable questions.

'Perhaps when he was a tiny little boy in Malta,' said Dionne, 'he would sit on the floor and wonder what his family looked like with no clothes on. Now he is in a strange land and has unlimited money he can find out. I think it's rather sweet.'

Dionne was to fulfil Jesus' prophecy and end up as the widow of a senior government minister in Paris. The nearest she got to playing Lady Macbeth was to pose in *tableaux vivants* like Nelson's Emma Hamilton, striking classical attitudes based on Greek sculptures for the pleasure of important guests. No one thought the worse of her for any of it, any more than they did of Pamela Harriman in her time or Carla Bruni today. Dionne was content.

Dionne is old now, and arthritis has got her bones, but she has, as they say, her memories, and quite a lot of love letters from important people which she can, if necessary, sell.

Beverley at thirty

'Now Bev,' said Winter. 'I think we are going to call you Rosa. Beverley is not the right name for you. It's dismissive, throwaway, colonial. We are revolutionaries. We are calling you Rosa after Rosa Luxemburg – last night's vote was unanimous. The same beautiful eyes, arched brows and springing hair over that high domed forehead. But why do you wear that dreary green shapeless sweater all the time? One of the comrades turned up last night in a topless dress. They're not exactly topless, just come down in a V to the middle of the waist. Women need to do what they can to cheer the men up, as vice versa; we are gender equal. Who's Rosa Luxemburg? Good Lord, Bev – Rosa – You are so ignorant. They didn't seem to teach you much at that Holloway College of yours, but then it is a woman's college. I expect they make it easier to get a first. I got a third deliberately. As Gramsci pointed out, the crisis in the educational process of differentiation and specialisation has taken place chaotically, without clear and precise principles, without a well-thought-out and consciously fixed plan, and the more one adds to the chaos the better. If your obvious firsts get thirds, and vice versa, that undermines the whole bourgeois educational conspiracy. Rosa Luxemburg was a socialist revolutionary who was murdered by the fascists in 1919.'

Winter Max – born 1928, christened Julian Waxmann Maidment, nicknamed at school (Harrow) Earglue – was a good-looking young man with a Zapata moustache, not too much brain and a swaggering air. Beverley loved him very much, quite a lot of the time. She found a picture of Rosa Luxemburg and saw a horse-faced woman with a sour gaze and was horrified. But world revolution was obviously a must and everyone she knew believed in it, and the men had agreed that marriage was incontestably a form of exclusive private property and as such was to be abhorred.

But Winter was prepared to marry her and formally adopt Alice in spite of his principles, which seldom seemed to apply to him but only to others, if she changed her name to Rosa and wore a topless dress to a meeting or two. So she did, and he was then proud to own her, and she vaguely proud to be owned.

She had a job as a secretary at University College London where the mummified body of Jeremy Bentham sat in a chair by the doorway, but even her degree would not get her any further than that. The savings had long ago run out and she remembered what Rita said: in the end you will have to marry to get a roof over your head.

Jesus had bought a house in Paris more suitable to his wealth and status, and the girls had been roofless once again. Dionne followed him to Paris; Beverley had Alice to think about and stayed in West London where the child was doing well at Holland Park Comprehensive. Here Alice was taught by Gramsciist ideologues who'd studied Fromm and Marcuse and saw a new way to the 'dictatorship of the proletariat' in things like teenage consumer culture. At any rate Alice had been a top-notch little gymnast until six months previously, when she was told that competition was a tool of capitalism, whereupon she had suddenly grown sultry-eyed and started buying lipsticks and refusing to wear tennis shoes.

It seemed to her mother that the spirit of competition, deprived of its natural sustenance, simply turned to acquisition instead. She tried to say as much to Joey Matthews the cell leader when the matter came up for discussion. Joey Matthews – born 1914, christened Josef Maybaum, later of Trinity College with Blunt and Burgess – sighed and said in his perfectly modulated voice: 'The long march through the hegemony is very long and slow indeed, I fear. When it is feminised it becomes more a limp than a march,' which Rosa took as a rebuke. She, a woman, was holding up the long march by quibbling with doctrine. He then quoted Adorno: '"Sport is the liberation of the body humiliated by economic interests, the return to the body of a part of the functions of which it has been deprived by industrial society,"' and advised, 'Wean the child off it, Rosa.'

Tell that to a ruptured hymen, thought Rosa, rudely, and quite went off Marxism for a bit, especially when Joey, who had been particularly charmed by the topless dress, came into the kitchen while she was making coffee for everyone, and made a pass at her with his trembling hand.

The wedding to Winter had been a big posh do in Gloucestershire with a lot of Maidment family and titles on his side and only little Alice and Dionne on hers; which rather relieved everyone, she thought. The roof over her head was now Robinsdale, in North London, spacious enough for meetings and for party members to be put up for the night, and was not too far away from the Soviet Trade Delegation in Highgate.

There was much coffee to be made, and now she was married Winter had gone off the idea of topless dresses, or indeed parties, and open, companionate marriages – so nothing was much fun, but at least she could put her past behind her, and be, just a bit, like anyone else. There was now nothing wrong with her life except boredom, and so she spent a lot of time worrying about whether Trotsky was the villain or Stalin, and copy-editing the far-left magazine *Black Hole*. She was soon pregnant with Richie.

Beverley at thirty-four

'Rosa, I've been thinking.'

'Have you, Winter?' He had taken LSD the day before. He still seemed slightly dazed and complained of flashbacks.

'You and I have been very close to each other for some time. Practically pro-hegemonistic; it isn't good.'

'I like it.'

'Yes, I know you do. But it is lazy. A woman needs to be free, to be liberated. Marriage is like prostitution, you are a slave, providing sexual, domestic and child-rearing services in return for board and lodging.'

'I'd earn if there were any jobs.'

'I wouldn't want you to be working. You are quite busy enough. The children need you. I just want you to be sexually free.'

'Ah, sexually.'

'Joey's going to be staying over tonight. We all owe him so much. He's moving to Moscow. He's appointed me leader of the cadre.'

'I thought it was going to be Clive?' Clive was the only working-class member of the North-West Cadre. Others tore their jeans, went unshaved, and tried to look poor and oppressed but it seldom worked. Clive wore a tie and polished his shoes, edited *Black Hole*, was an agent for left-wing writers, and was followed everywhere by MI5. He had great street credibility.

'Joey says I'm probably a better bet,' said Winter. 'He'll decide tomorrow. I really want this, Rosa.'

He grabbed her hand and squeezed it and looked at her imploringly. What was this about? She realised.

'You mean you want me to join him in the bed tonight?'

'Well, yes. It's a matter of revolutionary progress, liberation from old bonds of tradition. No one has to worry about getting pregnant any more. Why not? We should offer ourselves to each other freely. I don't mean you sneak in, nothing furtive. I'll show you to the bedside myself. He's expecting you. He really wants you, always has. What do you say, Rosa?'

'Actually, I'd rather not, Winter. He's too old. And my name is Beverley.'

'You bourgeoise cow,' he said, and slammed out of the house and stayed out.

She called Dionne in Paris and said, 'Why? Why?' and Dionne said men did that. It was a status thing. Pack behaviour. A dog with a bone will step back and release it when top dog comes along and wants it. That was what executive dinner parties were all about. You were there as a potential offering to the boss.

'Oh,' said Beverley, 'I see.'

Joey arrived, assuming Winter would be there in the house. He did not seem to mind that he wasn't, other than remarking that Winter always chickened out of group sex. Beverley did indeed join Joey in the bed. Winter was right: why indeed not? And he was not too old; he was a randy old goat. She told him so and he said he had been anointed by the blood of the workers. He fucked for all of them. She had not heard this one before, though she could see it was true enough.

She asked Joey not to tell Winter the details but he said one had to be open about these matters and tell the truth, otherwise in his experience there was trouble.

'Ah yes,' she said. 'Trust between comrades is imperative to the struggle.'

'I always feel you're laughing at us,' he complained, as Butt, Crossly, Ferguson and Barker had felt so long ago.

'Good Lord, no,' she said.

Winter came back about midday. Joey told Winter the liberating deed was more than satisfactorily done and at length, and he was very pleased. He formally bequeathed Winter the cadre there and then, and, more, left a briefcase stuffed with cash behind, to go towards the big *Rock Against Racism* demo. Then he flew back to Moscow, first class. Joey showed Beverley the tickets.

'There's no first class available on Aeroflot so I have to take the BA flight,' he said. 'Moscow always treats me well. The East Germans make you fly economy.'

Winter called her Bev from then on and screwed her nightly for a week. After that she was perfectly civil to him but more sensitive to the flaws in his character. On occasion, when he felt the need to restore his virility, he would search out people in the party he wanted or needed to impress and offer his wife to them, as a cat will drag in a dead bird and offer it to the one who fills the plate with cat food. She obliged, while feeling rather like the bird, a morally superior bird, of course.

Beverley at thirty-five

One Saturday Winter came back with a lot of gear from a camping shop and the famous army surplus store called Laurence Corner, and said he was on his way to Bolivia to join Che Guevara in the bitter fight against the imperialist lackeys. Beverley managed to get hold of Joey in Moscow and Joey only laughed.

'Yes,' he said. 'I know, they contacted me and asked for a reference for poor Winter, can you believe it? But those 26th July people have really got it organised. I wrote back saying: "Good on enthusiasm, poor on brains". They must have taken him on. Nothing I can do. Make sure he leaves a will.'

Beverley could have worked harder at dissuading Winter but she didn't. She didn't quite send him off to war, but almost. Like the brake cable she'd almost cut all the way through, but not quite. Winter was shot and killed in the jungle within days of arriving in Bolivia, by quite whose side it was never made clear, nor in what circumstances. Che Guevara himself was shot and killed within a month.

Winter had indeed made a new will, and had left a copy with his solicitors, without telling her. He had left Robinsdale to Beverley but the bulk of his money to the Movement. The Maidment parents and family shunned her, believing it was she who had led their Julian astray. She thought perhaps she had. Anything for a bit of excitement.

She remembered how before she left Coromandel, on the way to the ferry with her two suitcases, she had crept into Arthur's garage and lain on her back in the dust and sawed at the brake cable of the Mercury with a kitchen knife. It hadn't gone through but had probably weakened it a good deal. For all she knew Arthur was dead and she had killed him. It had been simpler when she was called Rosa. If she was Beverley there were too many things to remember. On the other hand she realised she felt more like herself.

Richie, aged nine, wept copiously for his father for a time and she had to make herself weep too, to keep the child in good face. He was a good-looking, bouncy, cheerful boy, but more Maidment than McLean, as obsessed by sport, cricket in particular, as his father had been with world revolution. She was fond of him but not involved with him and the feeling seemed to be mutual.

'Why? Why?' she asked Dionne.

'Because if you don't love the father why on earth should you love the child? I daresay daughters are different – but with the son all you'd see was the way their father slurped spaghetti, or scratched his feet, the kind of traits that annoy you if you haven't had enough sex with him recently. I'm never going to have children. It's all much too complicated.'

Beverley at once felt defensive of Richie: he was his own person, just in some way remote from her. As it was he drifted off towards his father's family, and seemed more at home with them than he did with her. She thought even then that when he grew up and left home he would go a long way but not have much to do with her, or only out of politeness.

In the meanwhile Alice, seventeen and unmarried, was pregnant and needed her attention, and was asking questions about her father.

Underpinnings

The inhabitants of the basement are getting really restless. They keep intruding into my thoughts. Scarlet in particular, of the fictional ones, is impatient. She has to get to her lover in Costa's. (I just wrote Castro's and had to go back and correct it – that's poor Winter coming through from the fictional dead. All that folly and virility gone to waste. I actually seem to mourn him.)

But I can't leave Beverley yet. I have a special duty to her. I can't leave her stranded and a widow, to play into the common belief that no woman's life is really interesting after they get to be forty, and that's pushing it. Why else are parts for women over thirty-five so thin on the ground, and novels about older women so hard to sell, though they are the bulk of the readers? No one wants to know is the brutal answer. I wrote my autobiography once and stopped when I got to thirty-seven. After that, really, who was going to care? Scarlet, Lola and the others will just have to wait. I'll proceed with Beverley, whom I have certainly set up for an interesting future life.

I have got Beverley the would-be parricide to Robinsdale and explained why she is as she is, and will certainly tell you presently about the other husbands: Batcombe, the architect, and Marcus Fletzner the famous right-wing journalist and drunk, and how Beverley was implicated in those deaths too, and how the kehua in the flapping of their wings can drive one to drastic action, more sometimes than just an imprudent running away.

It is suddenly really hot up here. We are in the middle of a heat-wave, and I've been going out into the garden sometimes, and walking amongst the daisies; yesterday I was brave enough to look in through the window of the basement room and see the mauve wrap which Vi gave me still over the back of the typing chair which seems to be just waiting, and think, all that ghost stuff is nonsense, I'm going to go and work down there where it's cool.

But then I overhear Rex, who is talking to his old soldier friend Martin the picture-restorer, describe Janice as the kind of person who turns the milk sour when she passes by a churn. Where did he get that imagery from, I wonder? It feels a bit Victorian to me. It's the kind of thing Mr Bennett would say of someone. Worse, it's how I had Scarlet think of Lola. All this energy is bouncing about from person to person, the dead and the living, the fictional and the flesh-and-blood, and won't lie down. Like Arthur seeing little Beverley's bloody footsteps, I have the feeling it's all my fault.

Uneasy it makes me too that the floors of Yatt House no longer seem much of a barrier. Even that protection is dissolving. Lately there have been odd disturbing incidents upstairs: the whiff of a cigar once or twice in my lovely, airy office. It can only be Mr Bennett. This fine room was after all once his and hers, the very bedroom in which for a time he was not allowed, lest a further pregnancy should kill his poor wife; so that red-blooded man – I know, I got a glimpse of him, and he was certainly macho enough to even flutter my papers – will have stomped up and down smoking of an evening when she had retired, and then come up to force himself upon her instead of going downstairs to find Mavis.

I don't suppose Janice has to put up with cigar smoke in her nice new bungalow. At least she invites the other side in, they don't come unasked.

Another thing is that yesterday I heard the sound of panting from the corner, and looked up from my computer, and there was Bonzo, stretched out under the window trying to cool down. I looked out to see if Martin's old Rover was in the drive but it wasn't, so I thought oh, we must be dog-sitting again. And when I looked again Bonzo wasn't there. He must have slipped out, which was rather clever of him in the time available. When I went downstairs next I said to Rex, 'I see we've got Bonzo,' and he looked surprised and said, 'No, Martin's not been round.' So there you are, make of that what you can.

If these phenomena are indeed to do with global warming, sudden extremes of weather, snow or wind, storm or swelter, the deliverers are soon going to be doing a brisk business.

The deliverers, you will remember, are the ones the church sends in to do exorcisms. Knowing my luck, the one that turned up would probably be back from the Bennetts' time, someone wearing a top hat, sent from the now decommissioned church across the road, bell, book, candle and all. And they'll be trying to exorcise me. I don't suppose I'm in danger, but people do just drop dead sometimes, like young Michael Jackson.

And what about Cristobel Bennett? Now she's propped up in bed in my office, clamouring for attention. I can't see her, or hear her, she's just dictating what I write: *Oh, Mr Bennett, Mr Bennett, leave Cristobel alone!* Mary Stopes the birth-control heroine didn't come along till a decade or so later to explain that every time a woman has a baby she doubles her chances of dying. The men, bishops, judges and legislators, didn't want to know – you could go to prison for advocating contraception – so it was a brave thing for a woman to say. Childbirth is not a nice way of dying, and takes a long time. I expect this nice office of mine, so pleasant for me, once echoed to screams, and any number of servants could not help. Downstairs Mavis haunts, upstairs Cristobel.

Robinsdale, that gentle home, was so much younger than Yatt House and had not had much time to accumulate real distress in its walls. Though I daresay the kehua perched in its trees and looked mournfully around the Antipodean foliage and longed for the darker greens of home, and for Beverley and her kin to react as they should: that is, go home and perform the necessary rituals. Slim chance we have, they must have thought, but they were in no position to do much of anything but flap and rattle and precipitate action that might be as harmful as helpful. The Furies can chase you with guilt until you take to your heels and jump over a cliff, but the kehua are not like that. They just want you home where you belong, with the whanau.

Back to Beverley, and sanity

After Winter died the North-West Cadre dissolved and re-formed elsewhere – its members so well trained in the ways of Gramsciist entryism that now they hold positions of power in many of our institutions, playing a significant role in the non-elected European Council, turning Europe into the Soviet Union Lite, as was always their intent. Or so Beverley's third husband Marcus was to insist, and though bright and witty enough, he was a noted conspiracy theorist. In the end, indeed, his mind was so muddied with drink, drugs and paranoia that he couldn't even dodge a train when he saw it coming. Beverley could not possibly be blamed since she was in Paris at the time, but it is possible to manipulate events from a distance.

An eligible and attractive widow with a good house and an agreeable nature is never going to be short of suitors. Nor was Beverley. Some she entertained, some she did not. Like women everywhere she hoped that true love would come along and solve all her problems, sweep her away on waves of certainty and overwhelm her with transcendent emotion, that sort of thing, but when after a couple of years she had not been so swept away she settled for Harry Batcombe, a slight, good-looking man with no personal baggage to drag around that she knew of: kind, gentle and well read – not in fact unlike the man Scarlet would later choose as a partner

– and very useful when it came to controlling the builders Bev had just hired for her new conservatory.

Harry worked at Buckingham Palace and saw the Queen in person every month or so to discuss the redesign and restoration of the galleries there, and frankly, Marxist Beverley was as much a sucker for royalty as anyone, and impressed by his Palace connections. Another bonus was that Harry got along well with Cynara, Alice's daughter by the Unknown One.

Beverley could never quite forget Rita's dictum that most men would not want to take on another man's child. She'd assumed that Winter, in taking on Alice, had been a kind of enlightened exception – yet here was another one. Children, the Pill having created a shortage of the little creatures, had become prizes to be valued, rather than seen as an expense, a blight on a busy man's life, and a usurper of the mother's emotion.

When Alice became pregnant at seventeen, just as she was off to study marine biology at Leeds – she liked fish and was good at science – she pressed Beverley more closely about her father and her grandparents.

'Your father was a medical student,' Beverley said. 'I met him on holiday but he gave me a false name and disappeared. That was the kind of thing young men did, even nice ones, in those days. And your grandparents? Well,' and she told Alice a version of the truth, about murder and suicide and tiny bloody footprints. She didn't mention Arthur. She never mentioned Arthur. If she thought of Arthur these days, which was rarely, she imagined his Ford Mercury crashing down the hillside near Kennedy Bay and him meeting his death in a fireball. The fuel tank on those cars was huge.

How the kehua congregated, flapped and squawked that day when Beverley told lies to Alice. They have a strange soundless squawk which makes you think the pressure in your ears has changed, and which made Alice so fearful she ran to the abortionist. But Beverley ran after her and dissuaded her from the vile deed, saying she Beverley would look after the child for ever more if she let it live. Kill one, save one.

So now Alice lived in Leeds studying fish and little Cynara lived in Robinsdale, where the vibes were good, apart from the strange creatures hanging batlike in the trees, which I daresay would show up when lightning played over Highgate. But few would be looking. A stray one hung up on a beech tree near the biological sciences faculty at Leeds, but Alice was young and her immune system was good, and whenever it told her to run back to her mother she managed to discount it.

Why should I, she said to the voice in her head. The less I see of family the better. Forget the family in the past, the one in the present was bad enough: there was all that business with her stepfather Winter and the North-West Cadre: and she'd seen Beverley, with her nightie torn, leave the spare room where Joey Matthews was sleeping, one early morning when her stepfather was not home.

Not the kind of thing, if you were Alice, you could forgive and forget. But that unforgiving tendency could have come down to her from anywhere – Walter McLean, or possibly Arthur – Walter would have had a more broody kind of temperament to begin with, than his cousin Arthur. The McLeans were a family of dour Scots from Inverness, whose family had arrived in Dunedin on the good ship *Numidian* in 1863 (probably with a kelpie or two), and moved up to Canterbury and a gentler climate, there to farm sheep and multiply.

Alice declined to tell anyone who her baby's father was. What business was it of theirs? But mother love is strong, so she got down to see Cynara quite a bit, in a formal kind of way. She had a cool, observant, *Alice in Wonderland* nature, which suited her looks: wide-eyed, blonde and still, always the illustration, never quite the real thing.

Anyway Beverley married Harry and Harry moved in and all went well, in a sexless kind of way, which was something of a relief. She had to learn to put the tops on jars properly and remember to lock up and how to use the new alarm system, but these were useful virtues, she told herself. Richie drifted over to the Maidment side of the family where his cricket skills were properly appreciated, then he became interested in film, for which Beverley was blamed as representative of the artistic side of the family. Beverley, never having seen herself as particularly artistic, was baffled.

The *News of the World*, having taken an interest years back in the goings-on in the North West Cadre, and in Beverley, of whom they kept in the files a few 'compromising' snaps from her early days, just in case, were delighted by her new royal connections.

They took to following Harry about and unearthed the fact that he was having an affair with a young pastry chef who worked in the Palace kitchens. On and on the headlines went: '*Rent Boy Serves Up Royal Stew*', and so forth. Beverley 'stood by him' – she had long since guessed – but Harry was found hanged, fortunately not in Robinsdale but in the Garrick Club's men's lavatory. But it was all unpleasant enough. Beverley could see from those early photographs the tabloid had reprinted of her and Dionne at the Mayfair Photographers' Club – she in black bra and pants, Dionne in nothing at all – that if it hadn't been for her Harry would still be alive.

Cynara, at sixteen, was more than old enough to understand what was going on and certainly made it her business so to do. Richie went off to California.

But the funeral was good. Rock Hudson, that icon of heterosexuality, had just been revealed as gay, and the closet door was finally creaking open. The church was crowded; fulsome tribute was paid to Harry's talents and character; no mention was made of his gayness. Beverley stood up and made a speech. She scorned the congregation for its cowardice, society for its hypocrisy, the press for its scummy cruelty: Harry was gay and that was that and why should he not be? A society which made men like Harry marry women like her and live a life so full of dismal subterfuge they preferred death, just had to change. She challenged the congregation. Let those present who were gay come forward and admit it. She sat down.

There was a shocked silence, and if you could hear the sound of slowly flapping kehua wings it was probably only the wheezing of the sound system, which in churches always seems to have a life of its own. Then someone stood up, and another, and another, they were popping up all over the place – fourteen men, three women – amongst them a few quite famous and recognisable faces – seventeen people 'came out' that day. And then the congregation began to applaud. It was a great day, and a glorious moment. And if Cynara was later to ditch Jesper and go to D'Dora, Beverley had no one to blame but herself.

Kehua hang in the sooty plane tree outside 11 Parliam Road where Cynara lives to this day. The road name is admittedly strange. The terrace rows were built by speculative builders in 1904, and the belief is that one of the new breed of women shorthand typists erroneously left an 'ent' off the end of the word, but after the plans were approved it was cheaper to leave the road sign as it was and those who lived there soon got used to it.

Alice was so full of horror at the publicity, and what she saw as her mother's exhibitionism at Harry's funeral, that she managed to get pregnant again and give birth to Scarlet, presumably in an attempt to prove the basic heterosexuality of the universe. She brought this baby up herself, but rather in the manner of Briony, Jackson's ex, was a cat mother – the kind whose ambition is to acquire a baby and a house and then get rid of the tomcat. She was to marry a somewhat dull but respectable accountant called Stanley, disliked by Cynara for no good reason, who gave his wife little cause for complaint, until finally an affair with his secretary provided Alice with the ammunition she needed to be rid of him.

She was a good mother, and tried to instil proper values in her daughter, and might well have done so had the peer group not become so strong in society, and the eighties so consumerist – at any rate at the end of it there was Scarlet, making the best of what she had, restless, forever optimistic, oddly unquestioning, though always looking over her shoulder to see what better might be on offer. But she is my heroine, a product of her times and Beverley's past combined, so I'm not going to diss her. Just blame the kehua if she can't settle.

There are a few clinging to the top of the lofty palm tree in the atrium of Nopasaran – no wonder Scarlet hates the place – and back home there's one hanging in the grapevine which grows so lavishly and splendidly in the conservatory at Lakeside Chase, Rawdon, where Scarlet spent her first years.

Alice and her accountant husband chose the house so Alice could study the development of mollusc life in man-made lakes. Alice has never seen or heard her kehua, but is always going to the doctors with vague complaints about her hearing, and the flashing lights at the edges of her eyes. They can find nothing wrong.

Beverley and Gerry, an interlude

Gerry was a mate of Harry's from college days. It was only natural for Beverley and he to get together after Harry's death, for tea, sympathy and reminiscences. One thing led to another. She appreciated his raw, outland sexual energy, so unlike Harry's, but perhaps he reminded her too much of Arthur, and while she was humming and hawing about taking him on properly Fiona stepped in and nabbed him and that was that.

Then Marcus came along, and Beverley turned out to be just a bit-part player in that particular life. But then wives so often are.

My view is that in order for her to take her place in the GCGITS' scheme of things, Beverley needed to be unpartnered in order that the publication of Marcus Fletzner's best-seller, *Slicing the Salami*, should happen. Fiona was just the convenient and all-too-disposable tool which allowed this to occur. At any rate, when the book was published and Marcus, his use to the GCGITS over, was well dead, Gerry, minus Fiona, was allowed to drift back on the scene. But not until Marcus' death had made sure that his book found an immense and influential readership. Nothing, in the world of the GSWITS and the GCGITS, is coincidental. They conspire in the pub.

A conversation between Marcus and Beverley

Marcus came to Robinsdale by appointment.

'Thank you for seeing me, Mrs Batcombe, I know you're not too fond of the press. In the circumstances it's good of you. You'll be glad to hear that I don't want to talk about Harry but about the NWC, the North-West Cadre. I am writing a book about neo-Trotskyists and I have come to the chapter on Joey Matthews, and his effect on the institutions of this country and the consequent dumbing down of established culture –'

'We never called it the NWC,' she said. 'We didn't call it anything in particular. But yes, Joey wuz here.'

Marcus stands on the doorstep and in the trees the kehua stir and flap their wings – they've been quiescent since Gerry left, and I reckon they've quite caught Beverley's liking for events: with kehua influence seems to flow both ways.

Marcus is not the kind to catch the sound. If anything he's an atheist of the Dawkins school. The rain begins; not hard but a dampening drizzle.

He is a big, handsome fleshy man, carelessly dressed, bright-eyed and forceful, and has made a living for many years by a quick wit and a lively tongue, an eye for the controversial, and entertaining an old-fashioned conceit that Britain should be for the British and there are reds under every bed. He survived until entrapped by the *Sunday Times* and recorded saying at a drunken dinner party that all immigrants were welcome so long as they pissed on the Koran at Border Control. 'Then we could go back to the old days of free travel.' He was recorded and declined to say (a) that his remarks were taken out of context or (b) that he was sorry. The ensuing uproar lost him his job at the BBC and his column in *The Times*, so he was able to focus on *Slicing the Salami*, though his publishers wanted him to call it *The Gramsci Effect*. No one would understand salami slicing, it being a term invented by the Communist leader Rakosi in 1945. But then no one had heard of Gramsci either.

'What is the name of the book?' Still she did not let him in.

'*Slicing the Salami*,' he said, making the decision there and then.

'What does that mean?'

He had to make his pitch from the step.

'It means demanding a little more each day, like cutting up a salami, thin slice after thin slice, until you have the whole sausage. It was Stalin's tactic for winning control of Eastern Europe, country after country, by violence, lies and misinformation, and it worked. It remains the Islamic tactic for holy Jihad today. It was what Joey Matthews from Moscow was doing in London, in 1965, slicing the salami, funding the useful idiots. The only question is, quite whose sausage it was. May I come in?'

'No. You can't. Useful idiots?'

'Lenin's phrase. The young intellectuals, lefties, budding politicians, writers, artists, academics, prelates, all on automatic pilot, who still think it is their duty to destroy the old bourgeois institutions and build the world from scratch. Little by little the Commies still slice the salami of the West.'

'That sounds like us,' she said blithely. 'Transitional demands, that kind of thing. "Make Poverty History". Sounds good, feels good, looks good on a poster.'

The girls who belonged to the NWC were there to make coffee and provide home comforts, not because of their brains. But perhaps she had a few, thought Marcus. The widow Batcombe, previously Max – he was the freedom fighter who famously died in a shoot-out in a Bolivian jungle, and who yet might make a chapter – was looking promising. Women kept love letters if nothing else. And she had made that speech at Batcombe's funeral.

'It would be easier if we could talk inside,' he suggested.

He could see over her shoulder comfort, order, stability, cleanliness, permanence and prosperity within, all the things he thought he did not need and now suddenly did. It was drizzling, and he had no coat. His personal life was in disarray, his dandruff was bad, his shirt was frayed, even he acknowledged he smoked and drank too much, his girlfriend had left him for a Labour Party activist, his washing machine had broken down and he was hungry. If he looked at Beverley he saw a woman in her mid-sixties who had kept her figure, and had probably had a facelift or two: a smarter, slimmer version of his mother, whom he loved. But at the moment he wanted more than anything just to be let in. She might give him coffee. He hated damp clothes.

'No,' she said, 'you can't come in. I don't want to talk about Winter. I have my family to consider.'

'I'll leave Winter out of it. I promise.'

'Yeah, right,' she said. 'Bears don't shit in the woods.'

'I only want to talk about Joey.'

'As a matter of interest, what became of him?'

'He died in Berlin, in August 1991, on the day Yeltsin rode the tank and the old order collapsed, to be born again in Brussels.

Forgive me if I quote from my own book: "*The formal dissolution of the Soviet Union was announced four months later; two months later the final agreement at Maastricht was reached. Was this, for Joey Matthews, born Josef Maybaum, double, even triple agent, victory or defeat?*" You see the kind of book it is? No one is going to want to read it. It can do no one any possible harm.'

She finally stood aside and let him in, made him coffee, and even offered him some bread and cheese. She said she could always tell when men were hungry. They looked at you with reproachful eyes. Once it was sex they were after. These days it was food.

The coffee was strong, the Cheddar basic but good, the bread was Waitrose best and there was a linen napkin. It was not how his girlfriends served food. They tore off a section of kitchen roll. They did not eat bread. They always seemed too busy thinking or tarting themselves up to look after the finer things in life. She offered him whisky with his coffee, a single malt, and he accepted and she swigged one too. Then they both had another. Then she brought out the bottle. Better and better.

'How well did you know Joey?' He had his recorder on, his pencil out. 'Was he heterosexual? A lot of those Cairncross guys were ambivalent.'

'I spent the night with him just up there,' she said, and she pointed to the ceiling. 'He was a good fuck, and I still remember it.'

He felt shocked and excited. '*I danced with the woman who danced with the Prince of Wales.*' He had his chapter. Joey had come alive. Now it would be easy. He looked at her again and some kind of erotic quality seemed to have entered into her, to which he responded. If Joe had done it so would he.

'I was sold to pay for a *Rock Against Racism* event,' she said.

Better and better. He asked if the NWC had taken all their

papers with them: was there anything left? She said they took nothing; without Joe they were hopeless, without Winter they were distraught. All their stuff was still in her attic; they were always meant to be taking it away but no one had ever turned up.

'Would I be able to look through them?' he asked.

'No,' she said. 'There's too much of it. You'd be here for ever, cramping my style. I'm looking for a husband.'

He could see he might have to marry her. Which he did, selling his flat to pay his debts, moving into Robinsdale. She was ten years older than he. Her family was aghast, and stayed away whenever they decently could. Their mother had not only married a right-wing, racist, atheist fascist, but one notorious for his views, embarrassing in the very association. Their reaction pained Beverley, but she was busy again and her bed was filled. He was companionable but not particularly active in bed, which suited her, and he made her laugh, as she did him. The kehua hibernated. Laughter puts them to sleep.

It took Marcus two years to finish the book, during which Beverley helped with the research, and Marcus grew sleek and smooth, joined AA, stopped taking cocaine and won back a few friends. In the attic he and Beverley found membership lists, accounts, diaries and correspondence, and also £2,000 in cash. She found compromising photographs of comrades who had once been young and were now in high places, running universities, hospital trusts, prison reform, the media and charities. A couple were ministers of the Crown. No one had ended up poor. It seemed that to be a justified sinner – as Marcus categorised all 'lefties'; those who believed the means justify the ends – guaranteed worldly success and wealth, and that to have a secret agenda made a person effective in the world.

Beverley, categorising, listing, annotating, précising, handed the stuff over to Marcus without comment, other than to say she thought he should be careful. Marcus spent many hours with his publishers' lawyers: Beverley, ever practical, hired a security guard to look under the car every morning. Various interests tried to have the book banned. Hostile reviews came out even before publication. Marcus loved every minute of it, Beverley hated every minute.

She lamented the night she had spent with Joey: she lamented even more that she had invited Marcus over the doorstep. The past was the past, what did it have to do with the present? She rashly said as much to Marcus.

'Do you understand nothing?' he demanded. She thought he had taken to cocaine again. Worse, he had decided that the odd glass of wine would do him no harm. 'Don't you see how this country is being destroyed by these cancerous, lying scum?'

She did not read the proofs. He told her once too often that she was a stupid, provincial cow. She'd been getting terrible migraines, kehua wings beating in her head, visible in the vein on her temple, so her family worried. *Run, run, run.* She told him to find a wife who suited him better, and did indeed run to the divorce solicitors.

One-two, one-two, little knees up and down beneath the blue and white checked dress, little bloodstained footprints in the yellow dust.

She went to stay with her friend Dionne in Paris. The kehua followed her and took up residence in the hydrangeas out on Dionne's patio. Dionne was just selling the last of her Chagalls. The suitors had not dried up, but Dionne's interest in them had. She would rather read the books she had forgone in her youth. Beverley did not get to the launch of *Slicing the Salami.*

Marcus had done as Beverley suggested and found a young

woman who thought as he did – as it happened, a member of the BNP – and invited her to live in Robinsdale while Beverley was away. Then Marcus changed the locks so Beverley couldn't get in without breaking in. The lawyers advised her against this latter act. Perhaps when it was over, all agreed, Marcus would revert to sanity. They had really both got on very well until this happened. Marcus called her from a pub when she was in Paris and said he was sorry, he had put the new key under a stone beneath the lilac tree if she came home when he was out. He blamed Beverley for provoking him.

'Perhaps I did,' said Beverley to Dionne. 'I am not a nice person. I thought I was but I am not. Look at me, I have betrayed my friends. Why, why did I do it?'

'For a bit of peace,' Dionne said. 'If a man moves into your life you do all sorts of things you wouldn't do normally. It doesn't have to be love; it's the sharing of the bed that does it. Propinquity. You sop up their vapours, in every sense of the word. Besides, they were not really your friends. They were the companions of your youth, which is a very different thing. See them as Marcus sees them – satanic lefty scum – and absolve yourself.'

Dionne tended to share Marcus' political outlook, but then this was Paris and she was a courtesan and so oblivious to social censure. The kehua, lost amongst the blues and pinks of the pompom hydrangeas, chattered and squeaked and Dionne said, 'Do you hear something?' and frowned and Beverley said, 'No.' Her hearing was not as acute as once it had been. 'All the same,' said Dionne, 'it might be safer not to go to the book launch.'

It was touch and go whether the launch of *Slicing the Salami* would go ahead. There was litigation up to the very last moment. The media forgot their normal plea of the public interest, and betrayed one of their own, that is to say, Marcus. All noisily and passionately agreed there must be a limit to freedom of speech. Advance sales soared. The launch was on.

Marcus took the BNP girl since Beverley was not around. She was small, dark and pale and wore a lot of make-up. (She was a friend of D'Dora's as it happened. They belonged to the same rock-climbing club.) They were both very drunk. There were demos outside and scuffles with the police before, and it was touch and go whether they could get into the publishing house at all, let alone up to the penthouse on the fifteenth floor where the view over London is so great. But the GCGITS made sure they got there.

Marcus and the BNP girl then apparently had an argument as to whether the view from the Penguin Penthouse in the Strand was better, and they left the party together. After that their movements were uncertain – London was not yet so lavish with its security cameras – other than that they ended up on the track of the Docklands Light Railway, where it runs overground near Canary Wharf; and both were struck and killed by an automated train. There was no evidence of foul play. Book sales were stupendous, *Slicing the Salami* had a six-month triumph, stayed around for a year or two, and then was quietly remaindered. Whatever the GCGITS' purpose was, it was served.

There were so many if-onlies for Beverley to worry about, amidst tears – if only I had gone to the book launch, if only I hadn't provoked him, provided the research in the first place, driven him to drink and so on – that Beverley felt as guilty as if she had pushed Marcus under the train herself. She sometimes remembered what he had said to her on the doorstep, that the book could do no possible harm. But it had certainly created a fuss, and lost her friends.

But gradually, like her family, friends drifted back, as did her good spirits. Robinsdale was her own again. She had the whole place redecorated. The ceilings, once yellow from cigarette smoke and the after-dinner cigar that Marcus had so enjoyed, were pure virginal white once again. She had a vestigial memory of someone talking about virgins and cloning, but did not pursue it.

Let's get out of here

Lately Mr Bennett has been up and down the stairs rather too often for comfort. It is still terrifically hot up here – we're in a heatwave – and the whiff of his cigar smoke is so strong as to be offensive. I am a non-smoker. Marcus, I notice, once just a cigarette smoker, has taken up cigar smoking as well. Go figure, as Beverley would say. Time to get downstairs again, where it's cooler, and away from the unseen collie panting in the corner, and what I am beginning to construe as the squeaking of a double bed. I can't blame the central heating at the moment and there's no air-conditioning. I think I see Mr Bennett as very like Marcus, only without the brains. But then Marcus has no reality either, come to think of it.

The other thing is that the father of my oldest child appeared to me yesterday, smiling, and I was conscious of a great affection for him. He died fifteen years ago. I had not married him but chosen to bring up the child without him. Unkindly, and unthinkingly, I had barred him from the whanau. When I say 'appeared' it was not quite in the flesh, nor in a dream: somewhere in between. Just that I remembered what he looked like, how he was, what his presence felt like, so clearly he might as well have been there in the real world. Mind you, I had just had three teeth out and was somewhat medicated. Though I was pleased to see my first sweetheart, and so pleased to be pleased, it is always a little worrying when deceased family members appear at one's side.

I remember how when my mother was very old and in a nursing home the nurse phoned us early one morning. 'You'd better come now,' she said.

I asked in alarm what had happened and she said, 'Your mother's in her normal good health. But when she woke this morning she told me she'd had a vivid dream. Her father was coming towards her smiling and stretching out his hand for her. Back home in Jamaica, at the training college, they taught us that if the patient was summoned by a family member in a dream we were to call the relatives at once. So that's what I'm doing.'

We went at once, and by the next morning my mother had died; we were in time to say goodbye. So if my son's father comes to me in a dream, I am glad to know he is in the whanau in spite of me, but I am also a little nervous. And I have to finish this book before I go. The show must go on.

I'll do it downstairs in the cool, not upstairs. Upstairs, once so tranquil and benevolent, hasn't half got itself all stirred up.

PART THREE

Enchanted Scarlet

We'll take a brief look first at Scarlet, since she's so restless. The fates are with her: a parking space has opened up in front of Costa's. And she parks the Prius swiftly and neatly. She is a safe, confident, polite, alert driver – this is her New Zealand ancestry: this is Arthur in the Mercury, taking the hairpin bends in his stride, pulling to one side if there is a faster car behind him – not, once he had the Mercury, that there ever was. Arthur, as it happens, died in his bed, not in the fireball that Beverley – with that part of her mind which ever allows Arthur to surface at all – half fears, and half hopes for. He died of heart failure in 1980. Rita was at his bedside. She had been rising thirty when they married and had been all the more pleased to be taken off the shelf.

'Taken off the shelf' is a phrase not in common use today. It's how spinsters – those who had lagged behind in the marriage race and remained old maids by their late twenties – were spoken of. Rita, unmarried and thirtyish, having 'put on her bonnet' (in other words given up), had taken in little Beverley for company, in place of the child she was unlikely to have, and had been rewarded. Any husband was better than none. But back, briskly, to Scarlet.

Scarlet manoeuvres smoothly and efficiently into a tight space which would defeat many another driver. Jackson, in spite of his fears of being late, is in the café before her, sees her through the windows, and his heart leaps. She is the solution to all his problems, and his joy is amplified by the slight stiffening feeling in his pants, which suggests to him that this is indeed true love. His encounter with Briony had been bruising. She so despises him, and so lets him know it, that the shortest conversation with her can leave him limp for days and in need of Viagra even though normally he is all eagerness and activity and requires no chemical help. See, Scarlet can vanquish even Briony. Scarlet sits, they lean towards each other, they take each other's hands, they gaze into each other's eyes. Those around feel warmly towards them, and envious. Costa's becomes a magic place.

You may have realised, reader, as I have just done, that in comparing Arthur's driving excellence with Scarlet's, I have suggested a genetic connection between them. In other words Arthur is indeed Beverley's father, Scarlet's great-grandfather. I too have been unsure until now. Did it happen as the Christchurch Press would have it, that Walter killed his wife in a crime passionnel, and then shot his dog and himself? Or as Beverley suspected – that she was Arthur's baby born to Kitchie, and Arthur used the bread knife on Kitchie when she chose to stay with the long-suffering Walter, then took Walter's gun as Walter fled for his life to the quarry, and shot him and his dog. That months later Arthur stopped by and wooed Rita, in order to get his daughter back. Even to wait until she was grown in order to possess her, to mark his own – it was sheep country, even though he was a doctor – as he had possessed and marked the mother. Though he may have started with the best intentions and weakened on the way: of that even I cannot be sure, and Beverley was doing the provoking. But Arthur as the killer is now the true version. Scarlet has killer's blood, murderer's blood, in her veins, for all she appears so lightweight. Jackson had better look out.

Scarlet called me back down to the basement. She wanted attention and she got it. There's no cigar smoke down here, and no panting noises and all is quiet; I notice that the green grass the other side of the window-panes has faded to brownish grey, it's been so hot and dry lately.

Now, though, here's Samantha standing in reception at MetaFashion, a Yummy Mummy to dream of, dressed in Boden, sensible and smart. She's a much better bet for Louis and Nopasaran than Scarlet could ever be. A pity about her husband and three children.

But Samantha and Louis are just so right. Samantha would be fascinated by what went on at MetaFashion, able to follow the thrills and tensions of the business, never be fighting against Louis where his beloved Nopasaran was concerned; no, she would be with him all the way, outraged by the planning authorities, looking up in Google to prove that English Heritage had misunderstood the law, going to night classes on the Brutalist architecture of the thirties, getting on well with his mother – there were even family connections: her father had been at Bedales with Annabel's best friend, Samantha's mother becoming Matron only because of reduced circumstances. If only Samantha's mother had kept out of the laundry room that afternoon, how happy everyone might have been. Only the GCGITS would not allow it.

Yes, and most of all Samantha was so obviously fertile and happy to have more children. She'd have had them trained to climb the ladders to bed as soon as they could crawl and she would never utter a complaint. She was a brave, valiant girl and she had loved Louis all her life, her first and only true love. No accident that in later life she often wore shoes with the seam up the middle of the upper: she felt close to Louis when she did.

When Louis was warned by Beverley that Scarlet was running

off to her lover and the couple could be found in Costa's if he hurried, Louis failed to hurry and who could blame him? Because when he'd called Samantha on the mobile number he kept in his wallet, she'd picked up the phone. There, after years, waiting. She had not lost the phone or changed her number. The GCGITS knows what he's doing.

'Louis!' said Samantha. 'I dreamt of you last night; how strange.'

'It isn't strange at all,' said Louis, 'I dream about you all the time.'

And it was as if the intervening years had all melted away. Samantha was shopping in Liberty's: so she was round at Meta-Fashion in ten minutes in a Boden cord blazer, a well-cut white shirt and a pretty flowered skirt, made of a thirties fabric print with red poppies on a white background – so different from the designer jeans and T-shirt style that Scarlet favoured. Before they knew it they were reunited on a sofa, and the stretch marks on Samantha's tummy from the three pregnancies and the thinning hair on Louis' anxious scalp were as nothing.

Samantha's husband was one of those business executives who had spent a lot of time flying around the world first or business class, but now in the recession was reduced to making conference calls from his offices in Oxford. The close and continued proximity of his PA had proved too much for him and he had enjoyed a weekend break with her in a famous country-house hotel in the Cotswolds but had felt so guilty he felt obliged to tell Samantha about it, with contrition and apologies, and assurances that the girl, a redhead, was to be transferred to their branch in Edinburgh.

Samantha, though shocked, had accepted Stanley's apologies and forgiven, but perhaps not properly, because on meeting Louis an element of tit for tat may have encouraged her embraces. At any rate, when these were concluded, Samantha had sat up on the sofa, covered her ample breasts with her gauze scarf, the one she had just bought at Liberty's – one of their peacock prints, yellow and grey, with the eye a greeny-blue – wept, and said this must not happen again. She was a married woman and had to think of family and children.

And just then D'Kath burst in upon them and it was obvious what had been happening on the yellow-velvet sofa. Forget that Samantha, naked beneath the swathe of gauzy scarf, looked like a Lord Leighton painting, crossed with a Klimt, what with the fabric and the build-up of colour combinations and the way the curls of the patterns blended into the tendrils of her hair, D'Kath ignored the exquisite setting and reacted as Samantha's mother had all those many years ago, with a shriek which could be heard around the building. The couple, shocked, sprang apart hastily.

And now both of them could think only of poor Stuart, the art master, who on finding Louis unfaithful, had hanged himself in a classroom. It could not be allowed to happen again. They must part. The consequences of illicit love, both knew from experience, can be terrible. The GCGITS gives with one hand, takes away, often brutally, with the other.

A word about that early disaster. Louis was hardly to be blamed for it. Sheer embarrassment, in the face of the art master's protracted advances, his insistence that only through sex could genius flourish, had left Louis with little choice but to do what Stuart seemed to expect him to do, that is to declare lasting love. Louis had mouthed words without understanding them. But that had not been how the world had seen it, let alone his mother. It had been very little to do with sex, a great deal to do with love. In the few dreadful weeks before he left the school for good, he became known as Sexbomb the Murderer.

Lola waits for Louis

So it was in a state of considerable upset that Louis let himself into Nopasaran. Forget Scarlet – he had found his loved one at last only to lose her, on the way meeting a degree of sexual pleasure he had not known existed. More, he could only conclude from her reaction that his colleague, cousin and partner D'Kath was in love with him, and was a lesbian fellow traveller only. The D'Thises and D'Thats were a business ploy. Now he had offended her, and in her deluded mind betrayed her, which could only bode no good for Meta-Fashion. Without Scarlet to provide him with an alibi, how was he to fend D'Kath off? Supposing he got to work and found her dangling from the end of a rope? He had construed D'Kath's occasional embrace and glass of champagne as no more than friendly. So obsessed had he been by the general assumption that he was gay, he had fallen into the trap of supposing the same thing of others.

He needed time within these beloved and calming walls to compose himself, to work out what he felt and what had to be done about Scarlet's absence. She was hopeless but already he missed her, her irreverence, her delinquency, her ability to move him to fury. He thought it was good for him; repressing anger gave you cancer, he was convinced. She would probably be back; she had done this twice before, and he had taken her back; today he was not so sure. It was all too much to take on board. And he had forgotten about Lola.

He was struck first, as he let himself in through the door, by how orderly everything was. Scarlet's mess had been tidied away: there were no odd shoes on the floor any old where: no discarded magazines tossed lightly away, no uncased mascara wands to be trodden into the original carpeting and so on, no old coffee cups spilled and forgotten. Cushions were plumped. He realised the artless carelessness which once had seemed so charming in Scarlet had become a source of irritation. But at least today she had cleared up before she went. It was a nice gesture. He hoped that if Scarlet had indeed gone for good, he would be able to go on turning up at Robinsdale. He liked Beverley and she liked him; mind you, he was frightened of Cynara, sorry for Jesper, alarmed by the thought of D'Dora, fascinated by Lola, and even as she came to mind, here she was. Of course, she was the house guest.

Lola was wearing the transparent top with lacy frills which Scarlet occasionally wore to parties with a slip beneath it, just high enough to hide the nipples. Lola wore the same garment without the slip, together with a thong, and that was all. Her long legs and feet were bare. She was reaching up with the metal hose to suck up cobwebs and dust from high places. Partly Louis was delighted that someone was bothering to do it, no matter how they were dressed, and partly he found the sight stirring, fresh as he was from the feel of Samantha beneath her Liberty gauze scarf with its Pre-Raphaelite undertones. This seemed to be a Tracey Emin version of the same thing, but valid enough. And it had a cultural context. Had he not once seen a Godard film of the young Brigitte Bardot doing the housework naked?

'Your wife is a real pig,' said Lola. 'She left me to do all this and has gone off with Jackson Wright the vampire.'

'I heard as much,' said Louis, wincing. 'She is not technically my wife, only morally, and please don't talk of your aunt like that. Shouldn't you cover yourself up a bit?'

'Why? Do you fancy me?' asked Lola, disentangling herself from the period vacuum cleaner, neatly coiling its wires by hand – it was too old even to have spring-loading for the cord – and following him into the kitchen. The dishes which were normally piled into the sink had been washed and put away. Plates were in size order, saucepans ranged with their handles all pointing in the same direction.

'Looks nice, doesn't it?' said Lola.

Scarlet had no visual sense, but Lola had. She must have got that from her father Jesper – though of course we must remember her mother Cynara's father was Unknown – it said so on her birth certificate, and Alice had refused to speak more on the subject to anyone. In vain did Beverley beg, and later Cynara plead, and health visitors protest – what about genetic risks and so forth, and a child had a right to know the identity of both parents, on and on – but Alice wouldn't tell.

Alice's mysterious pregnancy

Beverley had always had a suspicion that the child was in fact Winter's – so had not pressed her daughter too hard. There was such a thing as too much information. Winter Max was no blood relation of Alice's, after all, just a stepfather, and Cynara had turned out a fine healthy child. If you thought about it there was a look of the Maidments about Cynara – the stockier build, the pig-headed-ness. Better, then, not to think about it: if you did the generations became too confused – Cynara became Richie's half-sister as well as his niece.

But if it was indeed the case, no wonder Alice had fled north: not because of the shock-horror of family history but because her daughter did not want to be reminded of the horror and confusion that she herself had created in her own generation, sleeping with her mother's husband. No wonder in the end she had confirmed her allegiance to Jesus – she could not shake off the need for ongoing forgiveness. And Winter's sudden flight had less to do with the struggle, with Bolivia and Che Guevara, than just getting away from the mess. He had welcomed death, as perhaps Walter had, in his time, as preferable to the disaster that was life.

'Invent a medical student,' implored Beverley when her daughter's pregnancy became apparent, 'if you don't want to tell me who the father actually is.'

'It's not that I don't want,' wept Alice. 'It's that I can't. Oh, Mum!'

Was she weeping for herself or Winter? From guilt or grief or distress? What's a mother to do except not give the matter too much thought? It was not as if Winter was around any more, to berate. And he had already made sure he had no exclusive demands on her, Beverley, or she on him, as is the manner of revolutionaries.

'Or if not a medical student,' said Beverley, 'try an officer on leave, who was killed before he could marry you. One hears that one a lot.'

But Alice felt she had a duty to the truth. And if the truth was not possible, silence was next best.

In the course of her heredity and genetics module at Leeds, she was told that since sex was no longer about reproduction but recreation, when it happened within the family it was hardly of consequence. It did not feel quite like that to Alice; she felt the Freudian version was more likely, in which, though the horror and revulsion when it comes to inter-family sexual relationships were a mere social construct, knowledge of its incestuous begetting would stunt the development of the child's superego so that it remained infantile, sadistic, perfectionist, demanding and punishing. Alice did not want her baby's superego thus crippled. Better perhaps no baby at all, remembering that every baby you give birth to keeps out the next one, who might have a better chance in life.

The same advice echoed through the generations. If you don't know who the father is, invent one. Buy a wedding ring from Woolworth's, otherwise it's Epsom salts from Boots or gin from the pub or both and try lying in a too hot bath. Today's equivalent being the morning-after pill, or if you're still too drunk the morning after, down to the doctor in a week or two, and to the clinic, and whoosh, baby's gone. The baby is like the puppy, not just for Christmas, the baby is for life and a whole string of other lives, and a kehua attached to every one; the trees are alive with the sound of flapping. No wonder girls get scared.

Alice made for the clinic, and would have got there only Beverley hauled her back and made her the offer: 'You keep the baby, I'll take it on.'

The baby was born, and at the age of three weeks christened Mary. It was there at the christening service, in the charming surroundings of St John's in Hampstead, moved by the hymns and sunlight gleaming through stained-glass windows, that Alice began her intense relationship with Jesus. Winter was by that time off to Bolivia, whence he would never return. The baby was left in the care of Beverley. Alice took the tube down to King's Cross, and the train back to Leeds and her studies. Beverley took it on herself to rename the baby Cynara. When Cynara was sixteen, Alice claimed the girl as her own, wrenching her from her grandmother's care, renaming her as Mary and taking her back into her own household. Cynara, or Mary, disliked her stepfather and the dislike quickly developed into a feminism of almost religious intensity.

And now here's Lola, Winter's granddaughter and great-granddaughter both, contemplating sex with her uncle, and seeing nothing wrong in it. The incestuous tendency, after all, has come down to her from both sides of the family. It must be a very aggressive gene.

Who does and who is done unto? When it comes to sex it can be hard to tell. Lola is young but far more experienced sexually than Louis, who had had only four loves in his lifetime, and the fourth, earlier in the day, was by far the most explosive and has emotionally exhausted him. He is just so tired.

'You look really bad,' says Lola now to Louis, 'but you'll get over it. It's not as if you two were married or had any children.'

Louis sits down on the sofa and begins to weep. Lola sits beside him and says, 'Can I make everything feel better again?' in the gentlest way, and Louis knows that after a few formal protests this is exactly what he will do. As well be hanged for a sheep as for a lamb and serve Scarlet right, and serve Samantha right too, for stirring up old emotions and then leaving him in the shit, and D'Kath for bursting in on them and bringing up memories of disgrace at school, and Lola too, for simply being there and daring to behave in this outrageous way. Sixteen is not too young for sex; anyway she claimed to be seventeen for Help the Harmed and if that's the way she wants it who is he to stand in her way?

He and Samantha had been sixteen when first they met and rolled together on the infirmary's beds. Louis shuts his eyes and does as he is told: he lets Lola take most of his clothes off – she has none worth removing – and it is like being a small child again: she pushes him so he lolls against the back of the sofa, his cock still half erect with memories of Samantha, takes it in her mouth in the most practised way, and then sits on top of him doing the splits so she has an ankle on both arms of the sofa, quite the little gymnast, and then bounces up and down with her skinny little thighs, wailing and gasping, therapeutically stretching her inner leg muscles the while, until she is satisfied. After which she abruptly removes herself with no thought for his coming at all.

Louis is astonished at the uneroticism of it all; he has not met it before, but then, as he realises, he has met so little before. He feels quite sorry for her. She is like a housewife, he thinks, who asks a guest for dinner, cooks the meal, and serves it only to herself. By comparison, Scarlet is generosity itself.

'I have you in my power now,' Lola says, looking up from her mobile, where she is already busy interconnecting with the rest of the world. 'I can cry rape and I'm bound to win and the criminal compensation board will give me £20,000 and I can go to Haiti without waiting for Help the Harmed to get their act together.'

Louis turns pale. He can see it is all too likely. He needs Scarlet. She will know what to do.

'Don't worry, Uncle Louis,' says Lola. 'Only kidding. I feel a lot better now. Thanks!'

And she goes off to her friends, saying she's more than paid for her keep by doing the housework. She says Scarlet can keep the top, she doesn't need it any more, there's only a small tear under one of the arms.

Louis says pathetically, 'But Scarlet has gone.'

And Lola says, 'Don't you believe it. It's on Twitter that Jackson Wright is all washed up; so she'll be back.'

And Louis hardly knows what to think. He goes to bed and sleeps and sleeps and sleeps.

The peace and quiet of the basement

At the moment it is really very eerily quiet and normal down here. No chatter and clatter from Mavis or Cook, no cigar smoke. The peace was making me uneasy. Then I realised I couldn't even hear the birds singing or the keyboard clacking. So I took time off and went down to the nurse at the clinic and had my ears checked, and yes, there was a lot of wax, which had to be softened and washed out. I am sorry to plague you with this really rather disgusting detail – bad enough when characters have afflictions, but one hardly wants the writer to offer hers up as well – but it is relevant. The nurse said yes, in the build-up to the blockage one could get all kinds of sound effects in the ears, and yes, sudden changes of temperature might well affect the wax, hardening or softening it, though she hardly thought the sense of smell would be affected. On the other hand – ears, nose, throat – yes, it was possible. So all is explained. Well, quite a lot of it. It doesn't explain the dog who wasn't Bonzo walking past my window. But the unlikely is not the impossible.

I walked back from the clinic hearing everything so clearly it was almost painful. I could hear the drains beneath the pavement gurgling; the sound of the church bell ringing a celebratory carillon was as clear as that of the men moving a skip and shouting each other instructions. My ears had temporarily lost the ability to sort out irrelevant sound from the relevant. Within half an hour my hearing was back to normal, and I was able to dismiss the thought that though I'd assumed the church bells were coming from All Saints, the bells had been removed in the seventies. My sense of near sound and distant sound had been confused.

But why do I have the sense that I am being laughed at, that they are playing grandmother's footsteps? One child goes ahead, and the others creep up behind, and if the one in front suddenly turns round and if someone is discovered to be moving, that person is out.

The weather's been heavy lately, full of thunder, and very humid. Today really black clouds are blowing our way and seem to be piling up just the other side of the *lonicera* hedge which marks the edge of the garden some sixty feet away. Well, more or less *lonicera* – in the manner of unkempt hedges everywhere it also includes attractive intrusions of holly, hawthorn and roses. A single red rose and a shower of white ones stand out clearly against the black backdrop of clouds. I am so taken by it I stop typing and just stare. I would go and get my camera except that this would mean climbing up the stone stairs, worn down by the footsteps of the likes of Mavis, and Cook, and the laundress, yes, and occasionally Mr Bennett and his kind.

A crack of thunder comes so loud it makes me start up from my chair. A zigzag of lightning leaps through the clouds almost without pause and makes everything as bright as daylight for a second: everything is visible except for some reason the roses. My computer screen blinks and cuts out. I panic. But when I turn it on again – fortunately we have a kind of surge cut-out gadget – every word is there. I saved, thank God, before I stopped to stare at the roses. Even better, the leylandia just the far side of the hedge was struck and split – I have never liked it because it's an unnatural heavy green colour and it has blocked the view out of my bedroom window, and now the leylandia is no more, it is gone. And the rain came pelting down and did the garden no end of good, and everything smelled of fresh wet grass. So all was well.

Almost well. I say almost, because I'll swear that in that instant flash of light I saw a cluster of kehua hanging from one of the trees in the hedge, swinging gently in the rush of cool breeze that came just before the rain started down. It was only the vision of an instant, but there they were. This is not good. This is outrageous – what are they doing in my life? They are a fictional conceit. I brought them to this country. They come and go at my behest.

No wonder the dead staff are bloody laughing: they know what's going on. The spirits of the world are in collusion. I knew it was dangerous walking the edge of the occult. The more you think about it, the more it's there. But I shan't give up. I am not so far from the end of this book. The kehua of the South, the kelpies and selkies of the North may unite and riot, I shall stay down here and write.

Upstairs is too unhappy at the moment. The carillon I heard, from the bells that weren't, was surely celebrating the end of the First World War, from which two of the Bennett sons, William and Ernest, never came home. What good victory now? I can't bear it. Mr Bennett and Mavis' carryings-on are bad enough but Cristobel's grief is too near me, as she roams these now-desolate rooms. It is every woman's grief. Perhaps that's what brought the kehua to my garden: they are bent on joining together all the sorrowing families of the world, the ones destroyed by violence. They are learning globalism.

And now for something completely different

When Beverley had done her bit at the prompting of her kehua and had called Gerry and Louis, thus stirring up their lives enough to wake the dead, she calls her granddaughter Cynara to point out that Scarlet has left Louis and that she hopes Lola is not going to be homeless, because at this time in her life the girl needs guidance.

'She can come and stay with me if she likes,' says Beverley. 'I'll take her on.'

The kehua move closer, fluttering from the hornbeam at the end of the garden to hang from the branches of the wild cherry or *prunus avium*, which rubs its branches up against the windows of Beverley's conservatory, and which in spite of Harry's advice she had declined to have removed. (Harry is the second husband, if you remember, the troubled gay architect.) Sooner or later the glass panes are going to start cracking and breaking under the pressure of foliage. Beverley, waiting for Cynara's reply, finds her ears are blocked and stuffy and blows her nose, which doesn't help, but just makes sound the more distorted.

The kehua love event. They sniff it in the air. It makes them chatter and clatter. They like the idea of the family massing together: ideally of course it would be in the marae in pakeha Amberley, the dead and the living at peace together, all the rituals done. As it happened both Walter and Arthur had Maori ancestry, albeit diluted, from the bloodline of the great South Island warrior Te Rauparaha, but that was something you kept quiet about in Amberley in the 1920s. But the kehua have almost forgotten their purpose: which is to get Kitchie and Walter, Rita and Arthur, and little Beverley and all her descendants back with the whanau at last. The kehua have come to like the flora of this northern Antipodean land, the oaks, willows, ashes and aspens, with branches which are far easier to hang from than the pohutakawas whose cheerful red fronds are scratchy, let alone the kauris so tall and smooth you have to find an updraught to reach even the lowest branch. The flowering cherry suits them very well.

Beverley says she can well understand that Lola might find it difficult at her age to lose a father and find a second mother, and needs a place to be where there is less tumult than there was likely in her new future, either at Nopasaran with a distraught Louis, or at Parliam Road with her mother and D'Dora. At which Cynara, emotionally and physically exhausted by a wild night in The Dungeonette, accuses her grandmother of being homophobic.

'Could you repeat that?' asks Beverley, whose ears are giving her real trouble now. Cynara does. Beverley is hurt and angry.

'Good God,' she says to her granddaughter. 'I was married to Harry for long enough. Have you forgotten that?'

'Yes but it was you who drove him to his death,' says Cynara, who believes in frank speaking – one of the reasons Lola is in such difficulty now. 'Poor man. D'Dora reckons that speech you gave at the funeral was the most remarkable piece of homophobic hypocrisy she'd ever heard in her life.'

Chatter, chatter, chatter, go the kehua. This is not going well. Their agitation is infecting all the members of the clan.

Up in the North Alice feels a migraine coming on and takes to her bed.

Lola, in a taxi on the way to her friend the party-drug dealer, feels stuffy in the head, opens a window and a cinder flies into her left eye, which spoils her looks for days and in fact never really goes away, like the ice splinter in the eye of the Snow Queen. It puts Lola off sex for years. Before she'd walked out on Louis she had left a message on her mother's answermachine to say she had just bonked her Uncle Louis and serve everyone right. Now she wishes she hadn't. She needn't have worried. D'Dora had picked up the message and wiped it. Information meant power; secret information meant more power.

In LA Richie is struck by a sudden violent sore throat, and is on the phone to his physician. His children Waldo and Merielle catch it from him: it seems to be some kind of antibiotic-resistant bug, and lasts several weeks.

Gerry had, I think, picked up some kind of plaintive kelpie water spirit of Fiona's on the shoreline of Kalsoy, now crouching unseen up there in the luggage rack on his flight to Aberdeen. Something at any rate caused a leaking bottle of water to drip from the luggage rack so that Gerry's trousers were drenched.

Louis' kehua – Louis still being an honorary member of the hapu until we know whether Scarlet's departure is permanent – crack a pane of glass in the atrium skylight and drop splinters down, which fortunately miss Louis. He doesn't hear but, traumatised by women, sleeps on.

Cynara's sight is blurry. Perhaps she is getting a migraine, for she has had a lot of stress lately; a lot of tying and blindfolding went on in The Dungeonette. Her grandmother has made her a kindly offer, and she has repulsed it. What had D'Dora done to her that she returns evil for good? Her kehua, sensing danger, move closer on the dusty branch of the plane tree. Run, run, run, *they plead.* Time to get out of here!

And all Cynara wants to do is not to have to listen to her grandmother, to have a quiet night's sleep without D'Dora, and not have to think about Lola: just run. But where could she go?

You can blame any number of injuries and accidents on the troublesome, and now globally peripatetic, undead. Kehua work in particular through ears and eyes, but with noses and throats in reserve. Their nature becomes clearer and clearer in your writer's mind now she's back in the basement and has caught an actual look at the kehua hanging upside down like fruit bats, leathery wings folded over their ears.

'None of this is a joke,' says Beverley, accused of homophobia, to Cynara, 'and I take that rather amiss. I may be a hypocrite but so far as I am concerned your feminism has always been a sham. You just don't like sex, and blame men.'

'That is simply not true,' says Cynara, and would have put the phone down but D'Dora, coming in (she liked to overhear Cynara's conversations), gestures to her not to and picks up the extension phone. Beverley does not hear the click; her ears are playing up. So Beverley carries on. She would have done better to shut up.

'If anyone's to be pitied it's poor Jesper. This absurd carry-on with D'Dora's made the whole family look ridiculous. Are you really so desperate for a bit of sexual satisfaction? As for Lola, the poor girl actually believes she comes from a sperm bank.'

'What do you know about it?' asks Cynara, taken aback.

'Oh for heaven's sake,' says Beverley. 'Lola talks to Scarlet and Scarlet talks to me.'

D'Dora, listening, makes a throat-slitting gesture – does she mean Beverley, Scarlet or Lola? Cynara fears for Lola, and is distracted. She doesn't want to quarrel with her grandmother one bit and can't imagine why it is happening. She tries to concentrate.

'Please don't let's argue,' she says. 'I'm sorry I said that about Harry. I know how upset you were when he died. If you'll take back what you said about my not being a lesbian?'

'But you're not any kind of lesbian,' says Beverley, dashing away the olive branch Cynara offered. 'I don't believe you're even a feminist. You're just another pig-headed, deluded Maidment. You're like your father, any old cause will do so long as it upsets everyone.'

Which of course was the one thing Beverley should not have said. This is the secret of secrets. That Winter Max, originally Julian Waxmann Maidment, somehow managed to impregnate his stepdaughter Alice and so begat Cynara, a disaster which Beverley has not until now ever quite acknowledged to herself. Alice similarly has resisted all efforts by Cynara to elicit proper identification of her father.

And if Cynara the committed feminist did indeed choose a sperm bank rather than her husband Jesper to conceive Lola, it would not be altogether surprising. Mothers do unto their daughters what has been done unto them. And Winter, after all, was only doing unto Alice what Arthur had done to Beverley way back when. Perhaps Beverley had even unconsciously anticipated the act, and in anticipating, made it the more likely?

Be all that as it may, as a secret kept for nearly fifty years it was not something to be lightly revealed, and in its sudden and unexpected revelation created turmoil and event.

How the kehua clattered and chattered. At Robinsdale their little bat feet pounded on the old glass and scratched it a little, and at Parliam Road they swung to another branch, of a lime tree nearer to the house, and a spatter of stickiness descended from the leaves on to D'Dora's yellow Smart Car. The stickiness was due to a scale insect infestation and needs treatment, but Cynara has more to worry about today than this.

Cynara puts down the phone, stunned, to think about what had just been said. She calls her grandmother over and over but gets only the busy tone. She calls her mother Alice and gets the answer-machine. She tells herself it doesn't really matter who her father is. If it is indeed her grandfather, then he is dead, and she is who she is, just short of a quarter of the genes normally imported from another line of descent, and at least not the product of Alice's rape at the hands of some psychopath, which she has sometimes imagined to be the case. The Maidments are a wealthy and respectable family. Her father was a hero, who died fighting a revolutionary cause, and her mother was of age and no blood relation. It could be a lot worse. But D'Dora wants some attention.

'Who are the Maidments?' D'Dora asks.

Cynara says nobody, she doesn't want to talk about it. D'Dora has been throwing out some of Cynara's favourite kitchen utensils without as much as a by-your-leave – including the old aluminium pan Cynara kept especially for boiled eggs – and replacing them with her own, which look smarter but cook less well. She was talking of a civil marriage with Cynara as soon as the divorce from Jesper came through. She crushes all opposition before her.

'If you wouldn't mind just being quiet a little, D'Dora,' says Cynara now. 'I have various things to think about.'

This gives D'Dora great offence. A row ensues. Insults are exchanged. Cynara pleads for peace and quiet because she has just discovered who her father is; D'Dora says Cynara is family obsessed. Cynara says S&M is a pastime for the sexually obsessed. D'Dora says Cynara is no fun at The Dungeonette and sexually repressed. Cynara says D'Dora is a sexual bully and emotionally repressed. D'Dora says she wishes she had never moved in. Cynara says she wishes she had never taken on the Pinfold & Daughters case and had never set eyes on D'Dora. D'Dora says it is a bit late now and grabs up the phone to ask Beverley about her homophobia and Cynara snatches the phone from D'Dora's hand and throws it across the room where it breaks. Cynara then advances on D'Dora and slaps her hard, once on one cheek, once on the other, hard.

'Shut up,' Cynara says, 'you perverted little cunt. What do you know about anything?'

'One thing I know,' says D'Dora, 'is that your daughter left a message on the answerphone to say she'd just had sex with her uncle Louis and it was all your fault. I'm not staying in this horrid, cramped, dirty, dull little house a moment longer.'

And she goes upstairs to pack.

D'Dora leaving home

Not only had both Cynara and Parliam Road been a disappointment to D'Dora, but the previous night she had encountered a beautiful, disdainful, young, handcuffed blonde with a big house in South Kensington who had raised her eyebrows in Cynara's direction and said, 'What, her? Why?' The answer to D'Dora was now clear: why indeed?

But before she started packing D'Dora looked up the Maidments on Google, and got from there to Winter Max and the Bolivian death which had made headlines, arrived at a few dates and reasonable conclusions and rang Alice. She didn't even need a kehua to prompt her.

D'Dora was from Llanberis in Wales, mind you, and had her own connections with the Cwn Annwn, the hounds of death. If she sometimes heard their growlings from underneath The Dungeonette club in the early hours, they could easily be dismissed as the noise of some repair train, heavier than usual, travelling and rumbling along the Northern Line where it runs beneath Charing Cross and the Embankment.

Dogs of the Cwn Annwn, the Wild Hunt, had barked loudly enough on the night another of D'Dora's 'friends', Gwyneth, had wandered along the tracks with Marcus the right-wing journalist, Beverley's third husband, on the occasion of the launch of Marcus' book, *Slicing the Salami.* Alas, poor Gwyneth had been too drunk to hear when the train approached, and Marcus was deaf to the sounds from the other side, and neither had leapt aside in time.

The Wild Hunt was out in force that night, it being St John's Eve, June 21st, and the moon was full. But no one takes any notice of this kind of thing here any more. In other countries the astrologers would have been out in force, shaking their heads at time and date, and insisting the book launch be on a different day.

The Wild Hunt no longer sticks to its own territory but rides the railway tracks of Western Europe on its appointed nights. When the moon is full and clouds race across the sky, and you can hear the wail of the hounds rising and falling in the distance, then it is wise to take extra care with your step on the platform edge. By comparison to the Cwn Annwn of the northern lands, the kehua are mild and peaceful spirits.

D'Dora digs Alice out of her hole

Mischievous enough, however, to have D'Dora on the phone to Alice. Alice picks her mobile from her pocket where she stands on the banks of the lake at Rawdon, soothing her migraine, and watching the plump silvery trout leaping for midges and missing.

'This is D'Dora, Cynara's partner... I sound like a woman because I am a woman... I thought you'd have realised by now your daughter was gay. Now I have a problem here – Cynara and I want children, and in order to decide which of us is to be the birth mother we need to know more about Cynara's genetic inheritance than we do now. Is it the case that Cynara's father is Julian Maidment, the hero of Bolivia, otherwise known as Winter Max?'

And while Alice clung to her mobile wondering what sort of nightmare she was in, D'Dora went on to explain that it was more damaging to a child to be kept deliberately ignorant of the father by the mother she was entitled to trust, than to know she was the daughter of an incestuous relationship. She, D'Dora, was a psychiatric nurse and knew about these things. The concept of incest was a social construct: it took many generations of family interbreeding before faulty genes became dominant. Alice should not worry; Cynara was healthy enough other than a few sexual inhibitions, and Lola, Alice's grandchild, whose father was from a reliable sperm bank, where donors were properly screened, certainly did not inherit these, on the contrary. Lola was currently having it off with Alice's son-in-law Louis. D'Dora went on to explain that Beverley had confided in her, D'Dora, about Cynara's parentage.

'I've no idea who you are, but you're just poison,' said Alice to her unknown caller, 'and I don't believe a word you say. Just stay away from my Cynara.'

Alice threw her mobile in with the fish, who splashed and darted off. And she prayed to Jesus for strength, and also to the Jesus of Malta who had looked after her and babysat her when her feckless mother Beverley and her friend Dionne were off at the cinema, modelling nude for the Photographers' Club or making money as best they could.

Alice had more stamina than you might suppose. If she kept away from the family it was not because of lack of love for them, as they assumed, but because of an excess of it. Incest, according to her further studies, was both an inherited tendency and a learned one. So normally she stayed away and hoped for the best. But she could see that if this mad, vindictive woman was running round and upsetting everyone, she had better venture back into family territory. The kehua, who lived on the branches of the vine in her nice new conservatory, and could have been mistaken by the casual onlooker for a bunch of grapes, were pleased.

After the row was over

After the row was over and Cynara, unaware that D'Dora was on the phone to her mother causing as much trouble as she could, was quiet again, there now seemed to be two sets of voices in her head. One was crying *run, run, run,* in their familiar panic – and this was obviously absurd because the more D'Dora insulted her home the fonder Cynara became of it, and where was there to run to? The other was more cheerful, like a backbeat now, a call to acceptance and a kind of mirthful exhilaration running along beside it, a delight in the wayward nature of existence, in the unexpected. The backbeat was, though Cynara was also unaware of this, the spirits, or wairua, of Cynara's two boy children who had never come to term.

The kehua are servants of the bloodline; they are really no more than spiritual sheepdogs, rounding the flock up, irritating and sometimes frightening though they can be. But the wairua are the real thing, spirits straight from the atua, the soul of the whanau, than which there can be no higher or more joyful level of existence. These unborn wairua, or noho-whare, brought into existence by Cynara and Jesper, though flushed down the loo by Cynara when their gender was revealed, are, once conceived, indestructible, immanent. They carry mirth and lightness with them, they are not angry with you: they understand your necessity; the unborn of the whanau are as strong as the undead, and they stay around to help if they can. 'Get her out of here,' Cynara's two male unborn cried, 'the bitch! How dare she!'

Scarlet had been right: Cynara had allowed only one child, Lola, the female from the sperm bank, to come to term. But here were the other two at Cynara's side, and the air around her shimmered with elation, as if she was in some deep dark-green kauri forest on the other side of the world where she had never been, where the clematis hung dazzling white and sparkling and the karimako, the elusive bellbird, suddenly sang its impertinent, beautiful song and was gone again. Really, 11 Parliam Road and the forest were one and the same if you let them be.

'I'm off,' said D'Dora, stomping downstairs with her backpack, hoping to be stopped. 'I've just had a really interesting phone call with your mother.'

'Go, go,' was all Cynara said, laughing, 'and take your crampons with you.'

'I'll come back for my stuff,' said D'Dora, 'when it suits me,' and went.

Cynara called Beverley, and apologised for putting down the phone and said yes, if Beverley wanted to take Lola in for a bit, she, Cynara, would be very grateful. D'Dora was moving out, but she, Cynara, needed headspace. She did not mention the Louis business. Lola was probably just trying to cause trouble, leaving messages on the answerphone in the hope everyone would hear.

Beverley in her turn apologised for her *faux pas*. The secret of Cynara's birth was not hers to reveal, but Alice's. But she had to go now. She had just had a phone call from Gerry saying he was at Heathrow and coming over.

How the kehua shrieked. In their excitement they fell off the cherry branch and crawled over to the kowhai tree and clung there, and felt instantly at home. It is a bushy tree endemic to New Zealand, and had grown from a cutting given to her by Beverley's old friend Dionne years back, planted on a sheltered sunny slope of Robinsdale's large garden, near enough to the stream to really flourish. The kowhai tree grows startling clusters of bright-yellow rattling seedpods, which hang and cluster for all the world like kehua, except the latter are a blackish grey. Hanging there, though, encouraged and invigorated by renewed contact with the once-familiar plant, now all but forgotten in this sooty land, Beverley's kehua quickly adopted a pleasant yellowish tinge.

Alice prepares to leave Lakeside Chase

Meanwhile, up at Lakeside Chase, shocked by D'Dora's phone call, Alice had decided to act. Her children needed her. She had no wairua, no unborn souls, hanging around to help and make her laugh – she was a serious and responsible person – but her kehua were calling her to action. *Run, run, run, time to run! Down to the South, lose no time.* Perhaps self-interest contributed to the kehua's vehemence, if they felt like lightening up a little and becoming a bit more yellow than grey.

Alice promptly organised her next day's flight from Manchester to Luton, from whence she would go back to Robinsdale, her childhood home. Then she called Cynara to say she'd had a nasty phone call from a madwoman but had taken no notice. All the same she thought perhaps Cynara needed her help and she was coming down to visit in the morning. She would meet Cynara at Robinsdale.

'But Mother,' said Cynara, 'are you sure? I am a lesbian. Your church will not approve.' And she began to cry.

Alice said that was irrelevant, it was only lesbian bishops who were a source of confusion to the Church; at least Cynara had a child, so now she was free to take her sexual pleasures where she liked; but she should just be a great deal more careful with whom she associated. Discarded lovers often knew where too many bodies were buried and could be vindictive.

Cynara stopped crying in astonishment and said, 'But you hate gays. You wouldn't even come to Louis and Scarlet's wedding. You thought everyone in the fashion industry were sinful perverts.'

'What an extraordinary thing to say,' said Alice. 'I didn't come to the wedding because I was too busy and it's a long way and registry office weddings aren't worth travelling to. They cancelled it anyway.'

'Because you wouldn't come,' said Cynara.

'That's absurd,' said Alice. 'Scarlet was looking for excuses not to tie herself down, and I provided one. She was far too young. And as for you, there are things I need to tell you.'

'About my father?' asked Cynara.

'No, no, no,' said Alice impatiently, 'about Luke.'

'Who is Luke?' asked Cynara.

'My son,' said Alice, always, like her mother, one for a bit of drama. 'Your brother.'

'I look forward to it,' said Cynara, faintly. 'Is he a full brother?'

'Nothing like that,' said Alice. 'A half-brother, younger than you, inconveniently begotten but nothing worse than that.'

From which Cynara was able to conclude that yes, indeed, it was true. She, Cynara, was the child of the forbidden union between young Alice and the wicked, albeit idealistic, Winter.

That done, Alice looked up a number in a file on her laptop marked 'personal: do not enter' and called it. After only three rings a man answered it, which seemed to take her aback a little. But he was healthy and quick, and sounded educated and rather pleasant.

'Are you a Luke Addison?' she asked.

'Yes. Why? Who is this?' He had an accent. She thought probably Australian.

'I think you've been looking for me. At any rate you were a

couple of years back. You may have changed your mind, of course. But I'm your mother.'

A brief conversation followed, after which Alice called Beverley and said she would be in London the next day because she had things she wanted to ask, and things she wanted to tell. Would Beverley be at home?

'Where else would I be?' asked Beverley tartly. 'You may have forgotten I'm immobile. But what do you want to tell me? There is such a thing as too much information. I was living a perfectly calm life until Scarlet turned up and told me she was leaving Louis. Since then it's been mayhem. I can't stand any more. Do you remember Gerry? He's just called and said he's on his way over.'

'I thought he was married,' said Alice.

'He's widowed,' said Beverley. 'Don't be so suspicious.'

'I'm not suspicious,' said Alice, 'I just know the kind of thing that's likely to happen next. I'll come over tomorrow afternoon with Cynara and Scarlet – '

'Cynara, perhaps,' said Beverley. 'Scarlet, unlikely. Your younger daughter is off with an actor called Jackson Wright unless Louis has managed to stop her – really, Alice, you should take more responsibility for your children.'

'I'm trying to,' said Alice. 'I'm coming over to tell you about Luke, my son.'

There was a pause, gratifying to Alice, before Beverley spoke again.

Out in the garden

Ah, yes, Luke.

In the back garden there had been a terrible row: a buzzard had brought down a jackdaw, and was squatting there on the lawn, treading the prey, tearing at its flesh with its beak, with that terrible defiant watchful toss of the head as it swallowed. The blackbirds were setting up their alarm, the loud chip-chip-chip they make when there's danger about – first one, then others joined in, perching on the back of one teak garden bench, fluttering off to the next, settling on the overhanging branches where I saw the kehua in the storm; there were at least eight blackbirds. The racket was arresting. I'd no idea there were so many blackbirds in the garden; it was a real gathering of the clan. And then they got their act together and tried to drive the buzzard off. It finished its feed and disdainfully flew away, as if it didn't notice the blackbirds mobbing and pursuing. I'd been watching from the basement window. Rex came down from the attic and we went out to look.

'Poor thing,' I said of the circle of black and grey feathers. They wouldn't be there for long. The wind would take them and any bony remains be picked clean by armies of mice, and insects and squirmy things one seldom saw. All would be as if it had never happened.

'We had duck for dinner last night,' Rex reminded me.

He went inside and I stayed out in the garden and thought about

Luke. He's come on board rather late in the day for a new character, but the whanau is calling. Who's the buzzard? Jackson? Lola? D'Dora? Luke will lead us to him, or her.

Luke is like Mr Mason in *Jane Eyre*, the pale stranger from the West Indies who suddenly arrives by coach to make everything clear about the mysterious mad woman in the attic. Cousin Clive, visiting the other day, observed that whereas Mr Rochester kept a mad wife in the attic, Rex lived in the attic and kept a sane wife (me) in the basement. I was reassured. Apart from this paranormal business, which has suddenly afflicted me, and with which I deal with admirable aplomb and scepticism for one who is its victim, I am otherwise perfectly, even notoriously, sane. But it helps to be told so.

Well, here Luke is, and here he'll have to stay. The long-lost child, waiting in the wings. Cousin Clive had suddenly appeared in my life one summer – adopted out of the family in an earlier generation – but still part of the whanau and now taken again into the bloodline.

My ears are playing up a bit, but at least there's no sign of kehua hanging anywhere in the branches. There's not a bird to be seen; they're keeping away, in mourning, shocked by the irruption of the buzzard into the routine of their lives. I'd clear away the grey mound for their sake, but it's too disgusting. It will have to stay.

It's a bright day: the weather has been really pleasant since the storm and I've been keeping the basement window open. It's a double window, badly in need of painting, and I reckon the ants have started in again at the crumbling filler where someone botched a mend. The sill is once again covered with black granules. The right frame opens; the left is fixed. When I push the frame out from inside it just clears the heads of the two straw birds Rex put outside on the grass to stare in at me from the garden as I work; he bought them in the bric-a-brac stall at the village fête to entertain me. Their eyes are beads, and catch the sun and glitter. I'm not quite sure about their friendliness, but they keep still.

The basement has been moderately noisy from the other side lately; the steam iron hissing, the clatter of knives as they go into the knife box; the slow clank of hooves as some old nag comes round to the coal-hole, then the clatter of coal down the chute. They're used to me: getting bolder, accustomed to me once again after my spell upstairs. But at least I've seen nothing, heard no voices. Now all I hear is *things*. That's okay.

But there is something strange. Both straw birds used to look at me from the left window. Now there's one on the left and one on the right. Why is that? Who's moved them? Why? They can hardly move of their own volition. At least they're not jackdaws to reproach me about not burying their dead when I can. They're ersatz birds, straw coloured, yellowy, not the strange pewter grey and black of the jackdaw. If it hadn't been for the detail of the frame previously just clearing their heads as I opened the window, I would have assumed they'd always been positioned like that.

But as it happens I do remember the detail. However, I will put it down, like so much else, disappearing keys, reappearing letters, as just one of those things. My computer, for example, is very prey to the 'just one of those things' syndrome. Why does the page-numbering suddenly disappear? Why does an extra blank page appear at the beginning of the text so there's nothing on the screen, nothing, when I ask Word to bring me this novel, scaring me out of my wits that I've lost the whole thing – until Rex suggests I try scrolling down and there it is. Just one of those things.

Decades ago when I lived near Glastonbury, not far from the overflow to the Chalice Well, where a trickle of sacred water dropped continuously from a pipe sticking out of the side wall on to a patch of ground – where, I must say, grew the prettiest wild flowers – I'd fill one of those green plastic watering sprays you use for pot plants with the sacred water, and use it to spray anything that went wrong – like the computer, or the Hoover, or a burnt saucepan, or a needle that refused to thread – and it always worked. Rex used to fill his car radiator from the sacred well overflow but I always thought that was somehow sacrilegious. It needed to be used for small things. Needles, house keys, letters, straw birds – even the vacuum cleaner is too large. Poltergeists prefer dustpans they can spill when no one's looking. One moment the dust is in the pan – turn your back and the whole lot is scattered again. At least it is up here at Yatt House. I take it these things don't happen in Oxford, where Professor Dawkins lives, and domestic objects all obey the immutable laws of physics. Enough.

Just one of those things. Back to Luke.

The convergence of the clan, the convening of the whanau

Where's everyone? Louis is sleeping. Scarlet is in bed with Jackson; now she has what she wants she is not sure that she wants him. She is, do remember, very young, and has been bothered by kehua since her birth. Don't lose sympathy for her.

Scarlet's kehua has already settled in the alternating green and white leaves of the ornamental kolomikta kiwi vine which grows up towards the skylights from its vast deep-blue ceramic pot – and very pretty and exotic it is. Jackson's penthouse was designed and furnished as a show flat for Campion Tower, and the designers forgot to take their show plant away, though they meant to. Rather like the secret NWC files in Robinsdale which the members forgot to remove. People leave the oddest things behind. Ask anyone who moves house, or joins a train and finds a CD with a hundred thousand personal NHS details on it when he goes to sit down.

The kiwi vine started its existence in New Zealand so the kehua feels itself at home and is peaceful and sleeps when it really ought to be vibrating with *run, run, run* advice, as it was so eager to do when she was with Louis. The kehua so often get things wrong. They try, but are out of their depth.

Scarlet lies awake while Jackson sleeps and snores out of his perfectly sculpted nose, and his full lips (are they surgically enhanced?)

tremble as the breath escapes, and she feels lonelier than she ever has in her life before. She thinks of the two babies she didn't have but destroyed in the womb, one at seven weeks, one at ten. Perhaps she did wrong? Perhaps if they'd been born these odd things wouldn't have happened to her? She would have ended up in an ordinary house, not Nopasaran: she might have been happy with Louis if it hadn't been for the house. And he'd probably have married her even if she'd had two children with two different men and couldn't go through with either. She should have really and truly married Louis; he might even have been prepared to change his life for her. Her breath caught and she had to try not to cry and wake Jackson. She preferred him asleep than awake. She was crying, she realised, not so much for herself as for her lost babies, and what they were missing. All the crap, true, but all the other things as well: sex, love, music, special-effects films – you needed children to go to films with, not children like Lola, but ordinary kids – they'd miss just being alive. Just being alive was pretty good.

Thinking this, she felt comforted and suddenly less alone and in need of the mother who'd never seemed to want her. She could hear the rustle of leaves as the automatic air-conditioning switched itself on and played through the ornamental kiwi plant. No, reader, it was not for once her kehua stirring, but the arrival of reinforcements from the iwi: a couple of wairua, the spirits of her aborted babies, hanging around until their mother could rejoin the tribe and they could all be together again. Or perhaps it was that the attraction of the familiar green and white leaves had tempted them and they were prepared to nestle up against the whanau kehua, spirits of the unborn and the undead united. You have to be a bit careful of the wairua of the interrupted – like the kehua they can be tricky. If a bad tohunga got hold of them he could corrupt them and use them to damage Scarlet. But bad tohunga – or shamans, or medicine men, or witches, or wizards: those with malicious intent, anyway – are rare. Jackson may be bad, though he, like the buzzard, is hardly to blame for doing what it is in his nature to do, but he is no tohunga, no expert in sacred rites. Scarlet falls asleep.

Louis' mother Annabel is in France, looking through MetaFashion's books and wondering if it is time to sell it, or alternatively Nopasaran if anyone would buy it in its crumbling state. A pity he couldn't have married a girl with some money or background, instead of getting snared by this bright, brash girl who would do nothing for him except keep others more suitable out. She liked Scarlet, but she could not admire her.

In Paris Dionne went out on to her patio in the moonlight and watered her plants; she felt they needed watering, but at ten at night? That was unusual. She gave a little to the kowhai bush, but not much: *just a little*, it would say to her, *only a little, careful!*, feeling apparently as Dionne does when a hairstylist advances on her with the scissors. Dionne talked to her plants: she got on well with them and they with her. The kowhai bush was the one from which Beverley took a cutting fifteen years back, which has since grown into a proper tree in Robinsdale, almost as attractive to the kehua as the green and white kiwi vine in Campion Tower. Dionne's kowhai is still in a large pot, and somewhat root-bound. Twenty years back it was presented to a diplomat lover at a civic reception, when France was trying – not very hard – to repair relationships with New Zealand after the nuclear tests in the Pacific and the *Rainbow Warrior* affair.

During a 'cultural tour' of the South Island they had stopped off at a small town called Amberley for afternoon tea – a meal unknown to the visitors, consisting as it did of various elaborate types of cake – and at the civic centre had been presented with a cutting from a kowhai bush, New Zealand's national plant, in a pot made by a renowned local potter out of local clay. New Zealand does not in fact officially have a national plant, but New Zealanders know it to be so.

Do you see where I am going, reader? Saving us a trip to New Zealand for which I have neither time nor energy just at the moment? I have to get out of the basement soon; it is becoming apparent that I am the haunter here, not the hauntee.

All kinds of things conspire to stop one writing a novel – idleness, babies, alcoholism, men trouble, but this is a new one. It went suddenly dark in here just now and then I saw a flickering candle flame and heard a single bell struck and I'll swear a man's voice said something like, 'We judge her damned, we declare her excommunicate,' and a book thudded closed – a heavy Bible? – and the heavy male voice said, 'So be it.' They've been down here exorcising me with bell, book and candle! I feel really indignant. And rather angry, and thought, 'I've a right to be down here as much as this lot, bugger them,' and resolved to stay.

The light went on again: Rex came down to ask was I okay? A fuse had blown all the lights in the house but he had fixed it. I've just got to get on. I am not as easily got rid of as they think. If my hair turns white overnight, these days one need only go to the hairdresser. Where were we?

The diplomat offered the plant to Dionne on their return, since his wife might not appreciate it, and Dionne, who really loved him, put it in the sunniest, most sheltered corner of the patio, where it did well enough, but perhaps with not enough root space, and so remained comparatively small.

'If I truly love a man,' Dionne once said to Beverley, 'I like to grow something in his honour. I can't have his children – for me children simply will not do: I don't want to upset the wives – but I can nurture what I have left of him.'

When Beverley came to stay after Harry's death they sat and drank their coffee outside on the patio, and Beverley marvelled at the wild tangle of flowers and creepers Dionne had created; tendrils crept into the apartment, under windowsills and beneath the door. Even Dionne's hair, now she was old, clung like thin tendrils against her scalp.

Falling in love again, never wanted to, what's a girl to do, sang Dionne then in her already cracked voice, can't help it. Beverley remembered then how when they had gone to the pictures when they were young, and had left Baby Alice in Jesus' care, and happened to go to the thirties' film *The Blue Angel* because there was nothing else on, Dionne had said, 'That's what I want to be, that's how I want to live.' Dionne had made Marlene Dietrich her idol, rejoicing as she did to see the old man in love humiliated, made to crow like a cock to prove his love, then spurned. Beverley had been rather appalled, but Dionne had slapped her on the wrist for being so provincial. It was the only quarrel they had ever had. As well Dionne had not had sons, Beverley had thought then, she would have given them a terrible time. Just as well she had plants instead.

When Beverley came to stay her kehua chose the kowhai bush on which to hang amongst familiar yellow seedpods, naturally enough. They do so long for home; who of us doesn't, the living and the properly dead, the unborn and the undead, all of us, whatever mode we're in, spirit or flesh? And of course Beverley, moved by some childhood recollection, once took a seedling from Dionne's patio home in Paris to Robinsdale, wrapped in damp newspaper, with some wet earth still clinging to its roots.

On the day little Beverley ran one-two, one-two from the red death kitchen to Rita, the kowhai had been in yellow pod, and the whole dusty road alight with gold. Death is often accompanied by beauty: nature celebrates the passing by making the sunset more glorious, the moon more mysterious – or perhaps it's just that in the presence of death the senses become more acute, and shock makes time seem to change its pace.

But Gerry is coming

Beverley has limped to the bathroom and back – she is more mobile than she lets on – and done her face; not much make-up, it can make matters worse at her age, changed her wrap to a silky one by Natori and fluffed up her hair. She is really grateful that Scarlet washed it for her this morning, and hopes the girl is getting on all right. Beverley even gets to the front door and puts it on the snib for easy entry before getting back on her sofa, looking as delightful as anyone of nearly eighty can. How old is Gerry? Sixty-seven? Well, she has the house and a life; he hasn't. Will she turn him away, or will she forgive him for Fiona and take him in? She'll see what she feels like when he gets here.

And then the doorbell rings and she calls, 'Come in,' and a man enters who is not Gerry. He approaches cautiously and politely, stretching out his hand. It is shaking with emotion. He is long and lanky and in his mid-thirties, has a domed forehead and for a moment Beverley is reminded of her stepfather and possibly, probably, father. Taller, rangier and quicker moving, but still Arthur.

'Are you my grandmother?' he asks. 'Mrs Fletzner, née McLean?'

'You must be Alice's Luke?' she enquires, cool as a cucumber. *Run, run, run,* rattle the kehua in the kowhai tree. *Cucumber sandwiches equals knife, equals blood on the sand.* But Beverley can't run; bad knee.

'That was quick,' she says. 'I've only just got to hear about you. But that's Alice for you, she never tells you the important things.'

'I'm glad she's called Alice,' he says. 'A pretty name. She said she'd be at this address tomorrow. The kids and I are staying around the corner, isn't that a coincidence? I just had to be sure. I don't want her to get away. She could change her mind.' He has a New Zealand accent.

'Quite a coincidence,' Beverley says coolly. 'But I don't think she'll change her mind. My daughter is a very consistent kind of person. Why don't you go back to them now and come again tomorrow at the time she arranged. I may say without consulting me.'

'I have three children,' he says, unabashed, as he leaves. 'That's three more great-grandchildren for you; aren't you pleased?'

The whanau are gathering. The clans are coming home. Their energy is restoring Beverley. It is just as well because when the phone goes yet again as she undresses for bed it is Lola on the other end, and she will need every scrap of strength she has, both morally and physically.

Lola is weeping on the other end of the phone. Beverley is accustomed to her whining, moaning, yelling, sniggering, jeering, reproaching and snarling, but she has never heard Lola actually crying, let alone in terror and panic, as she is now. Beverley has reared innumerable children but has never heard anything quite like this. She is at once alert.

'Geegee,' pleads Lola. It is her childhood name for Beverley, short for great-grandmother. 'Please come, I can't get through to anyone. Please, quickly. I'm frightened.'

Last chance saloon, thinks Beverley, that's me. In the background she can hear discordant music – 'post-technobitch', she supposes; confined to her bed as she has been, she has been much charmed and educated by YouTube – and desultory singing and shouting in the background. At least Lola is with people. Lola's voice, as she croaks to be heard, is both slurred and over-modulated; God knows what Lola has been taking, to pull her down or perk her up or both at the same time, or quite what level of existence she is inhabiting. There is so much on the market. Whatever it is, thinks Beverley, it can kill you. Pray God it is legal so someone will call an ambulance.

'Where exactly are you?' she asks.

'Down the steps,' says Lola, 'you know where. I keep passing out and my hands have gone funny. Look.'

'I can't see your hands,' says Beverley. 'You're on the phone. Pull yourself together and call an ambulance.'

'I can't do that, they'll kill me,' says Lola.

Beverley hears the clatter as Lola's mobile falls to the floor and then there is only the sound of the music and random shouts and squeals, which could be pleasure or rage or both. And then there is no more speech from Lola.

Now as it happens Beverley does know what Lola means by 'down the steps', though Lola is pushing it to suppose that Beverley would. Beverley fund-raises for a charity called Young Sympathy, whose mission is to train young people in empathy for unfortunates. To this end school parties set up stalls in deprived areas to hand out advice leaflets, cups of tea and slices of cake to anyone in need of help. Lola's school, as a result of a certain amount of string-pulling by both Beverley and Cynara, supported the initiative: in return participating pupils received certificates which could be mentioned in CVs.

Beverley, coming to visit with a PR team to take photographs for the Young Sympathy newsletter, and finding Lola slicing cake and pouring cups of tea for those who seemed to be her friends, stayed on to help. The street friends were young and excitable, dressed eccentrically, colourfully and barely decently, à la Lady Gaga. Their gender was indeterminate, but those who had breasts showed them. Lack of money did not seem to be their problem, but they clearly liked the cake. Lola's charitable school friends, a well-behaved and virtuous lot, were evidently much impressed by Lola and her social circle.

Lola found the presence of her great-grandmother embarrassing, to the extent of introducing Beverley as her grandmother ('I used to call her Gee for Gran,' she went as far as saying), though she was polite enough and allowed herself to be helped pouring tea. Beverley asked her if her friends lived in a commune, and Lola nodded to a basement café called Down the Steps. The streets had once been residential but were now a curious mix of bazaars, shops, houses, tattoo parlours, travel agencies for less familiar foreign parts, and banks of unknown provenance.

'Live and partly live,' Lola said. 'Let's just say we hang out down there.'

And she went back to cutting slices of chocolate cake. Beverley had wondered at the time if she should say something to Cynara and decided there was little point. She would only lose what scraps of good opinion Lola had for her. She knew at the time it was a betrayal of principle, that what renders the old ineffective is their desire for the good opinion of the young, but she remained quiet.

Now here she was at an advanced age, barely able to walk and faced with Lola in evident need of rescue. Nor was there any time for thought, or time to ask for help. No time to direct an ambulance to a street she knew by sight but not by name, no will to ask the police: her past had put her outside the normal law-abiding community. In this Lola was her kith and kin. No matter how dire the circumstances, the theory ran, never trust the police. The kehua were in her ears, loud and imperative. *Run, Beverley, run.* Beverley ran. She pulled her clothes back on, found her purse and ran. Had she not done this a dozen times in her extreme youth, in the Jesus days she hoped she had forgotten. Pulled her clothes back on, grabbed her purse and run, from whatever danger threatened, sometimes less than she supposed, no doubt, sometimes more. Death, pain, humiliation of one kind of another. Girls were so trusting now for all they were so easy.

She found running easier than she thought. It hurt, but it worked. The body did what you told it to. She had been too protective of it, she could see. She got down to the crossroads and saw the yellow light of a taxi coming. She hailed it. It stopped. She directed it to Lola's school. The driver was local; she was lucky: he knew where the school was. He knew where the high street she described was. She took him to the corner and paid him off and waited until he disappeared. It was precious minutes wasted but she did not want to be traced. She was not sure why, but she remembered the lessons of the revolutionary days. Leave no trail. Not that anyone else ever remembered. And look where it had led Marcus. To a drunken death stumbling down a railway line. And where had her longer life led her? Standing outside the closed door of some low-life slum café with voices in her head, having to go in to face whatever her family, fate and the new society thrust at her? Was she not she too old for this kind of thing? Was there no one left capable of taking over?

She went down the three concrete steps which led to the front door. Light seeped from cracks beneath it and around it. She could hear the same nerve-grating music that had come through on Lola's mobile. Why were the young so desperate that only unmelodic music appealed? She stopped to recover. She had managed to hop out of the cab onto one leg okay, but when she was going down the steps she could not work out which of her legs was the burden-carrying one, made a mistake and paid for it in pain. She hoped she was doing it no permanent damage but oddly enough thought she probably was not.

The door was made of reinforced glass and looked as if it belonged to a warehouse, not a café. It appeared locked but when she pushed it opened. There was a rushing smell of alcohol, piss and smoke mixed, which took her aback. And then a mob of young people barged her aside to get up the steps and away. They seemed anxious to be off. They were very noisy, and gave little yelps of panic and confusion, which seemed to add up to 'Let's get out of here.' There was a flurry of young skinny limbs, bright colours, strange clothes, thigh-high boots, feather boas, pale faces, mad eyes and platinum hair tortured into strange peaked heights. When they had gone Beverley went on into what seemed as much a barn as a café or a bar. Such light as there was came from candles still fluttering on the tables. There seemed no one in charge – there is usually someone who safely extinguishes flames when everyone else has gone – but no. There was a lot of litter and broken glass and spilled drink on the ground; and the odd used condom and broken syringe. Whatever had happened had frightened even a clientèle accustomed to this kind of thing.

There were two people in the room. One was Lola, lying slumped over a table, semi-naked; a little form which seemed to have so little substance she could have been painted and not in real life at all. Too thin, too pale arms; little pathetic breasts. It was odd, Beverley thought, to think how much destructive energy could emanate from so small an entity. She was not dead, as Beverley had at first feared; she was making little snoring moans.

Beverley sat Lola up – she was half conscious – opened her mouth and thrust her fingers down her throat. Lola retched and vomited over Beverley. Not enough, but it would help. The other person in the room was unconscious, lying on the floor next to where Lola sat. He too was making little moaning sounds, little plaintive demands on the world. He was in his mid-forties, solid, saturnine, prosperous and thuggishly good-looking. His nails were well manicured, his shirt and suit expensive, his shoes handmade, and he was naked between socks and shirt. Beverley thought the socks were probably cashmere. His parts were large. Erect and in action they would have been impressive, but now lay limply. They seemed almost too large for Lola, and though she could not see Lola as an innocent victim, Beverley felt a maternal jab of rage on her behalf. Misbegotten though Lola might be, living evidence of Beverley's failure to be a proper person, a proper mother, she was family.

The man lay in a welter of £20 notes, which had fallen from his hand as he lost consciousness. Beverley kicked him with her sensible shoe, forgetting the pain it would cause her, and, feeling it, blamed him for inflicting it. She felt thoroughly disengaged from what she was seeing and doing. She seemed to have no context for her thoughts and actions. There were urgent voices in her head but she had no idea what they were saying. The mass of feather boas which had brushed by her face as the crowd left seemed to have some sort of repetitive quality: she kept seeing them when they weren't there. Her thoughts seemed to be coming in sequence; first this, then that, quite orderly though without an underlay of emotion, as she realised her thoughts normally were.

The man had clearly collapsed suddenly, and it was perhaps his collapse that had triggered the departure of the other guests. More was going on than they had bargained for. Perhaps he was the drug supplier. He was dressed as one. Only dealers did not usually take drugs themselves; they were too sensible. Perhaps the drugs supplied had been doctored, perhaps he had simply taken too much. OD'd, like Lola. Perhaps the fumes of whatever was in the air were affecting her. The music changed; a flapping sound mixed with the beat: the lyrics seemed to be directed at her. *Kill, Beverley kill.* This was what song lyrics were all about these days, kill, fuck, rape, steal, rejoice: the Devil's song.

Lola's BlackBerry lay on the floor. So did a rather old-fashioned real glass syringe full of a colourless liquid. Whatever it was it would do no one any good. One obvious thing to do was to use the BlackBerry to call an ambulance. Help would come. The other thing to do was use the syringe to jab in the raised vein in the calf of the semi-naked man where his bare leg lay fallen to one side, and kill him, and take Lola out of Down the Steps, in the hope that she would never go back there or anywhere like it, ever again. No one would know. This time she would make a better job of it than cutting the brakes; it had taken her a long time to get round to it.

She had forgotten so much. She supposed you had to, the better to survive. She felt anger ebbing away as she pushed in the syringe. Metal went more easily into flesh than you supposed, seeming almost to welcome death in, eager for it. She remembered Arthur saying as much, long ago and far away, when he was joking about killing her mother. She plunged it in for Rita who should have done it to Arthur. She thought perhaps she was doing it for women everywhere, to save them from having to. She did it to the punters who had taken pictures of her and Dionne when she was a girl: to all the men she had fled from, grabbing her purse and running downstairs: to the men who had loved her and left, to the men she had wept over, to the men who shouted and bullied to drown her out, to Winter for having sold her, to Harry who insulted her by preferring men, to Marcus who had robbed her mind, to Gerry for Fiona.

She killed them all, and as she did so thought she heard *kill, kill, kill* turn into *run, run, run,* and by the time the liquid had run out so had her hate. She remembered what she was about, wiped the syringe with her sleeve, dropped it on the ground amongst the banknotes, put the BlackBerry in her pocket, slapped Lola hard on both cheeks, got her to her feet and walking, and steered her out the door. Beverley no longer noticed the pain in her leg.

She looked back and the man lay unmoving on the floor; she felt fairly sure he would not wake. If he did, what would he remember? If he did not, who would care? He had invited death and he had got it. She had got Lola. She would give the matter no more attention.

There was no one about. It was three in the morning. She half pushed, half dragged Lola up the steps. This is the uphill struggle that children always are, she thought. What's new?

It had started to rain. She stopped supporting Lola when she reached a spot it was unlikely surveillance cameras could observe, and let her fall to the ground, which Lola did quite readily. Beverley was amazed at her own cleverness. Lola was half naked but it couldn't be helped. Beverley turned and walked away and hailed a taxi. She looked back and already a group of people were clustering around the fallen body. Someone put a coat over her. They would get her to hospital. Lola would have enough nous not to get herself identified. She would be just another anonymous drug victim who accepted treatment and then disappeared into the night. Lola had

Winter's paranoiac blood in her veins, and evidently, and fortunately, more brains than he ever had. Lola would survive. Beverley got the taxi to drop her on the corner and walked to her house: she tried not to limp but her command over her body was fading fast, and by the time she got to Robinsdale she was holding on to fences and hedges for support.

At seven-thirty in the morning the doorbell rings. It takes a long time for Beverley to get to the door. It is Gerry. This is the way things happen within families, she thinks: all coincidence. She sees her fate is settled. Gerry too is a natural claimant to the whanau. He has no one else. He's soaking wet when he comes in. The rain seemed to come out of nowhere. But then he brings Fiona's truly damp and dripping kelpie with him. The kelpie will appreciate the stream, the last visible tributary of the River Fleet, and with any luck will take up residence there, harmlessly. Let Beverley not believe she will ever be rid of Fiona.

The kehua is now looking for a good branch somewhere near Jesper's house to cling to and recuperate. It is exhausted. It had to move on with Lola from the comfortable quarters of Nopasaran but could find only an old branch sticking out of a dustbin in the squat where Lola's friends lived. Then Lola OD'd in the night, to blunt the remorse which beat about her head like the wings of the Furies, but she got the message *run, run, run*; or at least the passers-by did, and they got to A&E just in time.

Lola so nearly died she can't even remember it, but your writer knows how near a thing it was. Now she's gone to her father's to recover, and weeping she tells Jesper about her and Louis, while blaming Jesper for abandoning her and making her do it, while he tears his hair out and paces the room. She suddenly pulls herself together and sits up straight, and says, 'Well, actually, I did it not you. And at least he wasn't a blood relation.' She then says she's decided against going to Haiti. She's too young and she's going to be good and go back to college. Or she might stay on a year at school and try for Oxford.

The kehua finds a home under another diseased lime tree which is dropping its sticky stuff all over the parked cars, and folds its wings over its ears and hangs like a bat. It quite fancies Oxford, where at least they know how to look after trees.

The gathering of the kehua

The garden needs children. With Luke's lot joining, I can see the place might even become a marae in its own right, a rather strange, pakeha version of one in a foreign land, and about as far as you can get from home, but there are more than enough hapu, living, deceased, unborn and undead, from McLeans generations back, clustering around the place to compose a quorum, a new colony for the iwi. The kehua are becoming quite acclimatised; just as flora and fauna disperse from country to country, why shouldn't they? And Robinsdale's large garden might just about pass as a urupa, a place of natural beauty that you can come back to from distant places and know that this is where you naturally belong. But there are of course still rituals undone, grievances unsettled, to be attended to before it can possibly happen.

Luke, having reluctantly left Robinsdale the night before, is already back in it, talking – how he talks: whom can he have got that from? No one will know before Alice appears. Cynara has turned up, but not Lola, who to everyone's relief has rung to say she is staying with her father, back unexpectedly from Dubai. He has 'flu and she must look after him. No one can contact Scarlet, and Louis will not answer his phone. Alice is late. Her flight from Manchester has been delayed and the roadworks on the M1 are disgraceful. How did she keep a baby secret from her family? Why and how did she have it adopted out?

Gerry, who has reckoned on getting Beverley to himself, sulks at not being the centre of attention, goes to his room – he will have to wait to share Beverley's – and starts searching the Internet for jobs in London, preferably North London. It has occurred to both Beverley and Cynara that Luke might be Gerry's son but neither will voice the suspicion for fear it is true. It is fairly clear from his sulks that if it is the case, Gerry has been told nothing about it. Luke is younger than Cynara, older than Scarlet. When did it happen?

Alice at last turns up and embraces Luke. Luke embraces Alice. It is a reunion which goes well. Alice wears the kind of clothes Rita long ago wanted Beverley to wear, decent, tweedy and unadventurous, reassuring to a long-lost son. She tells Luke she had no option but to give him away: her husband Stanley would not accept another man's child. 'The other man', Luke's father, was a good-looking medical student who abandoned her.

So that is why she went north, thinks Beverley, nothing to do with Harry's death or the scandal, just that she was pregnant by the wrong man. Sometimes it is difficult to think well of one's own daughter.

Luke lectures in anthropology at the ANU, Canberra. He tells Alice about the couple who adopted him. His dad is a doctor, his mum a nurse. He had been lucky with his parents. They are a kind and pleasant Kiwi couple (he refers to New Zealanders as Kiwis – which annoys Beverley at first; she thinks of Kiwis as shy, timid, insect-ridden birds, but Luke – like his half-sister Cynara, never one to mince words – says, 'You have to remember you're rather old, Gran, and have been away from home a long, long time'). When they were working for NGOs in developing countries, they sent Luke to Thames High School for Boys, where he boarded. And yes, he had gone on school outings to the Auckland Library: why, he asks?

No matter, says Beverley. Anyway it's all pulled down now, he says.

'Never mind,' says Beverley. So Luke presses her further and she tells him, and all of them, of her trips to the Auckland Library and how she had discovered her origins, and about the murder. 'My father murdered my mother.' It seems to her as if she is relating a dream.

'Oh Mum,' says Alice, 'don't distress yourself. I know all that already. I have done since I went on a school trip to Paris. I ran into Dionne at the Louvre. She was blonder than ever and standing on the plinth next to some dignitary or other who was cutting a ribbon, but I recognised her at once. She used to look after me a lot when I was small. She took me out to tea and told me all about Arthur and Walter and all that. We had brioche and apricot jam. It was a long time ago.'

'Dionne had no business telling you,' is all Beverley can say.

'No more than you had telling Cynara,' says Alice.

'Hang on!' says Cynara to Alice. 'Stop. You mean my grandmother Beverley had my mother, you, by my great-grandfather Arthur, and you had me by your stepfather? Is there such a thing as an incest gene? My God, supposing Lola gets pregnant.'

Luke is beginning to look quite put out. So is Gerry. They have come here on a momentous day to put their own lives in order and the women are upstaging them.

Politely the women desist, and turn their attention to the menfolk. There are no secrets left.

Down in the basement

How they're crowding around me now, these characters. They too want to get out of here. Time is compressing. They're trying to wind this story up. The kehua are back in the cherry tree at Robinsdale now, up against the window, attracted by event, and the promise of more, but looking over their batlike wings at the kowhai bush, which is in danger of getting too damp, developing mould. Gerry's dripping kelpie is perhaps making matters worse. Someone is going to have to do something about that, in time. The tree may have to be replanted away from the stream nearer the house.

Luke has decided it's warm enough to have a barbecue in the garden. Luke loves to cook. He learned from a tohunga when he was small. The tohunga was a Samoan, working as the cook in a refugee camp, a vast man who wore a ragged tie-dyed T-shirt in reds and yellow and greens which reached to his knee, and sandals on dirty feet. But he could cook anything even remotely edible and make it taste good, and the child watched and learned, and pattered after him as he performed the rites and rituals of his calling. Today Luke notices the wilting kowhai tree and fears it doesn't bode good. The habits of kehua and kelpies alike are not unknown to him, and come to mind; he has after all studied anthropology.

He is on a sabbatical in London with his wife and children, but even scientists are affected by the knowledge they pick up along the way. His wife is up in the Hebrides recording the folk myths of the outer isles, and the children are in the garden, running around under the sprinkler, fully dressed and avoiding the water rather than seeking it, because it is frankly not that warm, happy enough, if complaining from time to time that their ears are still stuffed up from jet lag, and claiming that boiled sweets would clear them.

If Janice from Glastonbury was around she could probably learn to see hanging kehua in the same way she has learned to see haloes and recognise walk-ins from the binary Dog Star Sirius.

Even Janice is down here in spirit, good God. At least there has been no more bell, book and candle stuff going on, though twice now the power for the basement has blown, but I had everything on the computer saved on its emergency battery, and the black-outs lasted only a couple of minutes anyway. Rex says there's a loose connection somewhere: the wiring is ropy down here and someone will have to come in to look at it. I say, not until I have finished the novel. He says, surely I can work upstairs, but how can I explain that upstairs now is even more disconcerting than downstairs? Rex was out last night and I didn't dare go up to my study to do another hour's writing, I was too scared. That hasn't happened before. When I can see and hear the past it's not so bad; when they're silent it seems more sinister. I took sleeping pills and went to bed.

But even through the pills I dreamed of Scarlet and Lola. I am getting fond of Lola. She's just into the madness that sometimes possesses teenage girls when they are allowed no escape into romance, and end up bouncing their skinny thighs on top of older men.

And then I dreamed of Cynara, Dowson's Cynara, not mine, a ghostly figure from a lost age.

I cried for madder music and for stronger wine,
But when the feast is finish'd and the lamps expire,
Then falls thy shadow, Cynara! the night is thine;
And I am desolate and sick of an old passion,
Yea, hungry for the lips of my desire:
I have been faithful to thee, Cynara! in my fashion.

Dowson's Cynara was 'Missie' Adelaide, the owner's under-age daughter at his favourite Soho restaurant. He was hopelessly in love with her. We know too much. It was a better world, I think, before we all became so cynical and knowing, before women wanted to be men, when sex was deep, mysterious and forbidden. I blame the men.

I had a good day's writing down in the basement, in spite of everything. By the evening hobgoblins and foul fiends had fled away.

Another's day's writing

This evening I went out into the garden, which at the moment seems the most neutral place around here. And also of course to get a little sun for my skin. They say you need ten minutes' exposure to sunlight a day, so your body can produce the vitamin D it needs. Let them say away, I am fair-skinned and burn easily and try to be in the shade whenever I can. Though thinking about it I realise the caution only set in when I was thirty-five and my sister died of melanoma, a skin cancer. It was after that that the sun suddenly stopped being my friend, and became a dangerous, glowing ball of light which didn't like me and I didn't like it, and I dived underground.

But it's evening now, and the light is beautiful and calm. I need have no fear of lightning strikes and sudden visions of kehua, at least for the next few hours.

The sun is too low in the sky to be dangerous; our hilltop is suffused with a golden glow; and the white clouds are rimmed with pink, and over to the west above the stone wall the whole sky is streaked with oranges and reds. It is like a child's colour wash of a sunset, but expertly done. The wall is old, made from nicely dressed blocks of stone taken from the ruined abbey – after the dissolution of the monasteries the townsfolk were allowed to carry off the stone to compensate them for what amounted to the sudden lack of social services.

Do not think the abbeys of this country fell gently into ruins; people as well as buildings were hacked to death. I don't know where the stone was originally quarried but it seems to throw back a grey-pink glow that's all its own when the setting sun strikes it, as if at any moment it was going to burst into flames. Everything carries memories of the past, and the past is a mixed blessing. What starts with violence turns into beauty, and vice versa. Thanatos, the death wish, is as strong as Eros, the will towards life: they seem to take turns.

There is a pets' graveyard in the garden patch near the stable block where once the Bennetts kept their gig. Just a row of headstones for family pets, dogs and cats, I daresay a rabbit or two, or even a parrot; though you wouldn't get too many of those in a lifetime. Lucky if they don't outlive you. You might find a few slim remaining bones of these once-beloved creatures if you dug, but the rooting wildlife will have had more than enough time to scatter the remains over a hundred years or so. This is the most neglected part of the garden: it is shaded and overgrown, and a little spooky, but I do want to see how the pear tree is getting on. It clings to the brick wall of the old stables: no claw-hold here for my own kehua, for I may well have collected a few on the way. I comfort myself with the thought that at least my sister had a proper funeral, and was properly mourned.

There is nothing inside the stables, when I pull open the creaky door and look, but spiders, a few glass windows still valiantly whole but clouded with murk, some garden chairs we forgot to take out last summer, and a hole under the eaves where swifts in search of spiders understand how to dive, retrieve and get out again as fast as they can. I think I may be getting the whiff of cigar smoke and a man's voice calling, *Here Patch. Here Patch.* Please no. I retreat, back from the step.

And then, looking down, I see what I never noticed before: that there are words engraved on one of the larger stones. I look more closely. *Patch the Collie, 1890–1904, RIP.* And I have just remembered that months back this was the name I pulled out of the blue to give to the McLean dog, which got shot back in the thirties for the crime of witnessing a murder. I don't quite see how, outside in the glowing air, and the sun setting so punctually, to timetable, rationality ruling, this is significant. I must have seen the inscription once upon a time and forgotten that I had.

And then I hear the sound of car wheels on gravel and know it is Martin and his collie Bonzo. I wonder if Bonzo is a descendant of the original Patch.

Bonzo makes his usual galloping inspection of the garden while Martin, Rex's friend, rings the doorbell. Bonzo doesn't see me. Nobody goes into this part of the garden. As soon as Bonzo's done the garden, he does the house, casing the joint, up first to the attic where Rex works, then to the basement where I do, making sure everyone is where he expects them to be, or has good reason for being elsewhere. But today he takes an extra turn around the garden and sees me and stops short, almost skidding, baring his teeth, like a dog in a cartoon, one who's just seen a lady with her head tucked underneath her arm. It is me he is looking at.

The bristles on the ridge of his back go up; he is growling, snarling as he backs away. I am hurt: I am upset. Does he see something unnatural in me? Am I still the ghost? Or perhaps the dog that comes bouncing towards me is not Bonzo at all, but Patch? He turns and makes for the house, and down the corridor into the kitchen, tail between his legs; which is nothing at all like his usual body language, but he is certainly Bonzo. I follow him into the kitchen, where he too seems confused, and has had to sit down to recover his composure. He recognises me as me, with a reluctant banging of his tail on the floor as if I had played some dreadful trick on him, and he is now prepared to accept me as myself, but only just.

Rex is on his way home from the market. I am glad to take a break and drink a pot of tea with Martin, whose presence is as always genial and reassuring. He is a calm man. He has faced enough physical danger in his working life not to be afraid of fancies. He chuckles at Bonzo, and reassures him too.

When they're gone I go back down to the basement. I might as well write some more.

The cleansing of Robinsdale

The purification ceremony was up to a point inadvertent. Luke's first thought on hearing of the murder/suicide in Amberley was to hope that at least the McLeans had been properly buried and their homestead cleansed. He was not a superstitious man, and believed himself to be perfectly rational, but respect is due where respect is due. The Maori had been well established in North Canterbury at one time – though few choose to live there today – and it remains a numinous place. The old religions break through everywhere. If both Walter and Arthur, or either one, had Maori ancestry it would not be surprising. A number of English missionaries had gone native and had had to be recalled, but not before their offspring were settled in the area. And the Coromandel and Kennedy Bay hapu were powerful enough to drag Beverley into theirs, and include any dependent kehua, which would be hard on her heels.

He'd never heard of kehua travelling overseas. Traditionally, sanctified spirits travelled north to join their ancestors in Tane. They slipped down the trunks of the pohutakawa trees of the far North-West, lined up on Three Mile Beach, and then followed the path the setting sun lays upon the glittering water to reach that golden land. But he supposed if a few were restless enough they could end up in England, land of the long grey cloud, or even Scotland. Luke wondered how they would get on with the kelpies, the water ghosts of the North, and he laughed, and the others joined in, out of family loyalty rather than because they found him funny; just very, very loquacious. But in family life you have to take the rough with the smooth: that is the point of it.

Your writer did not laugh as she listened. She kept her head down and tried to concentrate through the noises that were now coming at her through the walls from all sides. The dog barking, Cristobel wailing, Mavis giggling, Cook swearing, and still she was all too conscious of the change in the fall of the light, as something passed in front of the window where the little straw birds sat, and when she looked, they were at least in the same place, though now they were lying on their sides, so they were staring at each other and not at her. Which seemed to be slightly better. If things are impersonal one can cope. She thought perhaps her own wairua were passing by, not the grateful dead, but the helpful unborn.

Just as well, as it turned out, that Scarlet's wairua were there in the ornamental kiwi plant in the penthouse at Campion Tower, albeit snuggled up to her kehua, asleep. The children were clamouring for a barbecue in the garden. Luke nipped round to Waitrose to buy the best steak, though his new-found grandmother berated him for his extravagance. In his tour of the garden – a veritable urupa, he called it, the place you always want to return to, the beautiful place where you feel grounded and at home – he'd taken a twig of the kowhai tree to examine it closer. Now he placed it beneath the steak as it cooked to give it flavour. Beverley hobbled out of the house, helped by Gerry, with greater ease than she had thought possible. She had been reared in New Zealand, after all, and if there is something to be done, you do it, weakness or not.

Beverley thought Luke was overcooking the steaks and bent over the barbecue to turn them. At that moment the barbecue, behaving so far like a quiescent sunspot, suddenly went nuclear, and a surge of flame leapt upwards and singed her hair, and the kowhai twig caught fire instead of baking gently. This twig, remember, was child of a bush which had spent a long time in a pot crafted by a local potter out of Amberley clay, and plants too, like the birds and the animals, have their own wairua, or soul. At any rate the two flames mixed and as her hair burned and others screamed and ran around trying to put the flames out, the necessary oblations for Beverley were complete.

The kehua that had followed Beverley, pleading with her, since she was a tiny child, and all its descendants too, as the hapu split, and split, and split again, could now return home to the marae satisfied. But the marae was not there any more, the urupa, the beautiful place, was covered by bungalows, and TV aerials and mobile phone and police masts, and would be hard to locate even if anyone still cared. They chattered and quaked and covered their eyes against reason, and leapt back to the kowhai tree, which recovered from its grief at losing them and stood proud again. The kehua thought they might as well stay; the conservatory could be the marae, the urupa could be found in the garden, Winter, Harry and Marcus could be gathered in, and even Fiona and Gwyneth. And no contrary instructions being received, the kehua settled in, content.

Just how much of a drama it was no one noticed. They were too busy dousing Beverley and allocating blame. As it happened Beverley's scalp was hardly touched though her hair was noticeably thinner and frizzled at its ends. Gerry wound a tie-dyed scarf in red, blue and green around her hair, and she forgot about the damage to it. He did not mind how much or how little hair she had, Gerry said. He was after her mind, and her experiences, not her body, and she was rich in both.

It was a gallant speech. He said he wanted to marry her but she was dubious about that. It would interfere with the children's inheritance. He was whanau, she accepted that, but only a rather recent member. She was not sure whether she wanted him in the house. He was not as young as he had been, and his eyes watered.

Scarlet's brush with death

The anticipation of change and event was already reverberating through the subtext of the spirit world, and up in Campion Tower Scarlet's wairua woke with a start, and up in the decorative kiwi her kehua went into alarm mode, and just as well, because even as Alice's flight was delayed and the traffic on the M1 ground to a halt, Scarlet, her face disfigured by rage and hate, was advancing on Jackson with a serrated bread knife raised about to strike, slit and slice. The past had sensed a time slip and was seeping through as best it could.

This is what had had happened between Scarlet and Jackson.

After their first night together Jackson had brought Scarlet coffee and toast in bed and instructed her not to leave crumbs. Well, it is the natural habit of men to instruct young women. Scarlet had objected.

'Don't you shout at me,' said Scarlet.

'Don't you screech at me,' said Jackson.

Scarlet's kehua, always sensitive to raised emotion, rustled in the blissful comfort of the ornamental kiwi plant. They were half inclined to start up their habitual refrain as duty demanded, *run, run, run,* but did not. The wairua were snuggling up so close and cosy to them it seemed too much bother. Yet why, when of all times now she needed their advice, did the kehua not squawk and flap their alarm, as the blackbirds did when the buzzard got the jackdaw?

I just got up and cleaned the cobwebby windows. I used the Windolene, which is kept with the other cleaning materials and cloths in the old pantry. Don't ask me why I suddenly felt the need, after months of living and working down here with the spiders and the ghosts, to get round to doing this. I thought if I looked more clearly out to the garden I would see more of what was really there than what I thought was there. Spirits surely dislike dust and dirt and dereliction. I can see I have been colluding with them to make their life easier. The ammonia smell of the cleaner quite masks that of the drifting cigar smoke, at any rate. It was very powerful in the pantry just now. God knows what Mr Bennett had been up to down there.

Enough about cleaning. Back to the computer. Perhaps a bad tohunga had indeed got hold of the wairua of Scarlet's aborted babies? These wairua are apparently easily led. Perhaps someone was ill-wishing her? Perhaps someone who wanted her cushy job, or an ex or discarded wife? Perhaps Briony would have had Jackson back if she, Scarlet, had not been around throwing herself at Jackson, offering all sorts of sexual delights, apparently with love thrown in for good measure? Someone like Scarlet could not hope to live without encountering envy, no matter how hard she smiled.

After Scarlet had drunk her coffee she assumed she would get up and pop round to her office to catch up with an article she was writing on the new trend towards mineral face powder and whether it dried the skin, and also pluck up the courage to call Louis and explain to him what she had done and why and how they could remain good friends. It would have to be done sooner or later.

But Jackson had other ideas. To stop her leaving there was sex and more sex until she was quite dizzy, and work was out of the question. Around the time that Luke was buying the steak for the barbecue, Jackson asked Scarlet if she had any money with her because the rent was due soon and he assumed she would be paying her share.

'You don't own this place?' she asked in surprise. She could see herself contributing towards the community charge but rent was somehow of a different order. Men were meant to provide the roof over one's head.

'No I don't,' he said, rather crossly. 'I rent. I don't want my ex-wife getting hold of any more of my property.'

And then he had to tell her about Briony and the kids, and Scarlet did not seem to mind so much about Briony as about the fact that he had children old enough to be at university. In her mind he was still Jackson the young vampire.

Then he told her he was going to give up films and become a mature drama student again. She asked him how he meant to live and he told her money was immaterial; he hardly imagined she worried about it. He had taken a line of coke and was not watching what he was saying, so full of faith in the future was he. She was sitting up in bed, shocked, with her breasts bare. Jackson fell upon them in adoration.

It was unfortunate that the girl with the bionic legs, who still had a key, called by to see what Jackson was doing and, seeing Scarlet unclothed in the bed, advanced to join in their pleasure, stripping as she went.

It was at this point that Scarlet, tried beyond endurance, followed the path that her ancestors had trod before, and leapt out of the bed. And seized the bread knife and advanced on Jackson. Jackson cowered instead of trying to disarm her and defend himself and she hated him the more for it; the bionic girl screamed with manic laughter; she loved this kind of thing.

It was good that this happened an instant before Beverley's hair and the kowhai twig went up in flames together, and a good thing that Beverley's hair was fluffed up and so caught the flame, thanks to Scarlet, because the wairua and the kehua started into wakefulness at the same time, and all screamed at Scarlet, *run, run, run!* Or else it was that Scarlet caught sight of her contorted face in the mirror, and dropped the knife and grabbed a coat and ran, ran, ran, down the stairs, because the lift took too long, and out into the street, and into her Prius and back home to Louis, home and safety.

Scarlet's now redundant kehua and her fitfully attentive wairua made their way off to Robinsdale, there to join the others in their spiritual home in the kowhai tree, to wait for their ancestors to reach out to claim them in the land of the long grey clouds where they now belonged. It was not the best thing, the best urupa, but the best thing on offer. And I have seen the Westway overpass gleam and glitter after a rain shower in the setting sun, and look like a golden path over the sea to Tane.

As for Louis and Scarlet, the shock of her seeing him and he seeing her in the flesh was very great for both of them. The Louis of her imagination, the Scarlet of his, were suddenly swept away by the reality of the other's existence and they simply clasped each other.

'I want to move house,' was all she said.

'We're going to have to,' he said.

He had been on the phone to his mother. She said he had to choose between Nopasaran or MetaFashion, and he had chosen MetaFashion. And in so doing he chose Scarlet, who thought perhaps she had better not risk losing Louis again, but would have the children he wanted.

Down here in the basement a fuse burned out and I was in the dark again. I saw no flame: I heard no bell. I sat quietly in the dark, unafraid, and all I heard was the man's voice saying again, 'So be it,' and I knew that this time it had worked; we had all exorcised one another. The lights went on again and I wrote The End and closed the document and shut the laptop and went up the worn stone steps, and left them all to it, ghosts and characters alike.

But I worried about Patch. I was startled a day or two later to hear a dog barking but it was only Bonzo, visiting. All the same I took a hair Bonzo left on the sofa and laid it, together with a hair from my own head, on the top of Patch's gravestone and lit them with a match and said a prayer for him and his whanau while the flame frizzled and flared. I thought I heard a voice saying again, 'So be it.' It had taken him three goes at the exorcism, whoever he was, before all the ends were tied and finally there was peace.

Glossary

atua	the soul of the whanau, than which there can be no higher or more joyful level of existence
hapu	kinship group within the tribe
iwi	the whole tribe
karakia	prayers and rituals of exorcism
kehua	the wandering spirits of the homeless dead, whose task is to shepherd the living and the dead of the hapu towards atua
marae	the physical meeting places of the iwi
pa	the physical home village
pakeha	non-Maori people
Tane	the great God Tane, progenitor of all
taniwha	river monsters who guard the tribe
tohunga	priests, shamans, healers, experts in sacred rites and significant practical tasks
urupa	the beautiful, peaceful place all remember, usually a graveyard
wairua	spirits of the unborn, their lives interrupted
whanau	the extended family, the bloodline